"What are you doing?"

What was he doing? Well, he certainly wasn't thinking. Mia was like a salve to a wound, and since everything was all mixed up and tangled anyway... "Considering kissing you, actually."

She pulled her head back even more, holding out her hands like double stop signs. "You can't kiss me!"

It was such a strange response to him trying to kiss her, Dell was almost amused. Refusal he'd expected. Some kind of scathing comment, yup. A sort of weird panic complete with squeaky voice and bug eyes? It was kind of cute.

"Why not?"

Dear Reader,

I've been in love with farms since I can remember. The romantic side of me likes to think love is a gene, passed down from generations before. My grandfather had to quit farming long before I was born, but when I was a kid he bought back the farmhouse he'd grown up in. He's always told me that farmhouse is his heart. The poetry of that sentiment stuck with me, and I was determined to put that heart into a book. So I wrote a story about two farmers whose farms were their hearts.

I sold that book (and a second book in the series) to Harlequin E in 2013, and in 2014 that book came out as part of the Harlequin E Contemporary Box Set Volume 2, and then on its own in September of 2014 under the title *All I Have*.

When Harlequin E folded, the awesome Harlequin Superromance team offered to move the entire Farmer's Market series to Superromance. Since the original two books were shorter, this came with the caveat that *All I Have* would need an additional 20,000 words. So, here we are!

All I Have is longer than the original version, but it's the same story of two people whose hearts are their farms and belong to each other.

Happy reading!

Nicole Helm
nicolehelm.wordpress.com

NICOLE HELM

—

All I Have

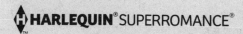
HARLEQUIN® SUPERROMANCE®

Recycling programs
for this product may
not exist in your area.

ISBN-13: 978-0-373-60919-2

All I Have

Copyright © 2014 by Nicole Helm

Printed in U.S.A.

Nicole Helm grew up with her nose in a book and a dream of becoming a writer. Luckily, after a few failed career choices, a husband and two kids, she gets to pursue that writing dream. She lives in Missouri with her husband and two sons and dreams of someday owning a barn.

Books by Nicole Helm

HARLEQUIN SUPERROMANCE

Too Close to Resist
Too Friendly to Date
Falling for the New Guy

HARLEQUIN E

All I Have

Other titles by this author available in ebook format.

To my Grandpa Beck. You once said the farm was your heart, so I gave Mia and Dell your heart.

Many thanks to the people at Harlequin, especially Alissa Davis for believing in this book from the beginning and making it even stronger, and Piya Campana for bringing it to Harlequin Superromance. I will be forever grateful for having the opportunity to work with both of you.

CHAPTER ONE

"Guh."

Mia Pruitt ran smack-dab into her sister's back, causing the pallet full of cabbages she was carrying to drop to the ground. Green spheres bounced against the concrete with a thud and rolled in every direction.

"Damn it, Cara." At least cabbage was one of the hardier vegetables Mia had for the early-spring market. The drop wouldn't really damage them.

"Sorry." But Cara didn't move. She stood frozen directly in the path between the truck bed and Mia's stand at the farmers' market, cabbage strewn about her feet.

Mia looked where Cara's gaze was transfixed and groaned. "Is he serious? It's not even fifty degrees. Can't he wait until July for that crap?"

"Who cares?" Cara fanned her face with her hand. "He can take his shirt off any day he wants. And if he gets cold, I will gladly step in to warm him up."

Dell Wainwright and his stupid shirtless antics had put a serious dent in their farmers' market profits last year. Cara didn't care, but this wasn't her full-time job. Mia was the one taking over the farm. Mia was the one making this stand into a living. She cared, and she was going to find a way to combat him this year.

Dell might look like a god among men shirtless behind his table full of spring vegetables, but she'd jump around naked in front of everyone before she let him put her out of business. This farmers' market was the best thing to happen to her share of Pruitt Farms and to her personally. In the past four years she'd been selling here, she had finally learned how to come out of her shell.

In its fifth year, the market had grown to fill up half a mall parking lot. Tables with awnings lined the outer lot. In early spring, there were only two rows, but by midsummer there'd be four. Each booth was made up of a variety of locally sourced items. From her and Dell's locally grown vegetables to people selling meat, eggs, local and homemade cheeses and honeys and breads, and a few craft and soap stands.

Each year they had more customers, and each year Dell's stand had directly competed with hers. She'd managed to build up her business to break even and was this close to making it profitable.

Yeah, Dell was not screwing that up. Six-pack abs or no six-pack abs. "Stop drooling and pick up the cabbage." She gave Cara a nudge with her boot. "He's the enemy, remember?"

"If the enemy looks like that, I'll gladly turn myself in. What kind of torture are we talking?"

"Gross."

"If you think that's gross, you need your eyes checked." Cara flipped her hair over her shoulder and bent down to pick up the cabbage at her feet. Her eyes never left Dell.

Mia set to unloading the early-spring haul onto the table under the Pruitt Farms tent. Meanwhile, Cara made no bones about watching Dell's every move.

Cara was always dating or talking about guys she wanted to date or pinning hot celebrity pictures to her Pinterest page. It wasn't that Mia didn't appreciate a hot guy. She just didn't understand obsessing over one.

Probably because twenty-six-year-old virgins didn't know what they were missing.

Mia set up the pallets, the price signs, made sure everything was just so, and maybe on occasion her gaze drifted to Dell and his broad, tanned shoulders as he hauled his own farm's offerings from truck to table.

He was still the enemy, but it didn't mean she couldn't *look*.

"So glad to see you girls back this year," Val greeted them, ever-present clipboard clutched to her chest. "You're going to stick with us all year, right?"

"Yes, ma'am. Couldn't kick us out if you wanted."

Val wasn't looking at her anymore, though. She was drooling over Dell, right along with Cara. Mia resisted the urge to hurl a cabbage across the aisle. Knowing Dell, he'd probably make a big show out of catching it.

"Uh-huh. Very good. See you next week." Val wandered off to Dell's table. In two seconds flat, Dell was making her giggle and blush.

"You can't stop staring, either."

"I'm picturing strangling him." If that picture included wondering what his skin might feel like under her hands it was curiosity, not interest. Or so she told herself, year after shirtless year.

"Hey, whatever floats your boat."

A group of women descended on Dell's table. Usually the first hour of the first week of the market was virtually empty, but today had a bit of a crowd. A mainly female crowd.

Not fair. What'd he do, advertise? *Male stripper does Millertown Farmers' Market.*

The group of women laughed and Dell made a big production of picking things up and putting things down and flexing and—ugh—he really was despicable.

"You're blushing."

"I am not!" Damn it. She totally was. Well, she'd come too far to be flustered by a pair of perfectly toned forearms. She was not the little girl who hyperventilated in the bathroom between classes if a boy even said hi to her.

It had always been a joke anyway. Say hi to Mia Pruitt and watch her self-destruct into a blushing, babbling mess.

Dell wasn't saying hi to her, joke or no joke, and he most certainly wasn't a boy. He was an adult man and she was an adult woman. A confident, strong woman no longer the laughingstock of her tiny Missouri farming community.

Every time someone bought a head of broccoli or cabbage from him, they weren't buying it from her. So, essentially, he was stealing.

Nobody liked thieves no matter how white their teeth were or how charming their grin might be.

"You know what?" Mia dropped the cash box onto the ground next to her chair with a loud crash. "Two can play his little game." She was done just…*taking* it. Maybe it was time to fight.

Cara laughed. "What does that mean? You going to take your shirt off?"

"Not exactly." Mia narrowed her eyes at Dell flirting with a young mom who carried a baby on her hip. Both mom and baby were charmed. Mom bought a bag full of vegetables. Probably wouldn't eat half of them before they went bad.

Mia might not have muscles and a five o'clock shadow women swooned over, but surely she could do something to undermine Dell's sex-sells philosophy.

If you couldn't beat 'em, join 'em. She wasn't sure how to join them yet, but she would damn well figure it out before next week. She was tired of being the passive taker-of-crap. She was going to act.

"MIA'S BORING HOLES through your skull with her eyes. Be afraid. Be very afraid."

Dell waved his brother off. "Please. Mia Pruitt is five foot three of all bark and no bite in a baggy sweatshirt."

"I don't know. She takes this farm stuff pretty seriously." Charlie stacked the last empty pallet on the truck bed. "Wouldn't want to get in her way. Besides, she's not bad without the glasses and the frizzy hair. Kind of cute, actually."

"I'm not worried about Mia." Dell pulled on a threadbare Mizzou sweatshirt. "I take my farm stuff pretty seriously, too." He spared her a glance. *Cute* was probably the right word for her. With her hair straight instead of a frizz of curls and the heavy-framed glasses gone, she no longer resembled Mia, Queen of the Geeks.

But in the baggy shirt and at-least-one-size-too-big jeans, even a sexy mouth and big green eyes couldn't push her beyond cute.

Charlie laughed. "Yeah, nothing says *serious* like taking off your shirt and flexing your muscles to sell a few extra cucumbers."

"Hey, a true businessman does what he has to do."

Charlie shook his head. "Whatever you tell yourself to sleep at night, man."

His VP of sales older brother could sneer at the farm and all that went with it as much as he liked, but with Dad making noises about selling instead of passing the farm on to Dell, Dell knew he had to kick ass this market season. That meant whatever tactics necessary, regardless of Charlie's approval.

If that meant taking off his shirt, so be it. A little harmless flirting and a few extra dollars in his pocket wouldn't hurt anyone, and it'd help him. Why did people have to assume that meant he was an idiot? He was raking it in.

"Can we hurry this up? I've got a lunch date with Emily downtown in, like, an hour."

Dell nodded and picked up the pace. Choosing a noisy, bustling dinner at a fancy restaurant downtown over the quiet ease of lunch at Moonrise in New Benton was beyond him. But then, the things he didn't understand about his older brother were too many to count.

Dell folded the awning and was tying it together when a pair of greenish cowboy boots stepped into his vision. He looked up, quirked an eyebrow at Mia.

"Wainwright." She was almost a foot shorter than he, so she had to tilt her head back when he stood to his full height.

He nodded, tipped the brim of his ball cap.

"Pruitt." Maybe he should have worn a Stetson hat. This felt more like high noon than a friendly greeting.

"Still lowering yourself to stripping for attention?" She crossed her arms over her chest, narrowed her eyes at him. "I thought maybe you'd grown up a bit since last year."

She had a dusting of light brown freckles across her nose. Kind of weird to notice it now, but then again he'd never spent much time looking at Mia. The girl who'd been the champion of awkward moments in high school, then come back from college quiet and unassuming. Of course, she'd never gotten up in his face and accused him of stripping before.

Dell grinned. That meant she thought he was a threat to her tidy little business. He primed up the charm and the drawl. "Don't worry, darling. I'm sure there'll be enough customers to go around. Not everyone is swayed by good looks and charm. Just most people."

She didn't cower. She didn't walk away. She didn't even dissolve into the Queen of the Geeks she'd been in high school. No, Mia Pruitt grinned at him—which had to be a first, even if she'd grown out of most of her awkwardness since she'd come back from college.

"Oh, I'm not worried. But you should be," she said. Then she sauntered away with enough confidence that Dell stared after her.

"Whoa." The saunter. The grin. Even with all her recent changes, he'd never seen that kind of… attitude from Mia before. Was it his imagination, or was it kind of hot?

Charlie slapped him on the back. "Told you not to cross her. Mia isn't the girl hiding behind the pony at Kelsey's birthday party anymore, if you hadn't noticed."

Dell stared after Mia's swinging hips. Apparently he hadn't noticed that at all.

CHAPTER TWO

MIA PULLED HER truck into the parking lot at Orscheln and tried not to be irritated by all Dad's sighing and grumbling. She drove too fast, braked too hard. The one and only place Dad ever criticized her.

Which was why, for the life of her, she couldn't figure out why he didn't drive himself. Or stay home.

"If you hate coming to town so much, you don't have to come. I could always get whatever you need."

"Have to ask Rick about this new vaccine."

"You could do that on the phone. I bet Rick even has email."

Dad harrumphed and got out of the truck. Mia trudged after him. Mostly, she loved spending time with Dad. He'd always been her biggest supporter, and one of the few people she felt understood her.

But going to Orscheln with Dad meant people didn't get used to her as Mia Pruitt, serious farmer. They still saw the girl who had cried when all the chickens had been sold, or accidentally let all the kittens up for adoption out of their cage because she'd been trying to pet them.

Daughter of the town hermit, the man who refused to talk to anyone except Rick when he came in. Should another employee approach him, he'd turn and walk away. If Rick was out sick, Dad would hop in his truck and go home.

Oh, who was she kidding? Even when she came in without Dad she was a Pruitt, and there was a *lot* of baggage that went with that.

But she could pretend when she was alone. Pretend she was your average twenty-six-year-old vegetable farmer. Or something.

"I'm going to…look at some plants. You go ahead inside." It was an excuse, a pathetic one at that, but maybe if she could pretend they hadn't walked in together…

Mia stared gloomily at some pansies as Dad grunted and went inside. She was being kind of a crap daughter, and that made her feel guilty. Especially having been on the receiving end of the "go ahead inside, I'll wait out here" line more than once.

"Of all the gin joints in the world, she walked into mine."

Mia closed her eyes. Apparently today was really going to make her feel as if she was sixteen again. She glanced over her shoulder at Dell. He had his beat-up Cardinals hat on, equally worn jeans and a black T-shirt that did unfair things to showcase the muscles of his arms.

If she was a cat, she'd hiss at him. Instead, she mustered her best fake smile. "You're wearing a shirt. What a novelty."

"No shirt, no shoes, no service." He grinned, and she hated that some part of her reacted to that grin. A weird flopping deep in her stomach; a floaty giddiness around her chest.

Yes, she was sixteen and still an idiot. "You got the quote all wrong, by the way."

"Huh?"

"It's, 'Of all the gin joints, in all the towns, in all the world, she walks into mine.' If you're going to quote something, it should at least be the right something."

"I have no idea what you're talking about."

"Figures," she muttered, turning her attention back to the plants. She had no use for flowers. She lived in an apartment in town, and even if she lived at the farm, she'd certainly plant something she could sell the produce of.

Dell did not seem to take the hint, still standing uncomfortably behind her. Uncomfortably because…well. He made her uncomfortable. Because he was a butt, that was why.

"Are you following me?" she asked, trying to sound bored. Succeeding, too, if she did say so herself.

"It's a small town, sugar."

She would not be irritated by the cocky way he drawled *sugar*. She would also not be…other things at the way his voice was all gravelly and sure of himself. Not hot. Not even cute.

"And yet, how many times have I run into you here before? I do these errands every Tuesday morning."

"Well, if you see me again, then you'll know I'm following you. For today, it's just an unfortunate coincidence."

Unfortunate. Yeah. She certainly got no secret thrill out of seeing him outside the market. Please. She hoped to *never* see him outside the market. She didn't even want to see him *at* the market.

"But while we're here, together, on this beautiful day, why don't you tell me what you've got up your sleeve so you don't embarrass yourself at the market Saturday?"

She glanced at him again, giving him a condescending look she'd been practicing in the mirror. "First of all, we're not together."

"I'm standing here. You're standing there right in touching distance. We're talking. Together enough from where I'm at."

"Why don't you stand *out* of touching distance?" Because words like *touching* made her even more uncomfortable than she already was. How could she pretend to be calm and collected when she had to think about…touching?

She had the petty desire to give him a little

push, but that would be silly and childish…and probably put her in contact with muscles she'd prefer to only fantasize about.

Except, no fantasizing.

"I don't know why you have reason to be so antagonistic with me, Mia. Fair competition and all that. Jealousy isn't an attractive quality."

She rolled her eyes. "The day I worry about being attractive to you is the day I go braindead." Jitters multiplied in her stomach. This was getting…weird. "Besides, if it's fair competition, you don't need to worry about what I've got up my sleeve."

"I'm just trying to look out for you. You've built quite a new rep for yourself."

She was not a violent person, but something about him made her visualize doing a lot of it. Unfortunately that also meant visualizing touching him. In a way that wasn't all…violent. "The day Dell Wainwright is looking out for my well-being is the day *I* start taking my shirt off at the market."

His eyes drifted to her chest, an almost considering look on his face. She crossed her arms over herself, the heat of embarrassment mixing with a different kind of heat.

"Go away, Dell. I am trying to do actual work here. I'm guessing you wouldn't know what that's like."

There was a beat of silence, a moment of tri-

umph that she'd shut him up, and then a twist of...
something not so nice in her stomach.

"Naw, I just sit around my farm twiddling my
thumbs." He stepped away from her, a weird energy in the tense shoulders and the hard line of
his mouth. "See you 'round, Pruitt."

Mia frowned after him. She had no idea why
she felt...kind of guilty and like a jerk. She hadn't
said anything too terrible to him, certainly not any
worse than him calling her Queen of the Geeks.

So the weird twist in her stomach was out of
place, and Dell was out of place for making her
feel it. She was about to stomp into the store, but
Dad's voice sounded from behind her.

"That boy bothering you?"

Mia snorted, couldn't help it. She turned to
Dad, who'd obviously come out of the feed exit.
It was nice Dad felt protective, but she did not
need to be protected. Or comforted. Not anymore.
"First of all, Dell Wainwright isn't a boy any more
than I'm a girl."

Dad harrumphed.

"Second, I'm not... That stuff doesn't bother
me anymore." Possibly because it wasn't the
same. Going toe-to-toe with Dell was less like
being made fun of, being called names. It was
more like battle. One she was more than equipped
to fight.

It was weirdly invigorating. It made her feel capable and strong. If she could take on Mr. Prom

King, she could take on anyone. If she could ignore the random bouts of misplaced guilt. Which she would.

She was going to take him on and win, and the more he poked at her, the more he'd find she didn't roll over and hide anymore.

"Let's go home."

It was tempting. Tempting to put off what she'd come for so she wouldn't have to run into Dell in the aisles, but not tempting enough to agree to.

"You can wait in the car if you want. But I have a few things that need picking up." Because she was not a wimp. Not anymore.

DELL HEFTED THE tarps he needed onto the dolly, trying to ignore the fact he could see Mia at the end of the aisle doing the same.

He'd been kind of a dick, and it wasn't his proudest moment, but she'd sure landed the knockout punch.

I'm guessing you wouldn't know what that's like.

As if farmwork could ever be anything but hard. As if he didn't work his ass off every day trying to compete with her.

Her very fine ass.

Yeah, he didn't want to be noticing things like that. So she wasn't a social mess anymore? It didn't mean he had any right or reason to be attracted to her. He didn't have time to be distracted by stuff like that. Not with Dad breathing down his neck for profits. Proof that his ideas could stand the test of time.

Dell looked down at the tarps. It was another expense he didn't need, but if he started cutting corners it would affect his crops. With both the weekly farmers' market and five families getting community-supported agriculture portions from him, he didn't have the option of risking product.

Life sure had been easier when he didn't care about this stuff. No one and nothing depending on him. Then again, if he hadn't been quite so laid-back, perhaps he wouldn't be in this position now.

If he'd been like Mia and gone to a tough school and worked hard and come back with all As, would it have mattered?

There was no answer for that. Nothing he could do to change what had happened. All he could do was focus on the present and the future and doing everything in his power to make Dad sell the farm to him.

Mia Pruitt was a competitor and distraction he would not let get in his way. He started rolling his dolly toward the cash register, realizing belatedly she was doing the same and they were now in line. Mia right in front of him.

So much for not being a distraction. Her baggy sweatshirt was pushed up to her elbows, revealing elegant forearms and delicate wrists. At least they looked that way, until she hefted a sack of sand as if it weighed nothing.

Her gaze landed on him and she rolled her eyes. "Oh, for heaven's sake," she said under her breath, tossing her sack of tarps on the conveyor belt.

"You're telling me." He crossed his arms, determined not to say anything else to her. Karl rang up her purchases and she stared resolutely at her dolly.

Karl rattled off a price and Mia dug a credit card out of her back pocket, and even while he was expressly ignoring her, it was kind of hard to ignore her ass.

Yes, he was a dick.

She blew out a breath, fidgeted as the ancient machine slowly printed out a receipt. Finally, she spoke. Because as much as she'd changed, there were still pieces of the old Mia in there.

"For what it's worth, I…" She raised her chin and looked him straight in the eye. Pretty green eyes. "I'm sorry," she said resolutely.

He was taken completely off guard, so much so he could make only a kind of "Huh?" sound.

"Holy moly, why am I doing this?" she muttered, snatching the receipt from Karl. She glanced at Dell, expression full of self-disgust. "I have my issues with how you sell stuff, and I'm going to use everything in my arsenal to beat you, but…I don't want to insult you in the process. It doesn't feel good to me."

"Are you insinuating it feels good to me?"

Her brows drew together. "No! I'm trying to be nice and apologize. Leave it to you to make that complicated."

"Leave it to me? Isn't that an insult?"

She grabbed the handle of her rolling tray. "Dell, you are the most annoying man I have ever met."

He had to work really hard not to smile. Something about riling her up was way too enjoyable. "Also an insult."

"Go to hell." She smiled faux-sweetly. "Please. Now it's an insult, but at least I'm being polite about it." Much like at the market last week, she sauntered away.

It made no sense he was smiling after her. Then again, he was beginning to think nothing about Mia Pruitt made any damn sense.

CHAPTER THREE

"How BADLY DO you want to beat Dell at the farmers' market?"

Mia looked up from the row of carrot seeds she was planting. Mia's youngest sister stood with Kenzie, Dell's little sister. Anna and Kenzie had been inseparable since kindergarten and Mia had never once felt weird about that.

Until now.

"Um."

"The jerk told my parents he caught me making out in the barn. I want him to burn," Kenzie said vehemently, clutching a book to her chest.

"Um."

"It's nothing all that bad," Anna explained, always the cool head wherever she went. "We just have some pictures of him, and we came up with this idea where you could post on the farmers' market page that you have pictures of the Naked Farmer in his underwear if people came to your booth Saturday morning or whatever. It would get you some extra customers, no doubt."

"You have pictures of Dell in his underwear?" Mia squeaked. "Not that I…" She closed her eyes against the embarrassed flush spreading up her neck. "I have no idea what you two are trying to accomplish here."

Kenzie opened up the book, revealing old photos in an album. Mia squinted. "Is that Dell?"

"Yes. In diapers. Underwear. It's a little harmless embarrassment."

Mia finally stood, trying to clap some of the dirt off her hands. The same uncomfortable twisting in her gut she'd felt yesterday at the store lodged itself there. "I'm not really into embarrassing anyone. I've kind of had my share of that, and it isn't fun."

"He walks around that market shirtless. Do you really think a few pictures from when he was a kid are going to embarrass him? I swear, he's embarrass-proof. And being-a-decent-human-being-proof."

Anna rolled her eyes. "Kenzie is overreacting."

"Jacob said we shouldn't go to prom together anymore!"

"You know he'll change his mind."

Mia tried to make sense of two seventeen-year-olds talking about things way beyond any experience she'd had in high school, but it was useless. *Boys* and *prom* might as well have been foreign words to her.

"The point is," Anna said matter-of-factly, "Dell thinks he can beat you with the shirtless stuff. So play a little dirty."

Mia had no idea why she was blushing again. "I'm sure our normal tactics are fine."

Kenzie blew out a frustrated breath. "I told you," she muttered to Anna. "Dell was right. She has no backbone."

"Hey!"

Anna gave her a sympathetic look. "She's kind of right. That's not always a bad thing, but if you want to beat Dell you're going to have to be a little meaner."

"I don't want to be mean. He's not being mean to me." Not really. It was nothing like high school, not when she could dish it back out.

Anna shrugged. "If he's telling Kenzie you have no backbone, he isn't exactly being nice. Regardless, if you're not willing to go after him a bit, he's always going to win."

"This isn't win-lose. It's...sell. Sell enough to be profitable. That has nothing to do with Dell."

Anna let out a belabored sigh. "Let's go back to the house, Kenzie. We'll work up some other revenge."

The two teens huffed off together, heads huddled, obviously discussing Mia's failings as a competitor.

Mia frowned and went back to her carrot seeds. The whole thing was stupid. More of the teasing and tricks she'd had to deal with when *she'd* been in high school. She was far more mature and worldly than Anna and Kenzie now. She did not need to feel peer-pressured into fighting dirty.

There was that annoying blush at the word *dirty* again. "I do not need to win, or be mean in the process," she said, combining the seeds with the sand and carefully spreading the mixture into the row she'd already tilled. "This isn't cutthroat business. It's just...vegetables."

She rocked back onto her heels. Cara always got on her when she caught her talking to herself. Or her vegetables. It was a habit. A habit of a lonely girl. She wasn't that girl anymore.

Dell was right. She has no backbone.

Mia scowled at that. She *had* a backbone. Being a nice person was not being backboneless. And if he thought her apologizing to him yesterday was lack of backbone...he obviously didn't know what being a decent human being was all about.

But he was clearly going to beat her in profits again, decency or not.

Mia got to her feet. She needed advice, and she already knew what Anna had to say. Cara would no doubt take the cutthroat side. So her only hope at getting a little reassurance was Dad. If she could get a few words out of him.

She trudged across her fields, making a mental note to stake the east tomatoes a little better. Dad was in his barn, studying one of the cows Mia knew had been sick. Dad had his beat-up spiral notebook in one hand, thoughtfully scribbling a few notes down.

Surely Dad of all people would agree with her. He hated conflict more than he loved his cows.

"Carrots coming along?"

Mia nodded as she took a spot next to him. "Yup. Sassy doing better?"

"Looks like."

Mia stared at the cow for a bit, trying to work out a way to ask without bringing Dell into the equation. There was no doubt her father would immediately bristle at the mention of a member of the male species, no matter how innocently.

"Do you think I have a backbone?" she asked, deciding the best route with Dad was to go for straightforward.

"Huh?"

"Like, if there's a problem or a conflict, do I stand up for things?"

Dad continued to frown at her. "This one of those things where you and your sisters ask me a question and there's no right answer except you all getting mad at me?"

"No, I'm serious. Do you think I have the backbone needed to be a businesswoman? To run my business successfully?"

"You're an excellent farmer, daughter."

Which was ignoring the question and made her feel sulky. But she didn't back down because she wanted to know. She needed to know what to do. "I'm talking about the business side of things."

Dad scratched a hand over his beard, then looked longingly at his cows outside the barn, but she wanted his opinion. She needed to know if even her father thought she was being the fool here.

"You keep an eye on your finances, and you make smart choices, and..."

"I'm a softie wimp."

"Aw, now, Mia." Dad clasped her shoulder, and if Dad was offering physical affection she was a sad case. Which meant she had to work harder to be...ruthless. Even if it felt kind of crappy.

The end justified the means and all that. That was what business—even farming business—was all about, maybe.

"You'll be fine. You're a good girl. It'll all work out."

But she didn't want to be fine or good; she wanted to be successful. She wanted a business that could sustain her for the rest of her life. She wanted profits and the confidence she'd built over the past five years.

So with a goodbye to Dad, she headed for the house and Kenzie's book of pictures.

"What's all that about?"

Dell frowned at the group of giggling women in front of Mia's stand. This was definitely not the norm. Especially for a forty-degree drizzly Saturday morning. But there were at least ten women with umbrellas and rain boots surrounding Pruitt Farms' stand, and the laughter kept building.

"Sneak over and check it out."

Charlie rolled his eyes. "Yeah, I'm sure there's a lot of cutthroat sabotage at the farmers' market. She stole the secret patent to grow broccoli. Oh. Wait."

"Bite me." Dell pushed Charlie away from the truck. "Stop being useless for once and find out what that's all about."

"I'm not useless. I only waste my Saturday mornings here to keep Mom off my back about karmic payment and family support and blah, blah, blah."

"Yeah, well, do some supporting." Dell shoved Charlie again. With a long, belabored sigh, Charlie walked over to the Pruitt side of the aisle.

A couple stopped by Dell's booth, obviously new to the market. Dell chatted them up, trying to keep his head in the game instead of across the aisle.

The couple left with some radishes and Charlie meandered back to their stand. He looked as if he fit more in with the customers in his dark jeans, sweater and some kind of loafer shoes. His brother, the yuppie.

Didn't make an ounce of sense to Dell, and

probably never would. When Charlie didn't offer anything, Dell nudged him. "So?"

Charlie shrugged. "She said check the market's Facebook page."

"Facebook page? That's her grand plan? Give me your phone."

Charlie rolled his eyes. "You even know how to use my phone?"

No, but did it take a rocket scientist to figure out? When he held out his hand, Charlie slapped the phone into his palm. Dell swiped his thumb across the bottom of the screen then stared. *Shit.* He didn't know how to use a damn smartphone. All he saw was a bunch of squares with *stock* or *finance* in the title. "How do I get to Facebook?"

"Give it back, moron."

"Just because I don't know how to use a smart-phone doesn't mean I'm a moron." Dell handed the phone back to his brother and shoved his hands into his pockets. He wasn't some dumb farmer. He had his ag degree from Mizzou.

But it was no MBA from Wash U in big brother's eyes. Or Dad's. No one seemed to want to let him live down the fact he'd been wait-listed, either, all because of his crap-ass standardized test scores. Who cared about those stupid tests anyway?

His family, that was who. Oh, and his girlfriend at the time, who'd dumped him for someone who could "intellectually stimulate" her.

He hadn't had a clue what that meant at eighteen. He had even less of a clue what it meant now.

More giggling echoed across the aisle and Dell hunched his shoulders, glaring at Charlie. "Hurry up."

Charlie waved him off. "Nothing on Mia's page."

"Well, what the hell are they laughing at, man?"

Charlie started laughing. Pretty soon he was laughing so hard he was slapping his knee.

"What the hell?"

Charlie passed the phone to him, and Dell squinted over the Millertown Farmers' Market page. The last comment was from Mia Pruitt.

"Pruitt Farms has an extraspecial treat this week, ladies. If you want to see pictures of our intrepid Naked Farmer, Dell Wainwright, in his underwear, do I have the goods for you. Stop by from eight to nine Saturday morning for a peek!"

Dell shoved the phone at his brother so fast Charlie nearly dropped it, but Dell barely registered Charlie's cursing because he'd already hopped the table and stalked over to the crowd of women. "Pruitt, you're dead."

The giggling didn't stop, but it did become more hushed as the sea parted, so he was standing face-to-face with Mia, only her table of goods—many of those goods in the bags of the women who normally bought from him—between them.

"Well, howdy, Dell," she drawled, flipping

closed a family album. Wait a second. *His mother's* family album.

"Where the hell'd you get that?"

"You look awfully cute in diapers, honey," Deirdre, one of his regular customers, said, giving his arm a pat.

It took every ounce of salesman in him not to shrug her off or growl at Mia. "Hand it over." She held it out and he snatched it from her hands.

"Careful. Your mother will kill you if you tear one of her pictures," Mia said sweetly. "And Deirdre's right, you do look awfully cute in nothing but your underwear."

He forced himself to grin. "Aw, sugar, don't be upset just because you've never seen me in my underwear."

She tried to grab the album back. But Dell was too quick. He flipped through the thick pages. There were indeed pictures of him in his underwear. Of course, he was under the age of eight in every single one of them.

"I particularly like the bare-butt one in cowboy boots. Adorable." Val pointed to the picture on the upper-left corner. He resisted the urge to slam it shut on her fingers.

"How did you get this?"

Mia smiled, flashing perfectly straight teeth. "Some secrets are meant to be kept."

"Trust me when I say I could get any little secret out of you I wanted."

Mia rolled her eyes. "Just because you're hot doesn't mean I'm going to— I mean…" Some of her bravado faded as her cheeks went pink. "You can't charm me."

But he kept waiting. Everyone they'd gone to high school with knew the key to unraveling any of Mia's attempts at social interaction was simply to wait. In silence.

"Oh, screw you. I got it from Kenzie. Have you forgotten our baby sisters are best friends? And she wasn't too happy with you apparently."

Damn it, Kenzie. "I'll kill her."

"You seem really obsessed with killing women today, Dell." Old Mia was gone, replaced by this surprisingly quick-on-her-feet, good-with-a-comeback version. Even knowing she'd gotten a little bit better with people hadn't prepared him for this, or the comment that came next.

"Perhaps you should seek therapy."

Dell shoved the album under his arm. "Don't think this is over." He pointed his finger at her, ignoring that she looked sexy with her hands on her hips. As he stalked away, Mia's laughter followed him.

She was going to pay. Big-time.

CHAPTER FOUR

THIS TIME WHEN Mia dropped a pallet full of vegetables, it wasn't Cara's fault. Instead, it was the sign under Morning Sun's stand: Morning Sun Farms. Home of the Naked Farmer.

The sound coming out of her mouth was somewhere between a screech and a snarl. Then Cara started giggling.

"Oh, my God. He's brilliant. Brilliant."

"Brilliant?" Mia sucked in a breath, tried to find some center of calm. All she found was more anger. "He's a glorified stripper!"

"A brilliant glorified stripper."

Mia bent to pick up the scattered radish bunches and cabbage heads. She couldn't believe he was using the title she'd come up with against her. And he wasn't even naked! Only half-naked.

Right?

Mia peeked above the table to make sure. Yep. He was still wearing jeans. Although they were loose enough to hang low on his hips and were liberally streaked with dirt and grass stains at the knees. He could be in a hot-farmer calendar with that getup.

All he needed to do was stick his thumbs through his belt loops, pull down the pants a little bit, maybe flex.

The image was not at all appealing.

Not at all.

Mia shook her head and focused on the vegetables. Putting them out in neat rows, hanging the pretty little price tags Anna had made for her in art class. Maybe Dell offered a certain kind of appeal to some women, but families would appreciate Pruitt's cleanliness, cuteness and overall clothedness.

She told herself that all morning, but woman after woman, regardless of the number of children they were carting around, fled to Dell and his shirtless idiocy. A few families came by her booth and bought some vegetables. A few of the women came over and bought a pan of Mom's cinnamon rolls, since Dell wasn't offering any baked goods at his table.

But mainly, Dell was winning. And she didn't know how to fight back. It was an old, familiar feeling. In the first grade, she'd accidentally tucked her skirt into her underwear and hadn't noticed for hours. Six years old, and she'd been forever labeled a geek. The teasing had escalated each school year, and her attempts to fit in had only made it worse.

She'd never known how to make herself above

the jokes, the snickers. She'd either tried too hard or stayed invisible. There was no in-between for her.

Mia took a deep breath and looked around the market. This space had given her the tools to be confident enough not to care what other people thought. To quiet the incessant voice in her head telling her she was doing everything wrong. She'd mostly found her in-between in adulthood and maturity, and that couldn't be taken away.

She might not know how to beat Dell yet, but she'd figure it out. Damn right she would.

As the morning wore down, Cara started packing up. "Anna texted me she won her event. She wants us to meet her at Moonrise at twelve thirty."

Mia muttered her assent, scowling at a grinning Dell as much as she could while they packed up the truck.

He sauntered over and Mia straightened to her full height. She wished for a few more inches so he wouldn't tower over her like some kind of Paul Bunyan. At least he had managed to put on his shirt before he came over.

He pulled his wallet out of his pocket. "I'll take one of your mom's cinnamon rolls." He grinned when Cara smiled at him, all but fluttering her lashes as she handed over the tin of gooey baked goods. "I sure worked up an appetite selling so much today."

"Yeah, I've heard stripping *is* really hard work. Maybe next week you can add some glittery tassels."

His jaw tensed, but then he smiled, his gaze drifting to her chest. "I wouldn't mind seeing you in some glittery tassels."

Wait. *What?*

He cleared his throat, shifting on his feet. "That's not…what I meant." He shoved the money at her. Mia grunted in disgust, trying to pretend she wasn't the darkest shade of red possible. She took his money and opened the change bank.

"Oh, don't worry about it, hon." He drawled out the *hon* until Mia ground her teeth. "Keep the change."

She needed one snappy comeback and she could forget this bizarre conversation had ever happened. But her mind was blank.

"It looks as if you guys might be needing the extra money after all." He winked, tipped his baseball cap.

"Of all the arrog—"

"Thanks, Dell," Cara said, stepping in front of her. "We appreciate it. See you next week."

"Sure thing, Carrie."

Dell sauntered off and Mia pushed her sister. "What the hell? He was being totally patronizing."

Cara shrugged. "So what? He's cute. He smiled

at me. Apparently he wants to see you in tassels, which, oh, my God. *And* he gave us five bucks. That's a two-buck tip."

"He called you *Carrie*."

Cara shrugged. "Hey, if he wants me to be a Carrie, I'll be a Carrie."

Mia slammed the truck bed shut and hopped into the driver's seat, fuming. *Keep the change. It looks as if you guys might be needing the extra money after all.* She'd show him where he could shove his change.

She would not, not, *not* think about the bizarre tassels comment. Of course he didn't mean it. No one could even see her breasts under her sweatshirt.

Even more important, she knew how Dell saw her. How everyone still saw her. She might have changed, but everyone from New Benton knew her as the girl who'd written and performed a one-woman play about cow milking at the school talent show in an attempt to get in with the theater kids.

No one wanted to see the girl who'd done *that* in anything other than a clown outfit.

Cara sang along with Carrie Underwood as Mia drove back to New Benton. The thirty-minute drive didn't calm her. She was still furious when she slid into a booth at the Moonrise Diner.

Anna was already seated, her hair in a wet ponytail from her swim meet, a New Benton High jacket across her shoulders. She looked over the menu. A menu that hadn't changed in any of their lifetimes. When she looked up, her head snapped back. "Uh-oh. Who crossed Mia? She's breathing fire."

Cara laughed, slinging an arm over Anna's shoulders. "I'll give you one guess."

Across the table, Mia sneered at them.

"Ah. Dell. I take it he got payback for the pictures?"

"Yup. He's still kicking her ass at the market. He even used the Naked Farmer thing to his advantage. Poor Mia isn't taking it well."

Mallory set their usual drinks in front of them. "You girls want the usual?"

"I want a salad instead of fries," Anna announced, putting the menu back behind the napkin dispenser. Mallory nodded and then disappeared to put in their orders.

"You need to up your game," Anna instructed, with the kind of surety Mia had never, ever had at seventeen.

She slumped in the booth. She was furious because she thought she'd gained the upper hand and Dell had proved that to be false without even trying. "How am I supposed to compete with beefcake of the month?"

"You have breasts." Cara pointed to Mia's chest.

Mia choked on the sip of soda she'd taken. "Excuse me?"

"I mean, you can't take your shirt off, but you could show off a few of those assets you insist on hiding. Women aren't the only ones who go to the farmers' market."

She couldn't even begin to formulate a response to her *sister* suggesting she use her breasts as some kind of selling device. Why were they getting so much attention today?

"Cara's on to something," Anna said, tapping her chin. "All you have to do is get some tighter jeans. Not even skintight, just ones that actually fit. A T-shirt instead of the baggy sweats."

"But—"

"We were right about the hair, weren't we?"

Yes, a year ago her sisters had finally convinced her the perm wasn't doing anything for her. Cara had gotten her an appointment with the hairstylist at the salon she worked at in Millertown. Shelly had made Mia's mousy, flat hair look decent with the right cut and highlights.

"And the glasses."

"Hey, I started wearing contacts for practical reasons." Mia folded and unfolded the napkin in front of her. She'd gotten to the point where she'd broken so many pairs of glasses and spent so much time cleaning them when she was out in the fields, getting over her eye-touching phobia had been downright necessary.

Losing the glasses hadn't been some lame attempt at being pretty. Even if she'd hoped the guys would magically start flocking once she went the contact route. Stupid movies giving girls stupid expectations.

Guys didn't flock. She could turn into Jessica Rabbit and everyone would still see her as Mia, Queen of the Geeks. She might have gotten over some of her shyness and social anxiety, but it certainly hadn't changed people's perception of her. Not here. Not when she'd accidentally set her hair on fire in chem lab freshman year. Twice.

"Whatever," Cara said with the wave of a hand. "The point is, guys are customers, too. Tight jeans, a low-cut shirt, you're good to go."

"I am not stooping to Dell's level."

"Suit yourself," Anna replied with a shrug. "But don't come complaining to us when his profits kick your profits' ass."

"You have a decent ass. You might as well flaunt it."

"You guys are nuttier than a fruitcake." Mia pushed out of the booth.

"Where are you going?"

"To the bathroom." Mia knew the bathrooms of every establishment in New Benton like the back of her hand, having spent many a hyperventilating moment in each of their stalls. Moonrise Diner had the nicest of the lot, so if she was going to do a little hyperventilating, there were few better places.

Mia shut herself in the first stall, took a deep

breath. She had a decent body underneath the baggy clothes, but she'd never felt comfortable showcasing it. She'd made progress the past few years in confidence and not caring what other people thought, but not progress enough to use her body as some kind of selling point. Wasn't that just a few steps away from prostitution?

Mia exhaled. Took another deep breath. Dell had kicked her ass today. It didn't take a look at his books to know he'd outsold her by almost half. All because he had a nice body and a swoon-worthy smile? How was that fair?

If she wore tighter jeans, a shirt that didn't hide every last curve, well, it wasn't as if she'd look any different than most of the women her age. It wasn't using sex as a selling tool. It was another step in being more like a normal twenty-six-year-old woman.

She'd gained confidence the past few years, finding her sense of self. It would be nice if the rest would fall into place, but maybe there were still changes to make to get to *normal*.

Maybe dressing the part would even bring her closer to that actual having-sex step. Or at least a real-kiss step. A date would be nice. Having someone look at her with the interest usually reserved for Cara.

So maybe it wasn't even all about the stand. Maybe this was a natural progression on the road she'd already taken. Start...dressing the part of a confident, successful young businesswoman who was possibly interested in a little male attention.

She would do this for herself, not just to compete, but to find her rightful spot in adulthood. Bolstered, Mia stepped out of the stall, head held high.

CHAPTER FIVE

IT COULDN'T HAVE been more than thirty-five degrees this morning, but sweat poured down Dell's back as he descended the hill in a steady jog. His entire family thought his three-mile-a-day habit was nuts, but few things were as refreshing as a morning run. Especially on cold mornings when frost danced on the grass and his breath huffed out in clouds.

He approached the small cabin at the edge of his parents' property. It had been built for his grandparents before Grandpa died and Grandma'd moved into the assisted-living center in Millertown. Now it was Dell's. Paid rent on it and everything.

Dell lifted a leg onto the wooden fence, stretching forward as he watched the sunrise envelop the sky behind the hill. On top of the hill was his parents' house. Mom and Dad would be long since up. Kenzie would be snoring—loudly—in his old room.

Sometimes he missed living in the big house. Always having someone to talk to or bother. He definitely wasn't solitary by nature, so living alone wasn't exactly a luxury. In fact, some days it downright blew.

But he was going to prove to Dad he was a responsible adult. Living on his own, paying rent, running the farmers' market and CSA parts of the farm, it was all supposed to show Dad that Dell was responsible and smart enough to take over, to run this place. That he wanted it for what it was.

So far, Dell had gotten a lot of skeptical looks and a reminder that he used to blow off chores to sleep off a night of partying. Or a rehash of when he'd wrecked the brand-new baler in an attempt to show off for a bunch of his buddies. Drunk.

Seven years ago. Was there a statute of limitations on blowing off chores or drunk baler-wrecking?

In Dad's world, probably not.

Still, the old baler story was less of a problem than when Dad lectured him about being more like Charlie, getting out of farming altogether, telling him to "see the future."

Dell inhaled the cold air, let it out, tried to blow the bitterness out with it. He'd been an idiot and a jackass for many years, for no particular reason other than he lacked direction and drive. Living up to everyone thinking he wasn't much more than a pretty face had seemed a lot easier than proving them wrong, but when Dad told him he was thinking about selling to a developer, it had snapped Dell out of it.

He loved the farm. He loved this place and doing this work. Losing it wasn't an option. Going into business, moving closer to Saint Louis. None of it appealed to Dell. No matter what it took, he was going to make his father see he had changed. He was going to make Dad see this place *was* his future.

Dell took care of the little cabin, even tried to keep it clean despite his messy nature. Occasionally he paid Kenzie to help him out in that department.

It was nice to have someplace that was his, that Dad couldn't look down his nose at.

And it was always nice to have a place to bring a woman home to.

Mia's image popped into his head. Such a strange intrusion he laughed into the quiet spring morning. A pig squealed in the distance and Dell jumped off the fence.

He had about fifteen minutes until Charlie would show up complaining about the early hour, and every damn thing, loading up the vegetables. It was nice to have company while he worked, but Charlie's nonstop bitching was starting to get old and they were only into week three. Charlie was helping out to soothe Mom's worries that his corporate lifestyle was ruining his karma. An idea she'd picked up from some corny TV show.

Dell didn't give much of a crap about his brother's karma, but the help was nice. If Charlie would stop complaining all the time. He wished he knew a way to make his big brother understand, to see the value of this place, to feel what it meant. So much more than just them.

On a sigh, Dell hopped into the shower. No more brooding over his family. He had work to do today.

What would Mia have up her sleeve? He doubted his turning around her Naked Farmer moniker to help himself had left her too happy. He probably hadn't helped the situation with his "keep the change" comment.

Nope. Not happy. If Mia could shoot lasers from her pretty green eyes, he'd be deader than a doornail.

Why the thought cheered him after his depressing inner monologue earlier, he had no idea. Something about going toe-to-toe with Mia was… fun.

Whistling, Dell pulled on a pair of faded jeans, the kind loose enough at the waist to hang a little low.

He was no dummy.

He shrugged on a button-up flannel shirt, finger combed his wet hair, then grabbed his keys and wallet. Maybe if he texted Charlie to meet him at the vegetable shed, he could cut down on the amount of whining he had to listen to.

But when he stepped outside, Charlie's sleek luxury car was already parked in front of the gate.

Along with Dad's truck. The two men leaned against poles of his fence, Charlie with a to-go coffee cup in his hand, Dad with his beat-up thermos.

They looked nothing alike. Charlie had Mom's height, her darker shade of blond. He was lean and polished. Dell had inherited Dad's bigger frame, light hair, dark eyes. But it seemed in terms of personality, Charlie had combined Mom and Dad to be the favorite and Dell was just…the odd man out.

He was the one following the old man's footsteps. Charlie acted as if the old man's footsteps were caked with manure. But of course Dad seemed to look at his own footsteps that way.

Not really the best comparison, since technically manure was a way of life around here.

Dell let out a breath and steeled himself for a round of disdain. They could keep trying this make-Dell-feel-like-an-idiot thing, but it wasn't going to change his determination. "Morning."

Dad and Charlie grunted in unison.

"Still doing the market thing, then?"

Dell didn't flinch, didn't scowl. "Yup. Told you I'd be doing it all year again. CSA stuff, too."

"Can't believe people pay money to come here and pick up a bunch of vegetables. What's wrong with the grocery store?"

"People care about where their food comes from."

Dad shook his head, muttered something about

hippies. Which was hilarious. Mom had been the one to suggest he start a CSA. In her own practical way, she was the biggest hippie in New Benton. "Has he let you look at the CSA profits?" Dad said to Charlie, jerking his head toward Dell. "They're pretty dismal if you ask me, but I'd like to know your take."

This time Dell did scowl. He jammed his baseball cap on his head in the hopes it'd hide most of his expression. His brother might be a VP of sales, but he didn't know a damn thing about Dell's business. "Charlie hasn't once set eyes on my spreadsheets. He sells crap, not food."

"You should let him look. I don't like what I'm seeing. Maybe we need a second opinion."

"He's not a farmer."

Dad rolled his eyes. "More power to him."

Dell didn't know how many times they could have the same conversation. Run in the same loop. Probably over and over and over, since neither of them could understand the other's point.

"Do I have to remind you *you're* a farmer?"

"I wanted something better for my sons. Look at Charlie. He went out and made a name for himself. Didn't get tied down to this burden. You don't know what you're getting yourself into."

Charlie had the decency to look uncomfortable, but he didn't speak up. Which was how things always seemed to go. Charlie was the great doer of what Dad and Mom wanted. Dell would forever be a disappointment.

If it meant the farm, he supposed he'd just have to suck it up and accept it. "I fell in love with this burden, Dad. This place. This work. I don't want better."

"Farming isn't love." Dad shook his head. "It's hard work and dirt and hell on a body." He drained his Thermos. "Head in the clouds." He walked back to his truck, shaking his head.

How could he feel that way? How could he still work this land and feel that way? Dell didn't understand it, wasn't sure he ever would.

In silence, he and Charlie slid into Dell's truck, drove up to the vegetable shack and loaded the truck for market. When they got back in and drove off Wainwright property, Charlie made a big production of tapping his leg, fidgeting in his seat.

"Spit it out." He'd rather hear all of Charlie's complaints than watch him try to keep them in.

"Look, Dell, you're not dumb."

Dell scowled at the stoplight in front of him. "I know I'm not dumb." Of course, Charlie had read at a kindergarten level at the age of three. And solved for x in elementary school. While Dell had enjoyed remedial reading *and* math all through middle school.

But that didn't make him dumb. Not in the areas that mattered.

"So, the thing is, you could have more than

this." Charlie waved at the farmland on each side of the highway Dell merged onto. "I know you like it, maybe you're even good at it, but how much longer is small-scale farming going to be a lucrative career?"

"I don't want more than this. This isn't some compromise or slacker job. It's what I want. It's important. I don't need lucrative."

"You need to survive. And are you so certain it's not that you want it just because Dad doesn't want you to do it? Remember how you didn't have any interest in playing basketball until *I* tried out, then suddenly it was all you wanted to do? And once I quit, so did you."

Dell shifted. "It's not the same." It wasn't, but he knew he couldn't convince Charlie of that. First, because Charlie thought Charlie was always right. Second, well, he wasn't about to admit he'd just been trying to get his older brother's attention.

He'd given up on that. Charlie was always going to look down his nose at him. They were too different, and for some reason Charlie didn't see the farm the way he did. Didn't feel the history in it, the belonging to it.

Charlie didn't say anything else, just shook his head and looked out the passenger-side window.

Dell watched as farmland morphed into suburbia. Tried to imagine living here, in a house all piled on top of another house, with nothing

but streets and strip malls and perfectly mani-
cured lawns.

He didn't belong anywhere here, even less so
in the packed-together city Charlie lived in. He
belonged on that farm, where he could look out
a window and see the swell of the hill, hear his
own footsteps, dig in the land and grow something. It was his heart, and the work he did *was*
important. Someday Dell would just have to
accept he was the only one in his family who
believed it.

MIA SAT IN the driver's seat, working on not hyperventilating. Some positive self-talk, some re-
minders that, in this space, people looked at her
as a professional, knowledgeable businesswoman,
not Mia, Queen of the Geeks, whose verbal diarrhea always meant saying the wrong thing at the
wrong time.

"Mia, get out of the car."

"I will." She nodded. Her feet ignored her.

Cara slammed her door shut. A few seconds
later she jerked open the driver's-side door. "Get
out, young lady."

"I'm older than you."

"Mia."

"Just give me a second."

"Mia, look at me."

Reluctantly, Mia met her sister's fierce stare.

"Do you think you're ugly?"

Mia frowned. "Well, no." She wasn't a bomb-shell, but she certainly wasn't ugly. Decent hair-cut, no more acne, body in good shape. She wasn't ugly. Didn't mean she was comfortable being seen as anything other than background noise. She'd worked so hard at being background noise since coming home from Truman four years ago. Worked on quietly doing what she needed to do, not babbling, not embarrassing herself.

This step seemed to scream, "Look at me," and as much as she wouldn't mind some male atten-tion, she wasn't ready for the screaming insecu-rity that went with it. If she was ready for that, she'd probably have had a date by now.

"Then, suck it up, sister. You're cute. No one's going to look twice at you except people who know you and wonder how you hid that body for so long. You look like a normal twenty-six-year-old woman. Of course, if a guy comes over to buy something, I'd make sure to bend over."

"Cara—"

"Just be you. Forget what you look like or what people think. That's how you've gotten this far, isn't it? You learned to stop worrying what peo-ple thought?"

That was true. Not an easy lesson to learn, or even one she'd mastered, but Cara was right. Who cared what people thought? She was wearing tight jeans and a T-shirt, for heaven's sake. Not a G-string and some tassels.

She certainly wasn't stripping, unlike *some* people.

Mia sneaked a glance over her shoulder at Dell. He hadn't taken off his shirt yet, but it was unbuttoned all the way. Moron.

With a deep breath, Mia hopped out of the truck, earning her a back pat from Cara. "Thanks."

"Anytime."

Squaring her shoulders, Mia focused on setting up the booth, including their newest tactic: free coloring pages and crayon packets for kids. Next week Anna was going to do face painting. If Dell was going to go the man-ogling route, she would go the family route.

Pants that fit and a low-cut T-shirt just meant looking less like the crazy, isolated farmer she was. It had nothing to do with sex appeal.

Of course, if a single guy was interested…

Mia shook her head. Idiot fantasies had never gotten her anywhere. Certainly not laid. She might *look* a little more alluring than she once had, but all her work at invisibility had certainly kept any interested parties away.

Well, maybe with her new look she'd work on that next.

This morning, though, she was concentrating on selling the pants off Dell Wainwright.

Not literally or anything. But, well, now that she thought of it…

Nope. Not going there.

Mia smiled brightly at a couple and their twin toddlers. "Good morning. Welcome to Pruitt Farms' stand. Do you see anything you like?"

She chatted with the mother about what kind of fertilizers they used and if they were certified organic. In the end, the twins each took a coloring sheet and crayons, and Mia sold one of everything.

She also made sure to tell them about the face painting next weekend, and they promised to return.

Take that, Magic Mike.

"Dell keeps looking at you," Cara stage whispered in her ear as Mia filled a bag with greens.

Mia refused to look over her shoulder. "So?"

"So? I don't mean he's looking at you like, oh, he happened to look over here. I mean, he's jaw-dropped looking at you. Like, 'damn, that girl is fine' looking at you."

She waved Cara off, placed the new bag onto the table. As another family passed their booth, she greeted, chatted and focused on her job. Once they were gone, she couldn't take the curiosity any longer.

She lifted her eyes over the aisle to Dell's table. There he was in all his shirtless glory, flirting with an older lady. Totally not looking at her.

Except when he handed the woman a bag of broccoli, his gaze met hers across the aisle. Something in her stomach flipped uncomfortably, and a warm sensation zinged down to her toes. Mia quickly looked down at her table, all too aware she was probably beet red from her shoulders to the roots of her hair.

From that point on, she promised herself not to look at Dell, and not to replay that weird moment his eyes had locked on hers and she'd felt *something*. Just from a look.

Nope. Not thinking about it.

She made it through the rest of the morning, pleased to see they'd sold more than last week. Some of that might have had to do with more people coming as the season went on, and that it wasn't raining today as it had been last week, but still, progress was progress.

"Uh-oh, here comes trouble," Cara said under her breath.

Mia looked up as Dell sauntered to their table.

She focused on packing up the leftovers. When he leaned his arms on her table and ducked under the awning, she was only momentarily mesmerized by the fine blond hair on his tanned, muscular forearms.

So not fair.

"That's quite a getup," he said, none too pleasantly.

She would not blush. She would not blush. She

would not blush. She stood to her full height, chin up to add a few centimeters. Fisting her hands on her hips, she managed her best intimidating glare, even if her cheeks were probably pink as she looked down at his hunched-over frame. "What getup?"

He stood, motioned a hand up and down her front. "That."

"What?"

He did the motion again. *"That."*

Mia cocked her head, folded her arms under her breasts. When Dell looked at the sky, she nearly giggled. "I never pegged you for the modest type. What with the stripping and all."

He scowled down at her, and it took a little extra effort to suck in a breath.

"I do not strip," he said through gritted teeth. He leaned closer and, by God, her heart nearly leaped out of her chest. But she stood her ground. Standing her ground felt really good.

"I see what you're trying to do here."

"And what's that?" Her voice wasn't even breathless. Go, her.

He held up his hand to do the gesture again, but stopped midway. His baffled look turned steely and grave. "I've got too much to lose to let you beat me. A nice ass and breasts aren't going to suddenly win you a bunch of customers. If you haven't noticed, most of the market's customers are families and women, not single guys looking for a hot girl to hit on."

Oh, she was so not flattered that he'd said she had a nice ass and breasts. Or insinuated she was the hot girl. She was not at all pleased he'd noticed. In fact, it was totally demeaning.

She'd work on her outrage later.

"Yeah, families, Dell." Mia pointed to the sign Anna had made her. Pruitt Farms, Family-Friendly Fruits and Veggies from Our Land to Your Table. "And I'm guessing a *family* with wife, husband and kids are going to come over to our booth with people fully clothed and kid-friendly activities. Free kid-friendly activities, at that."

Dell's jaw set tighter. "So what's with ditching the baggy clothes if you're so *family* oriented?"

Mia worked up her best dismissive smile. "Maybe I'm trolling for dates. Maybe I wanted to look different for fun. Maybe it's a business tactic. Maybe it's not. All you need to know is it's none of your business."

He took a deep breath, nostrils flaring with the effort. "You won't win, Mia." He shook his head and walked away.

Mia grinned. His words were a lie. He kept coming up to *her* demanding to know what was going on. He kept getting irritated by *her* tactics.

She was absolutely winning, and it felt awesome.

CHAPTER SIX

"Do you know how many calories are in one small square?"

"Moooom," Cara groaned. "Don't ruin this for everyone."

"Well, it's never too early to start being careful about your health," Mom said primly, taking a sip of her milk. Skim milk. "There are ways to make desserts healthier."

"It's Grandma's recipe!"

"Remember when Grandpa said they used to feed skim milk to the pigs when he was growing up?" Anna said with a grin, causing Mom to roll her eyes and huff out an annoyed breath.

"Yes, we did," Dad said, taking a defiant bite of brownie. Dessert was about the only thing he ever got defiant over.

Mia picked at the brownies Cara had brought over. Like everything Cara made, they were delicious, but ever since the market this morning she'd felt...weird.

Buoyed, yes. But, and she hated this *but*, Dell saying she was hot kept playing itself over and over in her mind, and her stomach felt all jittery and nervous and not at all interested in food.

She did not want to care that Dell said she had nice…assets. Why would she care? Why would that *please* her? It shouldn't. It was all very unstrong, unfeminist, unbusinesswoman of her.

But she was pleased. She couldn't help it. A guy thought she was hot. That had never happened before. At least not that she knew of. The fact it was Dell?

You are an idiot.

"Earth to Mia."

Jostled out of her annoying, embarrassing thoughts, Mia looked up at Cara.

"Ready to go?" She nodded toward the door, the international Cara symbol for "get me away from Mom before I lose it."

"Yup." Separation was definitely best when Cara got that squirrelly look about her. Mia didn't feel like playing peacemaker tonight. She wasn't sure *what* she felt like doing, but it wasn't that.

They got up from the table, offering Anna hugs and Dad goodbyes while Mom followed, the typical anxiety waving off her.

"Why don't you girls stay the night?" Mom engulfed Mia in a cinnamon-scented hug. She lowered her voice. "Sweetie, next time maybe you should wear one of those—what are they called?—camisole things under that shirt. It's a little low cut. You wouldn't want people to get the wrong idea."

"Maybe that's exactly what she wants," Cara whispered, earning herself a jab in the side.

"What, dear?"

"Nothing." Mia pushed Cara toward the door. "Ignore her. Do you want us to take the leftover brownies?"

"Oh, yes. Your father will inhale them before the night's over if you don't. Maybe next time you try my trick of making them with applesauce? Adding a little zucchini? It cuts back on the fat and—"

"It's Grandma's rec—"

Mia discreetly moved in between Mom and Cara. "Yes, Mom. Applesauce. Will do."

"Oh, I hate you two girls living on your own." Their mother wrung her hands, fretting next to the door as Mia and Cara shrugged on their coats. For two years Mia and Cara had shared an apartment. Still, every time they left the Pruitt farmhouse, Mom worried over the two young women living alone.

Cara rolled her eyes and groaned. "We're only ten minutes away, Mom. Two years, and a serial killer hasn't gotten us yet."

Mia pushed Cara again. "You're not helping."

Mom clucked her tongue. "Stay the night. Silly to drive all the way home when it's dark out."

"We're only ten minutes away," Mia repeated gently.

Mom took a deep breath and let it out, offering a pained smile. "All right. All right. We'll see you in the morning." Cara and Mia waved as they stepped out the door.

"Don't forget to get one of those camisoles, Mia!" Mom called after them. "And make sure to lock both locks on your door. Oh, and lock your car doors, even when you're driving."

Cara groaned into the evening quiet. "Seriously, how did we turn out normal? How did they even manage to produce three children? Never mind—I don't want to know the answer to that."

Mia climbed into the driver's seat of her truck. Cara and Anna were on that normal spectrum, but she wasn't always sure she was. How long had Mom's outer monologue been Mia's inner dialogue? She'd learned to manage the anxiety, push away the worry about what other people might think or do, but it wasn't as if the voice had disappeared.

Cara turned in her seat, smiling weirdly as Mia pulled out onto the highway.

"Okay, so hear me out before you totally shoot me down, 'kay?" Cara practically bounced in her seat.

"Oh, God."

"It's Saturday night. We rocked it at the market today. You look like someone I wouldn't be embarrassed to be seen with. I don't have to work at the salon tomorrow." Cara clutched Mia's arm. "Let's go to a bar."

Mia laughed, shaking off Cara's grip so she could have both hands on the steering wheel. "Right."

"I'm serious! It'll be fun. A few drinks. We find a few cute guys to chat up. Maybe you give a guy your number."

Mia's shoulders involuntarily hunched before she told herself to relax them. She was twenty-six, for heaven's sake. This was what she *should* be doing on a Saturday night. Not sitting at home with her seed catalogs. Maybe this was the *something different* she was wanting.

Still, the idea left her vaguely nauseous.

"We'll have fun! I promise! We can leave whenever you want. Please, please, please, please—"

"All right!"

Cara's squeal was ear piercing. "Let's go to Juniors. Way hotter guys there."

"Super." Mia tried to talk herself into some enthusiasm. She wasn't going to meet a guy holed up in her apartment, and she probably wasn't going to meet a guy working at the farm or even at the farmers' market. If she wanted to drop the virginity, she was going to have to put herself out there.

If she could control her blushing, quiet the anxiety, keep her mouth under control, there was no reason this couldn't be a fun evening.

And Cara wondered why she wasn't more pro-active in the dating scene.

Mia pulled into the crowded lot of Juniors. New Benton boasted only two bars, and Mia had never spent time at either, unless occasionally picking up a drunk Cara counted. Still, the whole town knew Juniors was where the young people went and The Shack was the old, townie bar.

Cara rummaged around in her purse as Mia parked in the back. She flipped down the visor mirror and began applying mascara, holding out a tube of something in her free hand. "Here."

"Oh, I—"

"Just put on some lipstick. Oh, and some mas-cara." Cara finished with the mascara, shoved both tubes of makeup at Mia. "Cara tip number one. Make sure to always wear lipstick. It makes a guy notice your mouth." Cara waggled her eye-brows.

Oh, this was so not a good idea. She did not belong here. Of course, there hadn't been any places she'd belonged growing up, outside the farm. Slowly, she was changing that. So maybe she needed to suck it up and try something dif-ferent. Sometimes jumping into the deep end was the only way to learn.

Mia took a deep breath and flipped down her own visor mirror. In the truck's pale dome light, she applied the lipstick and the mascara. She didn't wear makeup often, but Cara had given her enough lessons that she didn't look like a clown.

Hopefully.

"Ready?" Cara already had her door open. This really was her element.

She managed a weak smile. "Just give me a sec."

"Oh, God, not the Stuart Smalley routine."

"Just a second."

Cara shook her head in disgust as she hopped out of the truck and slammed the door. Mia looked at her expression in the mirror. Stupid or not, a little positive self-talk always helped calm her nerves and bolster her confidence.

"I can do this," she said to her reflection. "I am a confident, capable adult. Talking to a guy will not kill me. In fact, it'll probably be fun." It was time. Past time to fight anxiety and really go after this. Did she want to be alone forever without even kissing a guy? No. So she needed to make this work.

With one final "I can do this," Mia hopped out of the truck and met Cara at the door to the bar. "Okay, I'm ready."

"Because, gosh, darn it, people like you."

"Shut up and move."

Cara led her into the crowded bar. A few people greeted Cara and she waved. Even though Mia recognized a lot of the faces, no one called out to her. Her social circle was slim. Oh, sure, she talked to a few of the ladies at the market, had something passing as a friendship with some of the women there her age, but mostly her tried-and-true friends and confidants had the last name Pruitt. And did *not* hang out at Juniors.

Cara found a little table in a back corner. "You sit. I'll go order us some drinks."

"Just get me a soda."

Cara shook her head. "Yeah, right. An alcoholic beverage is exactly what you need."

Mia sat and looked around the room while Cara went up to the bar to order their drinks. People talked and chatted and yelled and laughed. In the corner, she felt somewhat separate from it all. Nobody looked at her. It was as if she wasn't even there.

Depressing thought. Funny how she'd spent so many years wishing to be invisible but always somehow ended up the butt of the joke, then finally getting the invisibility thing down and now she was wishing for attention.

Cara sauntered back over, two guys following her. Mia recognized one as C. J. Pinkerton, who'd been in her class. The other guy looked familiar, but she didn't remember his name. He unabashedly stared at Cara's ass as he walked behind her.

C.J., though, smiled and took a seat next to her. Mia froze a little. He was smiling at *her*. "Hey, I'm C.J."

Mia smiled, biting her tongue in time so she

didn't say something stupid like, *Duh, we went to high school together.* "Mia."

He squinted, leaning in closer. "No shit. Mia Pruitt." He didn't say the rest of it, but she knew what he was thinking. *Queen of the Geeks.* "You look a lot different than you did in high school, huh?" Then he smiled, pretty and white, a little crooked. He was definitely cute, if a little skinny.

"I guess I do." Mia took a sip of the drink Cara had put in front of her. She gave herself a mental high five. She sounded like a normal human being.

C.J. laughed. She'd made a guy laugh. Holy moly. For the next twenty minutes she managed to hold an entire conversation with a kind-of-cute guy without once hyperventilating. She might have blushed a few times, but maybe he didn't notice in the dim light of the bar.

She talked about the farm. He talked about working at the Ford plant in Millertown. It was going well. Hell, it was going *perfectly.* He even scooted his chair closer to hers.

"Want to dance?"

Hopefully the involuntary squeak she made was inaudible over the hum of the crowd and music. Who knew a little lipstick and some cleavage could make such a difference? Mia smiled, hoped her laugh didn't sound like some kind of nervous hyena. What if—? Nope. No *what-ifs.* "Give me a sec to run to the bathroom?"

C.J. leaned back in his seat and smiled. "Sure."

Mia stood, walked calmly to the bathroom. Where she would normally go into the stall and hyperventilate, she walked over to a sink instead. She washed her hands slowly, deliberately. Deep breath in. Deep breath out. She could totally do this. If she ever hoped of getting even remotely close to having sex, she *had* to do this.

Her stomach pitched, but she wasn't going to let that thought derail her. This wasn't about sex. This was about a dance. One dance. A step. Just like all the other steps she'd made to get here.

She looked at herself in the mirror. She looked put together and cute, and no one had to know all the anxiety in her mind if she didn't show it to them.

With a determined nod, Mia pushed out of the bathroom. Shaking her hair back, she put a little bounce in her step and walked back to the table. She faltered for a second when she realized C.J. was no longer at their table. Two new men had joined Cara.

Never should have given him a chance to realize what a colossal mistake he'd made by asking her to dance or the time to remember all her embarrassing moments. Well, that was fine. Mia swallowed down the hard dip of disappointment. Two new guys were sitting with Cara. From the back, they were pretty cute.

If step one had been talking to a guy without

acting like a goof, then doing it again didn't need to be a deal or a problem.

Mia stopped in her tracks when the first man's profile came into view. It wasn't *some* cute guy in her seat. It was Dell.

He lounged in the chair as if he owned it, the lip of a Budweiser bottle perched at his mouth. He must have seen her out of the corner of his eye because he turned and grinned.

"Well, well, well, this is a surprise," he drawled, setting the bottle back down on the table. He made no effort to move, instead hooked his arm over the back of the chair. "Come here often?" he asked with a wink.

Mia clenched her hands into fists. She wasn't sure whom she wanted to kill more. Cara, C.J. or Dell.

THE EXPRESSION ON Mia's face was enough to keep Dell from being uncomfortable with her appearance. It was the "if I could shoot lasers you'd be dead" look, and it amused him to no end.

Although, now that he noticed, he was about eye level with her breasts while she stood in front of him, and that took care of amusement. Dell cleared his throat, took another swig of beer. "Gonna join us?"

She mumbled something incomprehensible. With Kevin sidled up to Cara, Mia had no choice but to take the chair next to Dell.

She wasn't at all happy about that, and she made no bones about showing it.

"Buy you a drink?"

"I have a drink."

Dell raised an eyebrow at the fruity mixed drink and its floating cherry. "Want me to buy you a real drink?"

She smirked. "No." As if to prove a point, she took a dainty sip. She looked all around the bar, pretty much everywhere but at him.

Dell took another sip from his bottle, his eyes never leaving her. "C.J. said to let you know he was sorry, but he had to go." Not that Dell had realized he'd been talking about Mia. Not that C.J. had said it to him. His "let her know I had to go" had been said to Cara.

Her being Mia. Something about that made him clench his hand even harder on his bottle of beer.

Mia frowned. "Why'd he tell you that?"

Dell shrugged. Better not to say anything at all than lie or admit that C.J. hadn't told *him* at all.

She leaned forward, and Dell's gaze was drawn to the V in her T-shirt. He'd seen women show off a lot more cleavage than that before, but because he'd pretty much never seen Mia's cleavage, it was a little difficult to be a gentleman and return his gaze to her face.

She was blushing when he did. And scowling. "Why are you here?"

Dell nodded over to Kevin, who already had

Cara practically in his lap. "Kev asked me to meet him at Juniors. So I did."

"I mean, why are you at my table?"

"Kev was talking to Cara, so I came over. Then your boyfriend got a little peeved at that since he and I never have seen eye to eye on just about anything." Because C. J. Pinkerton was a grade-A asshole. Dell couldn't believe Mia would see anything in the guy. Surely she had better taste than that. "And since he's a big old coward, he moseyed on out of here."

"He's not my boyfriend." Mia looked down at her drink, and Dell was certainly not thrilled to hear it. What did he care? "And don't say *mosey*. This is Missouri, not Texas." She tacked on a "moron" under her breath.

He'd been enjoying her bluster before she tacked on the *moron*. He'd never much cared for being called that. Silence settled over them, and Dell tried to pretend she wasn't there, but it was just so weird seeing Mia look…well, hot. It kind of irritated him. God knew why. "So this new look isn't just for the market?"

She scowled at him, more death lasers shooting from her eyes. "It's a new leaf. Haven't you ever wanted to turn over a new leaf?"

Dell sipped his beer. Yeah, he knew that feeling pretty well. Only, didn't matter how many leaves he turned, the old one still stuck in his family's mind. "In a town like this, people see who you've always been."

She toyed with the napkin under her glass, eyebrows together. "I don't care what people see. It matters what I feel."

Well, that was a nice attitude to have. He wished he could duplicate it. Wished what Dad thought or did didn't matter, but when the guy telling you you're irresponsible held the deed to everything you wanted, how could you not care? Even more so when he was blood related. Dell took a deep drink. He didn't come to Juniors for philosophizing or talking to Mia Pruitt. He came for good company, pretty girls and a few laughs. To take his mind *off* all this crap.

Dell frowned. When had Mia become a pretty girl? He shook his head. This was all backward. He looked at Kevin, who practically had his tongue down Cara's throat. Why had Kevin called him at all if he was just going to try to get in Cara Pruitt's pants?

Dell would make his excuses and leave. He opened his mouth to do just that, but then realized he'd be ditching Mia with the make-out kids, and that didn't seem very fair. Especially considering how uncomfortable she looked. Besides, they might not get along, but they could always talk about farm stuff. Not exactly the best Saturday night, but he enjoyed it and Mia knew what she was talking about.

"You guys got any cold frames out at your place?"

She gave him a puzzled look, rubbed her tongue back and forth across her bottom lip.

Oh, Jesus, noticing her tongue was worse than noticing her breasts. Breasts could be innocuous if you tried hard enough to make them so. You could pretend they weren't there. You could pretend you didn't have any interest in finding out what they looked like. A tongue licking lips… yeah, not so much. It was…there.

Dell cleared his throat, started yammering on about the cold frame he'd built last year. She finally stopped doing the tongue thing and he breathed a sigh of relief as they spent the next fifteen minutes talking about farming.

Damn, she knew her stuff, and she seemed just as into it as he was. Anyone who listened to their conversation would think it nuts two twentysomethings were sitting around talking about fertilizer over a few drinks, but hell, he was actually kind of enjoying himself.

"So how did it start?" she asked, narrowing her eyes at him.

"How did what start?"

"The stupid take-off-your-shirt thing. You obviously care about your farm, so what gives? It makes you seem like you don't take it seriously."

"I take it plenty seriously." Oddly enough, it wasn't as insulting as when Charlie dinged him for it. When she said *seem like* it was almost as if she was willing to believe he *did* take it seriously. "Last year I was talking to some lady about how hot it was and she laughed and told me to take off my shirt. Said I'd probably sell a few more tomatoes that way. So I took her advice." Dell grinned. "She was right."

"You know it's totally demeaning, right?"

"Hey, you seem to be using my tactics." He pointed at the V of her shirt.

"I am fully clothed!"

Outraged was a good look for her. Her cheeks got a little pink and her full lips made a sexy little O.

For chrissake, *Sexy* and *Mia* did not belong in the same sentence, even if she was.

"Keep telling yourself that, darlin'." Dell touched her hand. Just the lightest brush of fingertip to wrist. She jerked it back so quickly her drink shook and barely avoided toppling over.

He'd blame it on the beer, except he'd had all of one. Maybe he'd just blame it on her antagonistic attitude. He had always liked to bother people. Good-naturedly, of course. Besides, if he flirted a little over the top, maybe he'd get her scurrying off and then he could stop feeling conflicted about being attracted to her. About enjoying the weird push and pull they gave each other.

She popped up out of her seat. "I have to go to the bathroom." Her entire face was beet red as she turned to walk past his chair.

Dell chuckled. "Same old Mia." The outside appearance might change, but deep down she was still awkward and geeky. Thank God.

She whirled around. "Wanna dance?"

He choked on his drink, sputtered and coughed as it burned down the wrong pipe. "What?" he croaked.

She smiled sweetly. Way too sweetly. "I said, wanna dance?"

Sweet baby Jesus, what on earth was Mia Pruitt up to?

CHAPTER SEVEN

MIA WAS PRETTY sure making Dell sputter over his beer meant she was winning at life. Same old Mia, her ass.

Then he grinned and unfurled from his seat like some kind of seedling in fast-forward time. Now he was this big, tall thing standing in front of her instead of safely seated with the table between them.

"Sure thing, sweetheart."

Damn it. Talk about backfire. Not only could she not dance, but she'd never danced with a guy before. Now she was going to dance with Dell in a bar blaring poppy country music?

What bizarro world had she tumbled into? He was supposed to say no and disappear, not tower over her with that smug smile on his face. Not put his hand on the small of her back and guide her to the dance floor on the opposite side of the bar.

Dell's hand was on the small of her back. Dell's very big, very warm hand. Dell Wainwright. If her mind repeated the information enough times maybe she'd process it enough to react appropriately, or at least stop the squealing in her mind.

What was she supposed to do? Where was she supposed to put her hands? Where *he* going to put *his* hands?

Dell stopped her on the dance floor, and before any more questions could circle in her brain, paralyzing all rational thought or function, Dell grabbed her hand and twirled her around.

On a breathless laugh, she ended up too close to the faded red cotton of his T-shirt, but he put his hand on her hip and guided her enough to the medium-tempo beat that she surprisingly didn't feel like an idiot.

He laughed with her, eyes meeting hers briefly. A weird humming second of—what? Attraction? Awareness? Mia frowned at their feet. This was a bad idea.

He cleared his throat. "So what prompted this new leaf?"

Mia shrugged, trying to ignore the reaction of her body to his fingertips on the curve of her hip. As if every one of her muscles was contracting, trying to stop time and soak up this moment. Sure, it was weird it was Dell, but a cute guy was dancing with her in a bar. She wanted to soak up that experience and remember it. The chances of it repeating were slim. "Well, lots of things, I guess."

"Name one."

She glared up at him. "No." Her...things were none of his business, and she didn't want him thinking he could boss her around. He was not her friend. He was more like her enemy. Why would she pour out her weaknesses to him?

He chuckled. "Prickly suits you, Mia."

She didn't know how to respond. Dell was about the only one who brought out the prickly. Usually being mean or snarky made her felt guilty, and every once in a while that cropped up, but mainly he deserved it. The only other person who goaded her was Cara. Mia peeked over her shoulder to see Cara still cozied up to Kevin.

"Don't know why he bothered to invite me if he was going to spend the whole night chatting up your sister."

"You're telling me. Coming here wasn't exactly my idea."

Dell laughed. "And here I had you pegged as a Juniors regular." When she glared at him, he only laughed harder.

"I imagine you've spent plenty of time here."

"Surely you can imagine me doing more interesting things than that." His grin was so pretty and wide, if she wasn't so embarrassed by what she *could* imagine, she might have smiled back.

Dell passed a glance over Kevin and Cara again. "Eh, probably for the best he's occupied. Shouldn't stay out too late anyway."

"Got a curfew?" Mia fake smiled up at him, mentally patting herself on the back for the flippant tone.

This time when he laughed it was completely void of humor. "No, just a business I have to go above and beyond proving I can run if I ever want it."

The information was so strange, Mia forgot all about the awkwardness of having one hand in Dell's and her other hand very, very lightly on his hip. "Your dad's not giving you the farm?"

"I'm working on it." His jaw set, twitched. Obviously a sore subject. How...weird. "Your dad giving the farm to you?"

Mia nodded. "Anna can take over the dairy part if she wants, but I started buying five percent of the cropland last year from my market profits. As long as everything goes according to plan, I'll own my share of the farm outright in twenty and Dad can retire."

"Must be nice." Dell stared at some point beyond her.

Well, who knew? The Naked Farmer wasn't quite as frivolous as she'd made him out to be. She'd always figured Dell the type to take over his dad's farm because he didn't want to work at anything else, but farming was hard. Generally not something you did only because you fell into it. If he was fighting to convince his dad he could take over, maybe he had a bit more at stake with the farmers' market stuff than she'd given him credit for.

Not that it mattered. The shirtless routine was

stupid, and she certainly wasn't going to let her guard down just because he had a few daddy issues or made her insides feel like melted Jell-O. Those were wholly secondary to beating him at the market.

"You know, I don't think I've ever met your dad. How is that possible in New Benton?" He smiled down at her, but the way his lips curved was tight and uncomfortable, as if it was a very forced smile. A forced conversation.

Well, darn it. Dell wasn't supposed to have hidden depths or be nice enough to force conversation. Mia looked at the faded logo on his chest. "Probably because he's a hermit."

Dell laughed, and she absolutely got no secret thrill from that. "No, seriously, outside of my family there are only three people he talks to. The priest at Saint Mary's, Rick at Orscheln and the guy who buys our milk."

The song ended, but Dell didn't let go of her hand. Mia's stomach did a weird flipping drop when he squeezed it instead.

"Wanna keep going until those two stop going at it?"

He gestured to Cara and Kevin making out in the dark corner. Mia grimaced. "Yeah. Sure."

"You know, you're pretty good at letting the guy lead in a dance. I thought you'd be trying to boss me around. It's a little shocking. You're not half-bad."

Mia smirked. "Coming from the guy who coined 'Mia, Queen of the Geeks,' that's quite a compliment."

His head snapped back. "I didn't make that up."

"Well, you're the first person I remember calling me it to my face," Mia returned. When his face fell into surprise and discomfort, and then guilt, Mia shifted uncomfortably in his grip. "I remember it quite clearly. Nothing like the homecoming king and queen laughing at you in the cafeteria when you're a lowly sophomore."

"Hey, listen, I'm sorry." When he moved to the music this time, the distance between them shrunk. He lowered his mouth closer to her ear, and Mia had to focus on the high school memory to keep her heart from escaping her chest and galloping out the door.

He made her stomach tie in knots, but it wasn't the kind she was used to. These weren't so much painful as they were…uncomfortable. Laced with a jittery excitement, a bizarre impulse to lean closer.

Oh, no, she could *not* do that. "Long time ago," she managed to croak. She moved to get a fraction of the distance between their bodies back. "Might have hurt my feelings at the time, but I got over it." Eventually. There were really only a few people she still harbored any bitterness toward, and Dell wasn't one of them. He'd been careless, but never malicious.

"Well, I'm still sorry. I wasn't big on thinking much beyond my own feelings at the time. Overhearing that nickname would be bad enough. Imagine it's worse having someone say it to your face."

Mia shrugged, more to hide the shiver as his breath danced along her neck. "High school. Most of us weren't thinking. I'm not worried about it. I *was* a geek. Either trying too hard to fit in or too hard to be invisible. Neither ever worked. In a town this size, you don't get to disappear." Why was she talking about this? Oh, yeah, because she never could shut her yap when she was uncomfortable.

When Dell didn't say anything, Mia bit her lip to keep the words from pouring out. She made it about five seconds before she couldn't stand it. "I'm pretty sure there's a statute of limitations on name-calling in high school. It ended a few years ago. Forget it."

Since she couldn't bring herself to look into his eyes, considering her face was probably red from the roots of her hair to the V of her shirt, she watched the underside of his stubbled chin move back and forth.

For the briefest flash she wondered what it might feel like, the whiskers against her palm. Against her face. *But, oh, my God, so not the time.* So not okay. This was *Dell.* Not some random guy.

"I'm not sure there's a statute of limitations on anything," he said grimly. "Mia, that was a really shitty thing for me to do. I know it probably doesn't make much difference now, but I am truly sorry."

"It doesn't matter." It didn't. She wanted to forget about it. Forget about him and him suddenly being all nice and repentant, and, no, she didn't want any of this. She *wanted* to hate him. He was making it impossible.

His mouth turned grim. "Right. Because you don't like me anyway. I'm just the dumb guy taking off his shirt. You can say it. Heard it plenty."

"I don't not like you and I don't think you're dumb." Mia squeezed her eyes shut. What a stupid thing to say. To admit. He was the enemy. Stealing her customers. Mia shook her head. How did she get to be on a dance floor in a bar dancing with the guy she was trying to beat in sales? Could *she* possibly get any dumber?

Just as Kenzie had accused her of, and Dad and Anna and Cara had backed up. She was a softie. Any sob story had her sobbing right along with the teller, sympathizing.

But this was Dell. Her enemy. Her only enemy. She didn't need to feel guilty or assuage his guilt, either. "Look, I wish you'd keep your shirt on and stop stealing my female customers, but I don't not like you." Yeah, that helped. Why didn't she just say, "I don't not like you" fifty more times so he really got the message? Why didn't she just lean right up against him and *really* show him?

The tap on Mia's shoulder almost made her jump, it was so startling. Cara was grinning, practically intertwined like a pretzel with Kevin.

"Hey, Kevin's going to give me a ride home."

"Oh, uh, okay."

"Keep an eye on her for me, Dell," Cara said with a wink.

"Catch you another time, man." Kevin offered Dell a goofy grin as Cara pulled him toward the door.

Mia looked back at Dell, realized her hand was still in his. He considered her for a second before speaking. "You, uh, need a ride home? Or I could buy you another drink."

Mia reminded herself it was pity or guilt over high school or eight million other reasons beyond Dell Wainwright wanting to spend a few extra minutes with her. It was none of the reasons she wanted to spend more time with him, and she could really not afford to want to spend more time with him. "No. No, I have my truck. You should head home. All that stuff to prove, remember?"

He grinned. "Right." Finally, *finally*, he released her hand, and she made sure to put more space between them.

"Bye," she offered lamely.

"See you Saturday, Mia."

She nodded, turned and tried not to scurry out

of the bar like a frightened animal. She looked back briefly to see Dell watching her go. Swallowing down the weird suspicion that he'd been checking out her ass, Mia let herself break into a jog once she got to the dark parking lot.

This was the absolute last time she ever let Cara talk her into anything.

CHAPTER EIGHT

"You can march right back out of here, because I do not forgive you."

Dell stared at Kenzie, curled up on his old bed, a laptop on her lap. What had once been sparse and filled with camo and John Deere decor was now all pink and sparkles and *girl*.

Even Kenzie's computer was pink.

She was, and always had been, a bit of a foreign object to him, but he hated when she was mad at him. Usually because she made him pay, but also because on more than one occasion she was his partner in crime.

Also, he thought his reaction to catching his baby sister making out in the barn with some *guy* was pretty tame. What he'd really like to have done was tie Jacob Masterson to a tree and shoot him with a BB gun.

"You know I'm looking out for you, right?"

"I can handle myself, thank you very much. Please don't act all pious as if you weren't doing way worse at my age. Charlie can give me that lecture. Not you."

"What do you think is 'way worse'—nope,

never mind. Don't answer that. You should be focusing on getting into a good school." *Not some idiot with a penis.*

Kenzie snorted. "Did you and Charlie swap bodies?"

"No, I—"

"Have never lectured me before. Do not start. I will not be held responsible for what I do to you." She slid off the bed, all grace and condescension. "The men in this family need to realize the women do not need to be told what to do. Being far superior to the three of you lunkheads arguing all the time. All because you can't just accept that people are different."

He hadn't ever lectured her before. Usually they were too busy pulling pranks on Charlie or the like. But he was starting to see what his wayward youth had created, and he wanted to make sure she didn't follow in his crap footsteps.

She shouldn't have to fight to do what she loved, and he trusted no man when it came to his baby sister.

As for being one of the three lunkheads who couldn't accept they were different… "I'd like to accept it. Surely you know that."

Some of her flip teenage know-it-allness slipped. "Okay, you're the least lunkheadiest."

"Thanks."

Charlie appeared in the doorway, clearing

his throat. "Mom told me to come get you two. Dinner is ready."

Kenzie shared a look with Dell. "Poor perfect Charlie. What a chore."

Charlie's eyebrows drew together. "What's that supposed to mean?"

"Nothing," Kenzie said in a singsongy voice, waltzing past him and down the stairs.

Charlie frowned after her, then turned his frown to Dell. "Aren't you two a little old to be ganging up on me?"

"Ganging up on you? How could we gang up on the infallible?" Before Charlie could speak, Dell pressed on. "Give her a lecture on guys, would you? She's not listening to me, but since you're the paragon of virtue, she says she'll listen to you."

"I doubt it."

"Well, so do I. It's worth a shot. They were not just kissing in that damn barn."

Charlie grimaced. "She's a smart girl."

"She is, but Jacob is a dipshit and Rylie got knocked up. I don't want her to be next. Not that she'd listen to me tell her that."

"It is a bit of a miracle you don't have any accidental progeny wandering around."

"Is it any wonder Kenzie and I gang up on you when you say such sweet things to us?"

"I'm pretty sure you started it."

"Now who sounds like a kid?"

Charlie let out an exasperated sigh. "I didn't

come up here to bicker with you." He scratched a hand through his perfectly styled hair. "I just wanted to warn you that Dad is going to bring up the developer stuff."

Dell swore.

"I know you don't agree with it and I know you want to argue with him, and I even get why. But it's a family dinner, and maybe you could let it go. This once."

"Let it go?"

"Yes. I'm not saying you have to agree, just don't argue. Mom asked—"

"Maybe Mom should do her own asking. You don't have to always be stepping in for them, Charlie. Last time I checked they could fight their own battles. And you're over thirty. You could stop acting as though their opinion on everything matters."

"And you are getting rather close to thirty to still be acting like a child."

They faced off for a few minutes, and it wasn't the kind of face-off he enjoyed, as with Mia. No, this was all tension and bad feelings, and he wondered if anything would ever change. Or would it keep getting worse? Until there was nothing left.

"I don't want to argue. I don't enjoy this. But I love it too much to let it go. To sit down and be the dutiful son. It isn't what I want, Charlie. I am not you."

"Because that is truly the worst thing you could ever be?"

"No. Because it *isn't* me. It doesn't make you wrong or bad. It only means I can't be something I'm not. I can't pretend. And I won't pretend this place doesn't mean everything to me."

"More than your family?"

"Maybe a piece of land can't call you worthless, ever think of that?"

"I never—"

But Dell wasn't interested in hearing what Charlie never said. Maybe he'd never said *worthless*, but they did their level best to make Dell feel it. So Dell went downstairs and sat at the dinner table with a smile plastered on his face, and every time Dad hinted around about *developing*, Dell shoved a bite of mashed potatoes in his mouth.

It wasn't any use, though. Family dinner was filled with tension, even more than usual. Charlie escaped the minute it was over, under the guise of business—because his business was so much more important. Kenzie had disappeared to do homework, taking Mom with her.

So it was just him and Dad and pie, and the inevitable.

"We'd make a good chunk of change going with a developer," Dad said, no longer beating around the bush. "Your mom and I could retire." Dad shoved a bite of cherry pie into his mouth.

He thought of Charlie asking him not to say

anything. Not to argue. But no one was here except him and Dad, and how could he pretend this didn't mean everything?

"You can retire by selling to me. I've got enough for my section of the farm right now. You sell your pig operation to Dean Coffey like he's been asking, that'll keep you for a few years while I make enough to buy the rest."

Dad shook his head. "Stupid," he said through a mouth of pie. "Why can't you get it through your head this place is nothing? Five years down the line you're going to be surrounded by subdivisions and malls. You can't hold on to this. Best let it go now."

"I don't care what I'm surrounded by."

"Foolish." Dad drained the rest of his milk, slammed the glass on the table. "You ever plan on settling down and having a family?"

"Christ." Dell shoved a hand through his hair. What would it take? He'd been having this fight for years, and he'd gotten nowhere. When did he give up?

He looked down at the table. His grandfather had built it, and just as it belonged in Mom's dining room, Dell belonged in this place. But maybe belonging wasn't enough.

"Well?" Dad prompted.

"I don't know. Not my concern right now. My concern right now is that this place belongs to me."

"You're a damn fool, and I'm not letting you

screw up by not seeing sense. I don't want to be bailing you out in a few years' time."

Dell pushed away from the table, his pie half-eaten. "Tell Mom I headed home." He tossed his napkin on the table and walked out. There was no way he was spending another hour beating his head against the brick wall of his dad's opinion. If everyone else got to escape, so did he.

As Dell stepped out on the porch, the family's German shepherd greeted him with a tennis ball.

Dell hurled the tennis ball, smiled as Colby ran for it, tongue lolling out of her mouth as she raced down the hill. Nothing like a dog to cheer you up after a nice, tense dinner with dear old Dad.

Was it always going to be this way? He couldn't be someone he wasn't and leave farming. He could go work for someone else, but then the land he'd loved his entire life would be built over into a subdivision.

With a grunt, Dell hurled the ball again, trying to take some solace in Colby's graceful strides.

The screen door creaked open and Mom stepped out. While Dell could see the years' toll on Dad's face every time he looked at him, Mom was exactly the same as she was in Dell's childhood memories. Sturdy jeans and boots, a flannel shirt folded up to the elbows. Slightly graying dark blond hair pulled back into a braid. She didn't wrinkle or change. She was just Mom. Strong, sturdy, calming. If it wasn't for her, he and Dad would probably have come to blows at some point.

Mom stood next to him on the top stair of the porch, watching Colby return lazily with the ball. "You can't let your father get to you."

"I'm not sure I have a choice."

"Of course you do. We always have a choice. I know it's frustrating, but he isn't trying to be the bad guy here, Dell. He's wrong, but that doesn't mean his reasons aren't right."

"That doesn't make a lick of sense." Dell bent down to scratch Colby's ears. "You know Mia Pruitt?"

"Oh, sweet little Mia. Poor girl."

Dell frowned, momentarily put off the point of bringing up Mia and how she was getting her family farm. "Why do you say that?"

"I just remember how she always seemed to be the butt of everyone's jokes. And no one I've ever met is in more need of stick-up-her-ass removal than Sarah Pruitt. The woman made being a co-room mother for Kenzie's kindergarten class a nightmare. That kind of stress from a mother can't be good for young girls."

"They seem fine enough." Fine enough to dance with him and infiltrate his dreams in ways he was not at all comfortable with. "Her dad's selling her his farm."

"You know, it's like that TV doctor says. Karmic debt."

"You really need to stop watching daytime TV." Dell took the slobbery tennis ball from Colby's mouth. He stood and hurled it again, farther this time. "Besides, I don't see how the two are related."

"It's not for you *to* see."

"Mom, no offense, but sometimes that crap is a billion times more annoying than you just coming out and saying I'm a jackass."

Mom laughed. "Maybe that's why I do it." She put her hand on his shoulder. "Dell, honey, I know there's a lot of tension over this."

"I don't understand why—"

Mom held up a hand and he stopped as he always had. "I can tell you what it'll take to change your father's mind. He won't like that I told you, and he'll still complain about you not wanting something more—which is silly, of course, because your roots are here, and what more is there?"

"Mom—"

"The point is, it's going to take some concentrated effort. He wants to see if this farm can support you and a family, should you choose to have one. Farming is changing. New Benton is changing. He wants to see this farmers' market and CSA give you the kind of security the pigs and corn and soybeans do. It's not wrong he wants to know you'll be taken care of. I want that, too."

"Did it occur to either of you that I can take care

of myself? Now. Five years from now. Twenty-five years from now."

"Of course you can, but no one wants to see their child fail."

Dell closed his eyes against the sharp pain. Why was his failure so inevitable to them? Had he truly been that big of a screwup?

"You have to prove to him that failure is impossible."

"How on earth do I do that?" How could he when apparently the fault was in him, not the changing face of farming or New Benton? "I showed him what we did last year. I've given him articles on the local food movement. I've done everything."

"Oh, sweetie, it's not everything until you've gotten what you want."

"Mom—"

"You need to show a bigger profit each month. Show him the market is growing. You can't grow the CSA right now, but you could start a waiting list. Prove to him that it's big and it's growing."

"I can't sustain that kind of growth. Trying to be too big *would* make me a failure."

"Just for a season. A few months of doing whatever it takes to increase profits, then once your father is convinced, you're good to go. Maybe one of those roadside stands. Maybe adding something to your booth. Maybe adding another market to sell at. Whatever it takes."

"I can't magically manufacture customers."

She patted his shoulder. "Of course you can. You know, Kenzie told me Anna Pruitt will be doing face painting for the Pruitt Farms table Saturday. Plus she designed special coloring sheets for kids."

Dell ground his teeth together. He may have been the one to bring up Mia, but he was ready for her to leave this conversation so he didn't have to listen to all the ways she was so much better than him. "So?"

"So they're offering fun and services, not just vegetables. Make it an experience. More people will come to the market if you're offering more than vegetables. More people equals more customers."

He was already walking around shirtless. What more did people want? Dell folded his arms behind his head, looked up at the sky. Mom was right, though. He needed to do something, and if he busted his butt extra hard the next few months to increase profits enough to get Dad off his back, next year he could focus on sustainability more than growth.

New customers to the market would be great, but it made more sense to work with what was already there. Since Mia was the only vendor at the market who sold exactly what he sold, that meant increasing profits had to be a direct attack against her.

It was a shame, but he wasn't going to let anyone get in his way. Nice ass, funny personality, didn't matter.

If Mia had to go down for him to get what he wanted, for maybe, just maybe, his family to stop being so fractured, well, then, so be it.

CHAPTER NINE

"I'M GOING TO make it my profile pic," Anna said with a giggle, tapping away at her phone.

Mia was about five seconds away from wrenching the phone from her sister and throwing it as hard as she could.

Preferably into Dell's face.

Mia glared at his newest sign. "Fifty cents for a picture with the Naked Farmer." It was a hand-scrawled sign, but it was doing the job. Both her sisters had forked over the change and were now giggling over pictures of them with Dell's bare arm over their shoulders.

Hidden depths, her ass. All that jaw clenching over his dad last weekend was probably some ploy to try to make her feel sorry for him. Well, she was not going to be a sucker. She'd played that role too many times in her life to repeat it when it mattered.

"Someone wants their face painted, Anna."

Anna bounced over to the mom and her kid, chatted for a few minutes, and then the mom wandered off while Anna began the design on the boy's face. When the mom ended up in Dell's line, Mia had to turn away.

"Oh, relax. It's all in good fun." Cara's nose was practically plastered to her phone screen.

"Yes. So much fun that mom is getting free babysitting while she gives Dell her money and I walk away empty-handed."

Cara had enough courtesy to look up and frown. "Well, that does kind of suck."

"You know what?" Mia looked around. There were plenty of guys. Some with women, some waiting for their spouses to be done with Dell's booth. There were even a few there on their own.

Mia shrugged out of the flannel shirt she'd worn over a tank top. It was a little cold to go around without sleeves, but hell, if Dell could walk around shirtless, she could bare her arms.

"Mia's busting out the big guns," Cara said with a laugh.

"Yes, I am. Why don't you bust out your big guns?"

Cara snorted, but always game, whipped off her T-shirt so she was wearing only a thin camisole. "Maybe you two could have a strip-off."

She slanted a look at Cara. "Just drum up some business, huh?"

"No problem." Cara skirted the table and went over to Anna. The two whispered about something, then Anna began to paint Cara's arm before she started walking around the market, greeting people, chatting, flirting when appropriate.

"You're next," Anna announced, grabbing Mia's arm. Anna began to paint, the Pruitt Farms logo taking shape on Mia's biceps.

Mia laughed. "Smart."

Anna finished up the green broccoli head of the logo. "I know."

Over the next hour, Cara managed to woo a few more people over to their booth. Mia chatted and smiled and even flirted. It was weird and a little uncomfortable, but she wasn't half-bad at stepping out of her shell these days. She wasn't quite keeping pace with Dell's crowd, but she was starting to cut into it, between Cara and her talking to people and Anna's free children's arts corner.

When Dell sauntered over, Mia knew he'd noticed it, too. But he didn't say anything, just stood outside the crowd watching her work. A little flustered, Mia focused on the man in front of her. He was probably pushing seventy, but she smiled and fawned over him and he ate it up. He also added a bag of greens to his purchases.

Once he was done, Mia realized her crowd was gone and Dell was still looming. "What do you want?" She skirted the table so she stood between him and their stuff. Not a very effective barrier, though, considering she barely came up to his shoulders.

"I thought you guys had a good idea. Maybe

I'll have Anna draw a big Morning Sun Farms logo on my chest."

"I think the muscles and chest hair would get in the way," Anna replied before dissolving into a fit of giggles.

"You're ridiculous." Everyone was being ridiculous. This whole thing had gotten completely out of hand. She needed to get back to a place of sanity and quiet Saturday mornings at the market.

"Don't be jealous, sugar."

Okay, screw sanity. "So help me God, you call me 'sugar' again, I will personally kick your ass."

"That's such a frightening prospect considering I could haul you over my shoulder like a sack of potatoes."

"Please, I'm just as strong as you are."

Dell looked her up and down dismissively. "Uh-huh."

"You guys should arm wrestle."

Mia glared at Cara, who only grinned in return. Without customers to distract them, Cara and Anna were all ears behind the table.

"Push-up contest?" Anna offered with barely contained glee.

"Is everything all right over here?" Val appeared, clutching her clipboard as she studied the situation.

"Dell and Mia are going to have a push-up contest. A little entertainment for customers."

Mia was going to kill Cara. "No, we are not."

"Chicken?" Dell smiled casually.

She was not falling for that. She was not biting. She was absolutely not going to embarrass herself just because he was standing there with that smug grin and his impressive arms folded over a broad, muscled chest. Nope. Nope. Nope.

"It's okay. Wouldn't want you to hurt yourself, darlin'."

"Okay, you're on." She'd find a way to wipe the smug grin off his face, and maybe shove the *darlin'* down his throat.

"So, what? Who can do the most? The most in a certain amount of time?" Cara rubbed her hands together.

"One minute. Who can do the most *real* push-ups." Dell emphasized the word *real* and Mia only barely resisted elbowing him right in the stomach. "Who'll judge?"

"We need someone impartial," Cara offered.

"How about Val?" Anna pointed toward Val's all-but-vibrating frame.

"Oh, yes!" Val practically threw her clipboard on the table and pulled out her phone. "I am so putting this on the market Facebook page. That'll be some publicity."

Mia stared at the small crowd gathering. How had this escalated so quickly? How was she in the middle of it? A push-up contest with Dell in the middle of the farmers' market. How on earth had this happened?

"I'll give you a five-second start...sugar."

That was how it happened. Irritating, smug *male*. Mia clapped her hands together, knelt down to the ground. "You're going down, Wainwright."

"No, that was just an uncomfortable dream I had last night," he mumbled, kneeling next to her.

Mia tried to ignore the double entendre, but heat spread up her neck. She stared hard at the ground. He was trying to psych her out, and she was not going to take the bait. The only going down was going to be literal. Or was it figurative? Aw, crap, she didn't know, but she didn't think push-ups and being turned on went together.

"All right, when I say, 'Go,' you go. Cara's got the timer. I'll count Dell, and Farrah will count Mia. All the way down. All the way up. Oh, man, this is going to be great. People are going to flood the market after this. We'll have to make it a weekly event." Val practically danced. "Okay, ready, set, go."

Mia started, paid no attention to Dell or if he did in fact give her a head start. At the farm she routinely lifted hay bales, weeded, hefted pounds and pounds of vegetables, raked, hoed. She might not be a man, but she was damn well strong enough to put in a good showing. Even against the guy who had shoulders and arms women drooled over.

Other women. Not her.

She focused on that instead of the screaming

of the muscles in her arms or the rough ground digging into her palms. She focused on making each push-up count, and ignored every last sound until Cara gleefully yelled, "Stop!"

Mia pushed back into a sitting position, trying to catch her breath. She glanced at Dell. He wasn't nearly as out of breath, but sweat glistened around his shoulders.

Oh, yum.

Oh, no. No "yum" thoughts allowed.

Val and Farrah conferenced over numbers. "All right, listen up, everyone. The winner of the first-ever Millertown Farmers' Market push-up contest is…a tie! Mia and Dell had exactly the same number!"

"What?"

Dell's incredulous question was enough to make Mia smile as she sucked in a breath and stretched out her tired arms. The cold of the cement started to seep through her jeans, but she was too tired to get up.

"A tie. That means you guys had the exact same number," Cara explained in what sounded like a preschool teacher's voice. "Maybe if you hadn't offered her a head start, you would have won."

Dell glared at her and Mia laughed. It was totally stupid, but this was the best thing to happen all season.

"Guess you'll have to rematch next week," Val said hopefully.

"Sure thing," Mia replied.

Dell shook his head, but as he stood he held out a hand to her. Mia hesitated for a second before letting him help her up.

He grinned. "All right. Rematch next week, but you're not getting a head start." When Mia was on her feet, Dell didn't let go of her hand. Instead, he drew her closer.

"This time, you'll be the one going down," he said, low enough only she could hear. Close enough she could feel his breath on her neck.

Oh, no, she was so not affected by that. Whatever shivery feeling in her core was some aftereffect of push-ups. Yup.

"I thought we established that was only in your dreams."

Go. Her.

Dell chuckled, completely unfazed. *Damn it.* "Sweet dreams, then." He released her hand and sauntered back to his booth, a trail of women following him.

"Great. All we did was make him all hot and sweaty so now even more women are flocking to him," Cara said with disgust. "I changed my mind on all this. I'm with Mia now. I hate Dell."

"I don't hate Dell. He was a good sport. We just…need a different tactic."

"Oh, God, you're not falling for all that over-sexed farmer-boy charm, are you?"

"Absolutely not!" Right? He *was* a decent guy.

She *hated* his tactics, but he wasn't…hate-worthy. And that was not the whole going-down conversation liquefying her mind.

"Good." Cara crossed her arms over her chest. "Ugh. I don't even know why I care about this. It's vegetables, for chrissake."

"Probably because you hate to lose."

"Oh, right. So, how do we win? Daisy Duke shorts and a car wash?"

"You know, you're going about this all wrong," Anna said casually, packing up her paints.

"What do you know, squirt?" Cara demanded.

"I know that if you want to win against the hottest guy in school, or in this case, the farmers' market, you don't fight with sex appeal."

"That's why we were doing the family angle, but it's barely registered. You were the one who told me to wear jeans that fit." Mia looked at the pile of coloring sheets no one had picked up. Anna's face painting had been glorified babysitting.

Anna shook her head. "The fitting clothes just make you look like someone to take seriously. And, sure, a girl's going to go for the hot guy nine times out of ten. The one time she's not? When it's boy versus girl. You want to win? You make this a battle of the sexes."

Mia gaped at her. It had never crossed her mind, but…Anna had a point. A really, really good point. Even Cara wrote off the hot guy if she thought she was losing to him. "She's right.

Holy moly, she is right. But how do we start a battle of the sexes?"

"You just did." Anna pointed to where the contest had taken place.

Mia laughed, laughed until she could barely catch her breath. "He'll never know what hit him."

"Way to get your ass handed to you by a girl."

"We tied. That is not an ass handing." But it didn't sit well, even if Mia looked awfully good rumpled and laughing. The way she'd smirked when she'd said, "I thought we'd established that was only in your dreams."

He couldn't keep the smile off his face. She was a pain in the ass, and he was enjoying it way too much.

"It is an ass handing when you call yourself the Naked Farmer and a girl the size of Tinkerbell beats you."

Dell glared at his brother. "She didn't beat me. We tied. And I sold an extra ten cabbages after that, so I don't really care." Profits were all that mattered. His pride could be bloody and broken before he'd give a shit.

Charlie shook his head, pulled his cap farther down on his head to shade the phone in his hand.

"Surprised you even noticed with your nose stuck to that thing."

"Hey, I'm looking after you. You know that's going to show up on the internet."

Dell loaded the truck with the empty pallets. What could be the harm in that? If women liked seeing him take his shirt off, surely they wouldn't mind watching him do some push-ups. Probably help him, actually.

Dell grinned at the thought. If Val used it for publicity, that meant more customers. New customers. New money. And, if they were women, he had a pretty good chance.

"Man, they don't waste time."

"Huh?"

Charlie held out his phone. Dell squinted at the screen. "Battle of the Sexes. Saturday, May 2, at 10:00 a.m." Dell frowned. "Battle of the sexes?"

"You're so screwed." Charlie chuckled. "They totally turned the tables on you with this rematch. You're screwed if you win, because they'll buy Mia's pity cabbages. Screwed if you lose, because no one wants a wimpy Naked Farmer."

"I am not screwed."

"This is a genius move. Man, maybe Mia wants a job. She's got this marketing thing down."

"Contrary to what you and Dad think, farming is it for some people."

"Yeah. *Some* people."

Charlie didn't say it, but there were a lot of descriptors hanging out in that *some*. Dumb people. Inferior people. *Worthless.*

"Get in the truck," Dell growled.

Oblivious to the fact that he was an ass, Charlie hopped in, still staring at the phone. Sounds of the crowd from earlier and Val yelling, "Go!" filled the truck as Dell maneuvered out of the parking lot.

"When did Mia get so hot? Or am I attracted to her now because she kicked your ass?"

Dell used some of his mother's meditation techniques to keep from wrecking the truck so he could wring Charlie's neck.

"Speaking of asses..." Charlie whistled. "Val got the perfect angle of Mia's."

"Would you shut the hell up?" It was bad enough *he'd* noticed Mia's ass; it was really not okay Charlie had. That made no sense, but he didn't care. He just wanted Charlie to shut up about everything, not only Mia's ass. Okay, but mainly about Mia's ass.

"What do you care?" Then Charlie huffed out a laugh. "Oh, man, you got a thing for your mortal-enemy farmer? Wait, what are female farmers called? Farmettes?"

"You're a prick."

Charlie clucked his tongue. "I don't see you being Mia's type. You know, even aside from all the trying-to-screw-each-other-over stuff. I think she went to Truman. Brainy."

"I'm not fucking dumb." But he was about to

bust his brother's lip. Or nose. Really, whatever was within reach.

"Don't get so bent out of shape. I'm just harassing you, man."

Dell swallowed down what he thought of that. He wasn't above harassing Charlie, and he wasn't the type of guy who could dish it out but not take it.

At least he was going to try really hard not to be that guy.

"Look, bottom line, you might need some advice from me if you want to beat the Pruitts. She keeps out-idea-ing you. I know everyone thinks I don't love the farm like you do, but... Well, I'm not unwilling to help you out."

"I don't need your help." He had a few more tricks up his sleeve. And they didn't include the farmers' market, which meant Mia couldn't flip it around on him. "Since when do you give a crap about the farm?"

"I can give a crap about it without wanting to make it my life."

"Then why do you keep telling me to sell?"

"Dad has good points. You, occasionally, have a few of your own. But when it comes to business, you can't let sentiment run your decisions. Dad's right about the love thing. Love doesn't make a productive, successful farm."

"What do you know about love, Charlie? Didn't

you just break up with Emily because she wanted to move in together?"

"I'm offering to help you, Dell."

"And I am telling you I do not need it from someone who doesn't love the place like I do." Or from anyone.

He would get the farm and his father's respect without help from anyone else. If Charlie helped, Charlie would get all the credit. Dell wasn't the screwup everyone seemed to think he was, and the only way to prove that was to do everything on his own.

Besides, Charlie was already back to his scowling stare-at-the-phone routine, so obviously he didn't really care. No, Dell was completely on his own.

Not his first choice, but at this point it was the only choice.

CHAPTER TEN

MIA SLAPPED HER gloves against the back of her jeans. The rain over the past week had been the perfect amount, but it had left her dirtier than normal at the end of the day. Mud caked her jeans, boots, shirt, nails, probably even her face at this point.

She grinned. Nothing better.

Tomorrow looked to be another great day. As long as tonight's predicted storms weren't too bad, tomorrow would be sunny and warmer, and that would be great for her seeds and plants. Plus there was a battle of the sexes to win tomorrow morning. Or lose. Didn't really matter. She already had a wave of support on Facebook. As long as people put their money where their like buttons were, she'd keep her profits where they needed to be.

A profitable year. She shouldn't count her chickens before they were hatched, but the excitement over that possible success was too much to completely combat.

Mia hiked up to the dairy barn. Looking the stereotypical farmer in manure-caked overalls and an oily old hat, Dad met her halfway. It was a habit born of nothing but doing it every day. Meet halfway and say goodbye to Dad.

"Calling it quits, Dad."

He nodded, moved the chew from one side of his mouth to the other.

"Daddy," Mia admonished, wrinkling her nose. Sunday dinner would be a nightmare if her mom found out he was chewing again. Not to mention it was a disgusting habit she wished he'd kick for good.

He patted her shoulder. "Gonna storm."

"Could be good."

"Could be bad."

"Always the optimist."

Dad's mouth curled just a little. He gave her shoulder one last pat and muttered a "See ya tomorrow, honey."

Pretty wordy for Dad, all in all. He returned to his cows and Mia walked back to her truck, stripping out of the muddy flannel button-up so she wouldn't totally mess up her driver's seat. She glanced at the sky. The clouds billowed on the horizon, dark and low. Too much more rain could be a serious problem for her crops. Dad was right, could be bad.

Unfortunately, Mother Nature couldn't be counted on to keep the crops' best interests in mind, and Mia had done all a person could do to safeguard her seeds and seedlings. She hopped in the truck, already turning her thoughts to a hot shower and a pot of macaroni and cheese. Weather couldn't be helped, so worrying over it was a waste of time.

She pulled the truck onto the highway and noticed a produce stand on the edge of the Pruitt property. Not the Pruitt produce stand Anna manned after school on Mondays and Wednesdays. Mia squinted at the sign, then screeched her truck to a stop on the shoulder.

She hopped out, read the sign three times before she kicked the stand. Morning Sun Farms Produce Stand. Mon–Fri 4–5, Sunday 12–3.

Mia studied the placement, groaned at the rumbling sky. Dell was a lot of things, but he wasn't stupid. Though right next to the Pruitt property line, the stand was firmly on county land, and no doubt aboveboard.

She was going to kill him. She would not stand for this…this…bullying was what it amounted to. She was way familiar with that. But she wouldn't cry over it. She wouldn't go whine to Cara or Dad. No, this time she was going to do something about it.

Mia hopped back in her truck and broke a few traffic laws to fly across town to the Wainwright farm. She'd picked Anna up a few times from the main house and knew Dell lived in the cabin on the edge of the property.

A little voice told her to calm down, but the anger only grew. Why was he screwing with *her*? There were other farmers at the market. Of course, she was really the only one in direct competition with him in terms of goods offered.

That didn't mean he got to go out of his way to piss her off. Putting his little stand right next to her farm wasn't necessary. It was petty. She wasn't going to take it. She was absolutely going to stand up for herself.

Mia pulled the truck to a stop in front of Dell's little cabin. Surrounded by a decorative if sagging wood-plank fence, the wrought iron gate a little rusty and ajar. Even with anger pumping through her veins, it was hard not to notice how cute and cozy the place looked nestled into the slightly rolling farmland behind it.

Too bad the proprietor was a dick. Yeah, he was a dick, and she was going to tell him that to his face. No pushover Mia anymore. She stalked up the charming stone walkway, fat drops of rain beginning to fall. Mia barely noticed.

She stomped up the stairs, lightening her steps only when the wood planks kind of creaked under her. Since she couldn't stomp, she put all her anger and effort into banging on the door so hard the windows rattled. The wind picked up, thunder accentuating her banging.

It took a few minutes, but Dell finally opened the door, his wavy blond hair wet from what she assumed to be the shower. And was it any surprise the guy wasn't wearing a shirt? She would not be distracted by that. Very purposefully she kept her gaze right on his eyes—nowhere else.

"Are you morally opposed to clothing the top portion of your body?"

He leaned against the door frame, unfazed. Of course he was unfazed. He'd have to care to be fazed. "Evenin', honey. Come by to get a peek? You missed me in my underwear."

She really wanted to give him a nice hard shove, but his bare chest made that idea too intimidating. If only she didn't have to crane her neck to glare at him. Even with the overhang, raindrops slid through the cracks and pelted her face, just a sprinkle, but enough she couldn't maintain eye contact without getting a drop to the eye. So she focused on his mouth. Definitely not the sexy stubble around it

She really had a problem. "You know why I'm here."

"Not a clue."

"Don't play dumb."

His easy smile faded. "I'm not dumb."

"I didn't say *you* were dumb." Why was he so touchy about that stuff? "Now put a shirt on and go pack up that stupid stand and get it away from my property."

"No."

He said it so simply, so matter-of-factly, her jaw actually dropped. "No? Just…no?" The rain fell harder and was starting to seep into her shirt. It was definitely not warm enough to be standing here in a May rainstorm in a tank top, but she was not backing down.

"Yeah. Just *no*. I checked with the county and I can put it there. It's got decent traffic and I needed another place to sell some of my leftovers." He smiled again, all straight white teeth. "Made a hundred bucks today."

Mia clenched her hands into fists. "I've been picked on enough in my life to know when someone is targeting me. This is crap, Dell. Don't be a jerk and a bully. I was beginning to think you were legitimately sorry for all the dumb high school stuff, but maybe once an asshole always an asshole."

"I'm not targeting you. It's not personal." He shifted in his easy stance against the door frame. He didn't look quite so cocky now, and at least that was something.

"Really? You popping little stands up next to anyone else's farm?"

He fidgeted more, but his expression remained grave and resolute. "Just back off, okay? You're doing fine. You're going to get your farm no matter what. I don't have that luxury. I'm sorry if that means stepping on your toes, but it is what it is."

Mia threw her arms in the air. "This is ridiculous. You're ridiculous. Actually, you're a bully and a selfish jerk and..." She trailed off, running out of insults. *Bully* and *jerk* and *asshole* were about all she had in her arsenal. "Oh, yeah, and a dick!" With a grunt, she turned on a heel. Of course the minute her boot hit grass hail began to pelt the ground. Not little pea-size hail, either. Big, golf ball–size hail.

Mia shook off the painful slap of ice against skin and kept walking to her truck. Maybe it was stupid, but she wasn't giving Dell the satisfaction of going back to his place for shelter.

The hail fell harder, growing in size, hard enough to probably leave a few small bruises. She'd never seen hail like this, but anger made the pellets' impact against her skin nothing more than irritating. As she reached out for her truck door, a softball-size piece of hail smashed through her windshield. Mia jumped back, screeching.

"Are you nuts?" Dell yelled over the thundering sound of hailstones hitting and bouncing off the ground and her truck. He grabbed her arm and pulled. "What the hell is wrong with you? Hail that size will give you a concussion if it knocks you in the head right."

He pushed her under the short overhang of the porch. The thudding of hail was drowned out by the heavy beating of her heart.

Mia let out a shaky breath, realized her hands were shaking, too. If she'd left the porch five seconds earlier, she'd have taken glass and hail right to the face. She squeezed her eyes shut and took another deep breath.

"You okay?"

Mia opened her eyes and managed a nod. "Damn it. My poor truck."

"Better than your head."

Which was true, and kind of nice, really. But she was mad at him. Too bad she couldn't muster any of that earlier anger. Hail this size wasn't just wreaking havoc on her truck; her crops would be trampled to hell.

"The corn. The tomatoes. My carrot seeds. Everything. God, Dell, this is terrible."

"I know." He pushed both hands through his hair, watched as the hail continued to fall, though blessedly diminishing in size.

"And the rain." The hail had petered out, but the torrential downpour that was following was going to be just as bad for everything. What would survive this?

He cursed. "This is the last thing I need."

She felt sorry for him. Then she remembered he was screwing her over. Unfortunately, she didn't have the heart to yell at him about it anymore. If this continued for much longer, neither of them would have anything to sell at their stands or the farmers' market after tomorrow.

Dell cleared his throat and looked at the top of the door frame. "Uh, Mia, with the rain and all, your shirt is kinda see-through."

Heat stealing up her cheeks, Mia looked down. Yup. Great. Her nipples were showing. She crossed her arms over her chest and prayed this storm was the apocalypse.

"Come on inside. I'll give you a sweatshirt to wear and you can wait out the storm. Once it calms down, I'll drive you home and you can figure out what to do about your truck from there."

"Why?" Why would he be nice to her after she'd come over, barrels blazing? Calling him names, even if he deserved them?

"Because it's the sensible thing to do." Then he grumbled something about people thinking he was the dumb one.

Mia followed him inside. What choice did she have? Her windshield was toast, her whole car probably flooding. She couldn't drive in this mess and she couldn't ask anyone to come pick her up in it, either.

Inside, the cabin was all warm wood and cozy furniture. Dell disappeared into a hallway and she stood dripping by the door. Thunder cracked, causing her to jump. Storms didn't usually make her nervous but she'd never, ever seen hail like that. Tornadoes could be right around the corner.

She was going to die in a tornado in Dell's cabin. Still a virgin.

Before she could roll her eyes at herself, Dell reappeared with a stack of clothes, duct tape and trash bags. "Sweatshirt, shorts—which'll probably be pants on you—and socks. I know they'll all be too big, but you'll be dry till it calms down. I'm going to go cover up your windshield."

"You don't have to—"

"I'm already wet, thanks to you." He stomped out the door before she could stop him.

Rude and nice at the same time. How was she supposed to know how to react to that? She looked down at the pile of dry clothes Dell had shoved at her, and realized she was shivering.

The last thing she wanted to do was put on Dell's clothes in Dell's house, but she didn't really have any other choice.

The tornado would probably sweep through the minute she took off an item of clothing. Her obituary would read "died naked and a virgin in Dell Wainwright's cabin."

"Oh, shut up, brain." She whipped off a shirt, hurriedly putting on Dell's sweatshirt. She was stuck, and somewhere out there Mother Nature was laughing her fool head off.

DELL GRUMBLED AS he secured the trash bags over Mia's windshield. It was likely already pretty wet inside the cab, and his trash-bag tent wouldn't hold forever, but it gave him an excuse to get away from Mia and her freaking see-through shirt.

Which hopefully gave him the chance to lose the most embarrassing erection of his life.

Totally normal. He'd been able to see her breasts, for chrissake. Right through the stupid white tank top and bra plastered to her skin. Her wet, chilled skin he had suddenly and earnestly wanted to touch.

He barely resisted the urge to hurl the duct tape across the lawn. He was not going to think about Mia that way. She'd been right about him being a dick and a bully, but *he* was also right about fighting her being his only chance.

So having her be all hot and…whatever, was not something he could afford. Her nipples could go to hell.

Along with him, because this storm was probably ending everything he'd ever worked for as it seeped into his clothes, cascaded down his hair and face.

He couldn't make a profit if everything he'd planted was beat to hell by hail or washed away by rain. At this rate, he wouldn't be surprised if a tornado took the whole place out.

Dell shook his head. This was farming. He knew that. You could do a lot to control things, but you could never truly control Mother Nature. He just wished she'd picked a different year to screw with him.

Dell stomped through the puddles on the lawn, wrenched off his boots, then left them on the porch.

When he stepped back inside, Mia was sitting on his couch in his oversize clothes, legs curled under her, watching out the front window. Worry creased her forehead, and something in the moment had a weird weight banding around his lungs.

She knew what was happening. What this storm was doing to him it was also doing to her. They were in it together, in a very strange way.

She turned to look at him. Not just worry on her face, but sadness. Yeah, he knew the feeling. One thing about Mother Nature, she didn't pick and choose whom she screwed over.

"I'm gonna go dry off," he said, needing to escape before he was tempted to feel as sorry for her as he felt for himself.

She would recover from this. He didn't know how he would. He stomped into his bathroom and shed the wet clothes, tossing them into the bathtub.

He pulled on dry boxers, an old Mizzou sweatshirt, a faded pair of jeans, dry socks. Then he sat on the edge of the bathtub for a second. Something about being alone in his house with Mia while the world practically washed away around them seemed like a really bad idea.

Especially when he was already feeling as if he was screwed. He tended to make bad decisions when he felt that way. Bad decisions when nipples and feeling like a failure were involved.

Dell laughed at himself. Right, Mia would totally go along with any bad decisions. He shook his head and pushed off the bathtub. The storm couldn't last much longer. He hoped. Then he'd drop her off and she wouldn't be his problem anymore.

His misery did not love or want company.

He walked out to the living room. Mia was still curled up on his couch, but she had a phone to her ear. "I'm fine, Mom. No. No. Fine. Yes. Well, I'm not alone." Mia glanced at him. "Mom, please, go…lie down or something. Everything is fine. I promise. Just have Dad get me Bob's number and—" She paused again, rubbing her tongue back and forth across her bottom lip.

Sweet Jesus. Dell stood awkwardly in the middle of his living room and stared hard out the window. Rain continued to pelt in sheets. It was enough of a distraction. Instead of lust, all he felt was dread and depression.

"Mom…Mom…Mom. I have to go, okay? I'm fine. You're fine. Everyone is fine. Just relax. I'll be by tomorrow. Bye."

Dell took a breath, hoping it was safe to look at her again. Her cheeks were a little pink and her shoulders were practically at her ears.

"Mom's kind of, well, anxious." She toyed with her phone. "Um, Dad will have someone over to replace the windshield tomorrow, then we'll get the truck out of your hair."

"Okay," Dell replied lamely. He needed to sit, but the only other place to sit not covered in seed catalogs and ads for farming supply stores was on the other end of the couch Mia was currently sitting on.

In his clothes. Her dark hair wet and clinging to freckled skin, cheeks pink, worrying her tongue over her bottom lip again. Dell eased as far onto the edge of the couch as he could, wrapped an arm around the back and focused on the rain pelting the ground outside the front window.

His yard already resembled a lake. "Still going." The sinking feeling burrowed deeper. "It's all going to be gone." He hadn't meant to say it out loud, and hearing it, even in his own voice, made his eyes burn.

"I know. I know." Her sigh was shaky. "What on earth are we going to do?"

We? He glanced her way again. As if they were in this together, as he'd idiotically thought. And it was idiotic. They weren't in anything together. She was on the other side of the world, and she looked way too close to tears for comfort. "House rules. No crying."

"I'm not crying." She said it with a little sniff, doing that raising-her-chin thing that made him think she could fight.

Mia Pruitt was a fighter, and he gave her credit. She was close to tears, but they never appeared on her cheeks.

"Well, there goes my life. I always figured it'd be my dad screwing me over. Didn't account for the weather to beat him to it."

In his peripheral vision he could see her studying him. Serious green eyes watched his face as if looking for some tell he was lying.

"You're really, truly that bad off with your dad that he would…?"

Dell laughed a little bitterly. "Depends on your definition of *bad off.*" He stared at the rain beating away everything he'd worked for. "We don't understand each other, I guess. He thinks this place is some burden he's saving me from, and I think…" What was he doing whining to Mia about his problems?

"You think what?"

He frowned over at her. The look on her face was something he couldn't quite read. She seemed…empathetic, which was something entirely foreign to him. Even Mom didn't seem to *feel* for him. She understood him better than Dad and Charlie, but she understood Dad, too.

Why did Mia care? He should laugh it off and pretend he didn't. But real, honest words tumbled out instead. "I think this place is in my bones and I don't want to lose it."

Her mouth softened into a smile. "That's kind of poetic."

He scoffed. "Whatever. Doesn't matter. Without better profits this year, there will be no next year. This will be subdivisions or strip malls."

She blinked a few times. "I'm sorry, Dell. That sucks."

He shrugged it off, not sure what to do with her sympathy. Not sure what to do with her being nice and kind. Like her apology, he didn't know what to do with these things. He kind of wished she'd call him a dick again.

"You know, it's not the worst-case scenario."

Dell laughed bitterly. "Right. A tornado hasn't blown us over. Yet."

"It's May. We've got time to do a little recovery. The market goes through October, and Val's talking about doing some winter dates. Yeah, it sucks and it'll kick our ass a little this year, but it's not the end of the world. We'll survive. Maybe you won't have better profits, but—"

Dell pushed off the couch, stalked the interior of the cabin, which felt entirely too small for him, let alone him and Mia. She was small, but she smelled like… He didn't know. Something aside from the cabin and the rain and the dirt. "I don't have a year. I have to excel, not survive." He had to kick *her* ass to save his own.

"Dell, your dad is a farmer. He understands how weather works. How some years are worse than others." She leaned toward him, all earnest surety. "He's not going to sell out from under you just because you had a rough year."

"You don't have a clue, honey."

She was quiet for a minute, and when he sneaked a glance at her, she had curled back into the couch, her eyes on the window or the rain outside it. "I guess you're right. I was just trying to…"

She didn't finish the sentence, but he knew. She was trying to make him feel better. Huh. She was trying to be nice and supportive. Weird how good that felt coming from someone who was supposed to be his enemy.

"I can't imagine it," she said softly. "It'd be like losing a part of myself. Like you said, it's in my bones. No one should have to lose that."

Her gaze stayed on the rain-splattered windows. Thunder clapped and she jerked just a bit, her fingers clutched around her phone as if it was some kind of anchor in the midst of all the chaos outside.

Like losing a part of yourself. Yes, that was exactly what it felt like. Even the prospect of losing this place. He knew every inch of ground. The swell of the hill, the ancient peeling red of the barn, the way the earth smelled a little different during each season.

If he lost it, even if he wound up on a farm somewhere else, it would never be the same. A part of him would be gone.

It made sense she understood. Their childhoods must have been similar, growing up on a family farm, going to the same schools except college. They'd both come back and taken over part of the reins.

He'd always believed her to be completely separate from him because he'd been popular and she hadn't. Because he had an ease with people and she had to work at it. She was so freaking smart and he was, well, not so much.

But they weren't so different after all, were they? She'd been the geek and he'd been the dumb farm kid who was the life of a party. Their reputations had reduced them down to some simplified version of people they really weren't.

He watched Mia watch the storm. She looked sad, but not defeated. Worried, but not devastated.

Why did that give him some kind of weird hope? That there was understanding and possibilities— things he'd almost, *almost* stopped believing in.

When he sat down on the couch this time, he didn't think about keeping a lot of space between them. Instead, he slid right next to her. Mia shifted and blinked a few times. "Um. You've got that cold frame, too. So maybe you haven't lost everything. It might provide shelter and keep some of the rain away. Definitely no hail damage to that stuff. Well, probably." She went on chattering about all the possibilities. About all the ways he might not be totally screwed. All the ways he could cut costs and still come out a little on top.

Every single possible chance he had. Dell laughed. The woman who had told him to go to hell not that many weeks ago was sitting on his couch in his clothes telling him it would be okay.

Not once making him feel like an idiot for still having an ounce of belief left.

He leaned in, invading a bit of her space. Hell, this day was already screwed, why not really screw it over? When he touched her cheek, she flinched, then her eyes went comically wide.

"What are you doing?"

What was he doing? Well, not thinking, and yet he couldn't help himself. She was like a salve to a wound, and since everything was all mixed up and tangled anyway, why not have it? "Thinking about kissing you, actually."

She pulled her head back even more, holding out her hands like double stop signs. "You can't kiss me!"

It was such a strange response to him trying to kiss her, he was almost amused. Refusal he'd expected. Some kind of scathing comment, yup. A sort of weird panic complete with squeaky voice and bug eyes? It was kind of cute. "Why not?"

She opened her mouth, a high-pitched squeaking sound escaping. She blinked at him a few times. "Because."

He grinned, liking the way the blush made her skin all rosy. She was…sweet. A nice change from the girls he usually tried to kiss. Well, not tried. He always succeeded. "Because why?"

"B-because. Because. I…I don't need a reason!"

But she wasn't scurrying away from him. Instead, she stayed right there. After blinking a few more times, some of the panic left her face and she actually looked as if maybe she was thinking about it.

Dell pushed a piece of hair behind her ear, fingertips brushing down the soft skin of her neck. Maybe it was stupid, but she was pretty and thoughtful and funny. It wasn't as if he had anything else to lose after today. What would be wrong with getting at least some enjoyment out of the evening? "Mia."

He liked saying her name. Watching her mouth open a fraction to suck in a breath. Yes, there were nerves there, but she was holding her ground. He'd spent a lot of time in his youth trying to figure out women, and while he didn't have it down to a science, he did know how to recognize interest.

Mia visibly swallowed, her eyes darting to his mouth and then back to his eyes. "Um." But she didn't tell him to back off or screw off, so he bent his head closer, slowly, to give her time if she wanted to bolt. She squirmed a little, but stayed in place, her eyes on his. She didn't even flinch when he rested his hand behind her neck, when the side of his thigh pressed against her curled-up legs.

When his mouth was half an inch or so from hers, he could hear her sharp intake of breath. Her hands tightened around her phone in front of her chest and her eyes were still wide.

But she didn't move. He went to close the last

distance between them, but before he could she squeaked and pulled her head back.

"I'm a virgin." She immediately clapped a hand over her mouth, apparently as surprised at blurting it out as he was at hearing it.

Dell pulled back. He couldn't help it. He swallowed, tried to process the information. Mia was a virgin.

Well.

What the hell was he supposed to do about that?

CHAPTER ELEVEN

MIA WAS FIVE seconds away from running out of Dell's cabin. Screw the rain. Screw her smashed windshield.

She'd blurted out she was a virgin like some kind of crazed moron. Would it have killed her to keep her mouth shut and let him kiss her?

Apparently. She'd done everything in her power to ignore the panic, to let him do it. Because why not? They were supposed to be enemies and everything, but he was cute and his comment about the farm being in his bones had really gotten to her.

He wasn't some idiot doing this because he didn't know what else to do. He wasn't screwing with her to get a few laughs. This farm was the world to him, and she knew what that felt like.

Dell really did have the depth she'd been a little too drawn to that night at the bar. It wasn't some ploy or some scam to mess with her. And now...

Now he was slowly inching his way to the other side of the couch. She couldn't read his expression, but it didn't take a mind reader to tell he was freaked.

Holy moly, why wouldn't he be? Mia, Queen of the Geeks, strikes again. She'd thought she was beyond freaking out the second a guy showed any kind of interest. She'd handled C.J. the other night at the bar. Danced with Dell. That was supposed to be progress.

Dell had erased it with one "I was thinking about kissing you." And surely she'd erased any interest he had in her with one crazed "I'm a virgin."

Mia covered her face with her hands. "Please, for the love of everything holy, forget I said that. Pretend the past five minutes didn't happen. Don't ever, *ever* bring it up."

He was silent. Completely silent. As the seconds ticked by and the embarrassed heat in her neck and face eased, curiosity crept in. What was he doing? What was he thinking? Why had he tried to kiss her in the first place?

Maybe if it had been right after the see-through shirt incident she could understand. She might not have any guy experience, but she knew enough to know that guys liked boobs. Probably didn't matter much whom they belonged to.

But he hadn't tried to kiss her then. He'd tried to kiss her when she'd been in his oversize clothes, talking about sad things and—

"Rain's letting up." His weight left the couch. "I'll drive you home."

It was a struggle between mind and body to uncover her hands from her face, but she did it. Her face had to be flaming red, but so what? Being embarrassed wasn't any more embarrassing than *why* she was embarrassed.

What woman blurted out she was a virgin the first time a guy tried to kiss her? Especially if she was twenty-six damn years old.

Probably the girl who managed to scare guys off before they even got to the I-might-want-to-kiss-you moment. The girl who couldn't even *get* guys to look at her like that because she couldn't shed that high school reputation. Or who'd worked so hard to be a confident businesswoman that she'd also inadvertently kept herself apart. Head down, no nonbusiness talk engaged, all so afraid she'd turn back into who she'd once been.

Mia forced her legs off the couch. She couldn't look Dell in the eye. She wasn't so embarrassed about being a virgin. The information itself couldn't be that shocking.

But the delivery...

Mia stifled a groan. She could not think of a way this day could be any more a failure.

"I'll get a bag for your things."

He disappeared into the kitchen briefly and returned with a plastic grocery bag. She held her hand out to take it, but he didn't notice. Instead, he picked up the wet ball of clothes next to the door and stuffed them into the bag before handing them to her.

"Guess your shoes'll be soaked, but they'd probably be soaked after a walk through the ocean out there anyway."

Mia held the bag limply in one hand. He wasn't going to address it. He was going to forget it, just as she asked. Pretend it had never happened.

The relief washed through her so hard she fumbled with her boots. Yes, a little soggy, but she managed to get her feet in and laced.

When they stepped out onto the porch, the rain had fallen off into a steady drizzle and the thunder was only a low, distant roll. Mia sneaked a peek at Dell. His face was expressionless as he stepped off the porch and into the puddles along the walk.

She scurried after him. Part of her wanted to hug him in thanks, but considering she'd blurted out she was a virgin when he tried to kiss her, she'd probably mention she hadn't been kissed next.

She had a lot of embarrassing memories, but this one really took the blue ribbon.

He pulled up the door of the ramshackle garage, then pushed it the rest of the way over. He was so good at pretending nothing had happened, she was beginning to think she'd imagined it.

He climbed in the driver's seat of his truck, and she clambered her way up into the passenger seat. He backed out of the drive, squelching through mud and rain. He was blissfully silent all the way to the highway.

He'd drop her off and she'd stay out of his way from here on out. She'd avoid his stand next to their property, never make eye contact at the market and make sure to send someone else to get her hail-damaged truck.

This was it. End of the line. No more bickering or bantering with him. No accidental meet-ups at the bar or impromptu visits to his house. Because every time she saw him she'd remember and relive that horrifying embarrassment, and every time he saw her beet-red face he'd remember, too.

"So is it like a wait-till-marriage kind of thing?"

His voice suddenly filling the silence caused her to jump. She put a hand to her racing heart. He hadn't seriously asked her...

"Your family's Catholic, right? So it's, like, a church thing?"

"No," Mia replied, surprised when her voice didn't squeak. "No. It's not."

"Okay, so..."

Mia squeezed her eyes shut. She was not having this conversation. She was not in Dell's truck. None of the past hour had happened. Not one second of it.

When she opened her eyes, she was in Dell's truck, driving through rivulets of water running down the street, the virgin issue hanging in the air.

No dream. No apocalypse. Just the cold reality of her crap way with men. Maybe with enough practice she'd get over that, but for right now her practice meter was at zero. "Look, it just…never happened, okay? Is it really all that surprising? You know me. I have two speeds—major embarrassment or totally invisible. And totally invisible has been preferable to getting laughed at on a date." Or after a kiss. Or a nonkiss because she blurted she was a virgin.

"Okay, so you were kind of a geek, and maybe you turned really quiet after you came back from college, but look at you. You're—" He cleared his throat. "Anyway, the point is…" He drummed his fingers on the steering wheel. "Actually, I have no idea what my point is."

She almost laughed but couldn't make it escape her mouth.

"So you're waiting for the right guy, then?"

"I wouldn't mind a few Mr. Wrongs along the way."

When he chuckled, Mia bounced her head against the headrest of the seat. Why couldn't she just shut the hell up?

She sneaked a peek at his face. He kept moving his mouth around. After a few seconds she realized he was trying not to smile.

"What?" she demanded, not seeing the humor in the situation at all. She hunched in the seat. "Seems only fair I get to have a bit of fun, too, even if I do get a late start."

"You're right. Does seem only fair." Now he was outright grinning.

What was wrong with her? Silence would not be the end of the world. Why could her mind never accept that?

Mia looked in the backseat.

"What are you looking for?"

"Tape."

"For what?"

She crossed her arms over her chest and let out an irritated breath. "My mouth."

He barked out a laugh. "I'll tell you what, Mia, you are funny."

"Fantastic."

"And you have a very nice mouth."

She blinked at him a few times before realizing her jaw had dropped. She snapped her mouth shut and looked out the windshield. The rain was down to a sprinkle, the streetlights reflecting on the dark pavement of the street as Dell drove into town.

Was that flirting? No. No possible way. Not after this bizarre evening. But he had tried to kiss her…

No. She was not letting her brain go down that train of thought. Even if he was flirting or complimenting or interested. He wasn't just a Mr. Wrong, he was a Mr. Embarrassment Waiting to Happen.

"What street?"

"Corner of Oak and Willow."

A few minutes later he pulled into the parking space in front of the old house turned into apartments.

"Thanks." Mia unbuckled herself as fast as she could.

"You already get your stuff put up for market tomorrow?"

Mia stopped halfway out the truck. "Um, yeah."

He nodded, staring at the windshield. "Good. Me, too. Guess I'll see you tomorrow."

"Sure." She hopped the rest of the way out, closed the door before her idiot mouth could betray her again.

She might see him tomorrow, but she was definitely not talking to him. Except for that whole battle-of-the-sexes thing. And getting her truck.

Crap.

DELL KNEW HE should push the truck into Drive and go, but...

He watched Mia hurry up the stairs of her apartment. *Let it go, man.* But how was she going to get to the market without her truck?

And how was he supposed to figure out what to do with her if she just scurried away?

Let it go. Didn't he have enough on his plate without worrying about her?

He'd never been very good at listening to the voice inside his head, though. He pushed out of the truck and jogged up to the porch. He called her name and she stopped just a hair short of shutting the door completely.

Slowly, warily, she pulled it back open. "Did I forget something?"

"No." No, he had. He'd forgotten his damn mind. "You got a ride to the market tomorrow?"

She furrowed her brow. "I'm sure I'll figure something out. Cara's car is too small, but maybe we can switch with Dad and—"

"I'll give you a ride."

"Huh?"

He shifted and looked at his boots. There was some little part of his brain saying the same exact thing. "I'll give you a ride. There's room in my truck and we're going to the same place."

Her brows furrowed. "Why would you do that?"

Because he was a moron, that was why. "It's pretty much on my way to Millertown anyway."

"I thought you were trying to put me out of business."

He was hugely uncomfortable with that assessment. Anything he'd done or would do wasn't about her, it was about him. And he wasn't putting her out of business. Her dad was giving her their farm. She didn't have to worry about…business. She didn't have to worry about anything, and he certainly wasn't worried about helping her.

Except this whole offering-her-a-ride thing.

That was all idiotic, brain-dead him. "I'm not trying to put you out of business. I'm just trying to keep myself in business."

She pursed her lips together, eyeing him suspiciously.

"Look, if you pay for half the gas I'm saving money, which is something I really need to do if everything looks as bad as I think it will in the light of day."

Her suspicion eased a little. "I guess it would be sensible."

Yup. Totally sensible. Except for the part where he was thinking about kissing her. Thinking about her comments about Mr. Wrong. He could definitely be a Mr. Wrong. He'd had ample practice.

Dell scratched a hand through his hair, trying to focus. "Right. So I'll load myself up in the morning. I can pick you up at six, head over to your farm, load you up. We're on the road by seven, there by seven thirty to set up. That way I don't have to listen to Charlie bitch and moan about getting up at five."

Her mouth curved into a small smile. "Guess it saves me from having to be Cara's alarm clock, which never ends well."

He nodded. "Good." *See? Mutually beneficial.* Didn't hurt him to be helpful. In fact, if she paid half the gas, it would help him. He wasn't making a mistake. He was looking out for himself.

"So, um, is that all?"

Dell cleared his throat. "Uh-huh." She studied him. Still wearing his clothes, her brown hair wet and hanging limp at her shoulders. His fingers itched to touch that damp hair, run through it. Itched to find skin under the layers of cotton.

He didn't get it. He really didn't. He'd known her most of his life, though not well. Still, she'd always been there, so it made no sense he suddenly found her irresistible.

"Dell?"

Totally insane, but screw it. He'd never been any good at listening to the voice of reason if reason didn't get him what he wanted.

He stepped toe-to-toe with her, and in one swift movement cupped her face and pressed his mouth to hers.

She was stiff at first, holding her arms still between them, enough that his brain was starting to tell him this impulsive move was the biggest in the long line of mistakes he'd made today. Then she softened against him, the distance between their bodies gone. Her posture relaxed and she kissed him back.

He slid his tongue over her bottom lip, just to get a taste of her. He kept his hands on her face because he didn't trust himself otherwise. Her palms rested on his chest.

There was something tentative and sweet about the way she kissed him, and he wanted to sink into it until there was nothing sweet about it. But this was Mia. Mia, who hadn't had sex before.

Dell pulled away, though he kept his hands on her face. He brushed his thumb down her cheek. Had he ever noticed how soft a woman's cheek felt or how pretty she looked right after being kissed? Flushed and breathless and excited. If so, he couldn't remember it. Usually he was too busy galloping forward.

There would be no galloping forward with Mia. He dropped his hands, took a step away and felt as though he'd been hit by a stun gun.

She only stared, her mouth parted slightly, eyes blinking at him as if he was some foreign object she couldn't identify. Considering he couldn't figure himself out, that seemed about right.

"Tomorrow. Six." He turned around and walked back to the truck, shaken by the sudden realization he was in way over his head. Kissing her was inviting all kinds of complication into his life, and he didn't need that. Couldn't afford it. Not if he wanted to find a way to fix whatever damage today had wrought.

He was so far from the right guy to be in such a sensitive situation. She was sweet and smart and funny, and he didn't know what to do with any of those things. But he'd kissed her and he wouldn't forget the way she felt, not for a very long time.

CHAPTER TWELVE

Mia stood stock-still long after the taillights of Dell's truck disappeared around the corner.

What on earth had happened?

He'd kissed her. Like, *really* kissed her. It was kind of awesome. No first-kiss jittery awkwardness or insane confessions. It was only fair. The universe owed her that after what had happened at his place.

But…how had it happened? *Why* had it happened? Where was she supposed to go from here? He'd just left. And was picking her up tomorrow morning and… What the hell?

Beyond all that, she had no idea what the damage to her crops was or what she was going to be able to do about it. She had her stuff put away for tomorrow, but what about the crops she sold to the restaurant in Millertown? What about the next few market weeks? What was left and what could she do?

Good God, this was a mess.

Cara's car headlights swung into the parking space in front of the apartment, and Mia realized she hadn't moved since Dell released her. Standing on her porch. Having been kissed.

Kissed. By Dell Wainwright.

It still didn't make an ounce of sense.

"Oh, my God. How many times has Mom called you?" Cara slammed her door and walked up the sidewalk. "I swear, it's as if she didn't even believe me there was no hail in Millertown. Where's your truck? At Mom and Dad's?"

Mia swallowed. "Well, no."

Cara walked inside, tossing her keys and purse on the ancient coffee table in their small living room. "Oookay. So where is it? Did you have hail damage? Mom said the hail was as big as footballs."

"Softballs, maybe."

Cara pulled a can of soda out of the fridge, studied her for a beat. "Okay, give it up. Why are you being so weird?"

"I'm not—"

"Gonna close the door?"

Mia looked at her hand. Yup, it was still holding the door open. *Wow. Close door. Take off shoes.*

Mia forced herself to act, all while Cara studied her intently.

"What are you wearing? Those are not your clothes. Where's your truck?"

"Well, my truck is at Dell's." She hoped if she mumbled the information nonchalantly enough, Cara would let the subject drop. And she wouldn't pick up on the fact Mia was wearing Dell's clothes and take that the wrong way.

"What? What is your truck doing at Dell's? Are you wearing Dell's clothes? Oh, my God. Oh, *my* God. Spill it!"

"My windshield is bashed in."

"Mia." Cara plopped onto the couch, and Mia sank into the cushion next to her.

"All right. I went over there to yell at him because he put a produce stand up next to the farm."

"Evil bastard."

Mia was about to defend him—*evil* and *bastard* were harsh—but defending him would give away more than Dell's clothes did. "Anyway, it started hailing and raining. My windshield got bashed, my shirt was wet and a little see-through, and he gave me some dry clothes and drove me home."

That was her story and she was sticking to it. Cara didn't need to know the rest. No sirree. She would not crack under Cara's speculative stare.

"And he tried to kiss me and I blurted out I was a virgin and then we got here and he really did kiss me."

"What!" The screech was probably heard by Grandma Phelps in Arizona. "You told him you're a virgin and he…" Cara shook her head, held up a hand. "Back up. Walk me through it. No detail left unturned."

Reliving her idiocy wasn't high on her to-do list. She had to start making some contingency plans for what farm damage awaited her in the morning light.

But…maybe Cara would know what to do about Dell, because after that kiss, Mia had *no idea* how she was supposed to act when he came to pick her up tomorrow morning.

Oh. God.

She went through the whole scenario. Her face overheated at the whole virgin-blurting retelling, and Cara's occasional screeched "what" or "oh, my God" didn't help, but Mia got the story out. With her face buried in her pulled-up knees, Mia groaned. "So?"

Cara was quiet for a few seconds. Mia peeked between her knees, trying to read her sister's expression. No such luck. Cara had her complete poker face on.

Mia was so jealous she could cry. Why didn't she have the ability to keep her mouth shut and look totally unaffected?

"Oh, no," Cara said in a hushed tone. "What if he has some kind of creepy virgin fetish?"

"Cara! Ew!"

"Well…"

"He said he wanted to kiss me before he knew that. And if you'd seen his face after I let that little bomb drop, you'd know you were wrong."

Cara's concern turned into a grin. "I totally thought there was something between you guys at the bar, but I talked myself out of it. I figured you'd never go for the bad boy."

"He's not a bad boy." Nothing she'd seen of Dell in the past few weeks was bad, per se. Sometimes a little underhanded, but seeing why he was acting that way changed her perception of it. He was in a really crappy situation, and if the tables were turned she couldn't rule out that she'd be doing the exact same thing.

"Kevin has some stories to tell. Apparently Dell and his buddies got drunk one night and wrecked his dad's brand-new baler. Kevin's brother was there and saw it all."

"How many years ago was that?"

Cara tsked. "Man, you've got it bad."

"I don't have anything, but I know what it's like for things you used to do to follow you long after they've stopped being relevant." Mia toyed with the sleeve of her—no, Dell's—sweatshirt. A warm, jumpy sensation pinged through her stomach, bringing her back to the important subject at hand. "What do I do tomorrow when he picks me up? If I don't have a plan I'll start talking about my period or something even more embarrassing."

Cara snorted out a laugh, then reached over and patted Mia's knee. "No idea, but think of it this way. He kissed you *after* you said, like, the most embarrassing thing ever. He must like you."

"That doesn't help me. He walked away, too.

And…you're the expert on guys. You're supposed to know what I'm supposed to do. Help me."

"Okay. Well, do you like him? I mean, more than in the middle-school sense? Is he a nice guy? Is he respectful? Do you want to jump his bones?"

Mia cradled her head in her hands. "I don't even know what bones I'm supposed to want to jump."

"Only one, kiddo, and even you aren't that naive. But, you know, are you interested?"

True enough, but she didn't want to think about bone jumping. She didn't want to think about any of this. "I don't know. He's a direct competitor and probably out of my social league, and the guy cannot keep a shirt on."

"That's not answering the question. Besides, when a guy looks like Dell, the shirt thing is a plus, not a minus."

"I…," Mia looked down at her clutched hands. Even contemplating sex with Dell seemed like a big leap. He'd kissed her once. And there were enough complications with the market and their opposite personalities that she didn't imagine she'd be magically falling into bed with him.

But if the situation presented itself…

The problem was, she did like him. Liked his dedication to his farm and his sense of humor. There was an inner decency about him. Getting her dry clothes, driving her home, not being a total ass in the face of her embarrassing confession.

But…but…but…

Ugh.

"Just be yourself. That's what you were doing when he kissed you, right?"

"Well, yes, but I could do without the verbal diarrhea. Whether that's being myself or not." But Cara had a point. It wasn't as if she'd been some better, more seductive version of herself at Dell's house. She hadn't been trying to be anything on the way home or while unlocking her door, and he'd kissed her anyway. Kissed her really, really well. Not that she had a frame of reference, but still. That was one damn good kiss. One she wouldn't forget anytime soon.

He didn't have to do it, and he didn't need to do anything else to try to embarrass her. She'd taken care of that. So, as Cara had said, the kiss meant he…liked her, in that non-middle-school sense.

Holy moly.

Of course, she also couldn't forget he'd left without a word right after. Well, except that he'd pick her up at six. Mia groaned and curled into the couch cushion.

Cara patted her shoulder. "Welcome to the real word, big sister. It kinda sucks. But hey, if you're lucky you'll finally get some sex out of the deal." Cara hopped off the couch. "I'll get the ice cream."

She didn't need ice cream. She needed a time machine. Not necessarily to go back and change it, but to fast-forward to a point where she knew what the hell to do about it.

DELL PULLED HIS truck onto the gravel driveway that led up to his garage, but Charlie's car was already parked there. When Dell glanced at the porch, a lone shadow stood in the dark.

He had no idea why Charlie would be here. It was almost nine thirty and Charlie rarely spent the night anymore. It would be a good hour's drive back to the city, then another hour's drive back tomorrow morning to help at the market.

If what was coming was another one of Charlie's lectures about giving it up, Dell wasn't sure how mature and forgiving he could be. Especially when he was already on edge. The weather. Kissing Mia. Everything was messed up and he didn't have the wherewithal to battle Charlie's condescension.

"I'm not in much mood for company," Dell said into the quiet evening. Quiet except for the squelch of boot in mud. That was not so quiet, and it managed to squish in time with the chorus of "fuck this" in his mind.

"I figured you wouldn't be, but I also figured…" There was a beat of silence filled by the incessant drone of spring peepers.

Dell stepped onto the porch and realized Charlie seemed…not himself. There was something tentative and fidgety about him, not the normal control and polish.

"Is that Mia's truck?" He nodded toward the vehicle.

"Yup." Charlie didn't need any more explanation than that.

"You didn't do that to the windshield, did you?"

Dell rolled his eyes. "If you haven't heard, there was a hailstorm. She was here chewing me out and her windshield got bashed in. So, I gave her a ride home." And saw her nipples, found out she was a virgin, then kissed her.

Could remember every second of that kiss from the shocked rigidness to the way she'd melted against him. Like a movie looping in his brain. Sweet, alluring Mia, cheeks soft under his palms and—

Maybe it was a good thing Charlie was here. He could stop thinking about Mia in completely inappropriate and desperate ways.

"Oh."

"Charlie, look, I mean it when I say I'll be shit for having any kind of conversations tonight. Whatever you're doing—"

"I've been thinking about something, and I thought tonight might be the right time to run something by you."

"On what probably amounts to the worst night of my farming career?"

"Yes."

Dell let out a belabored sigh and went to the door. He might not be in the mood for sparring with Charlie, but it was better than beating himself up over kissing Mia, fantasizing about Mia, *wanting Mia*.

He wanted the virgin issue to be a roadblock. A reason not to want her. But no matter how much he didn't *want* to want her, it didn't change the fact that…

That kiss had knocked him on his ass, and he wanted more. More from his five-foot-three farming rival.

"You haven't changed much," Charlie offered, waving an arm to encompass the open living room.

Sure, Dell had lived here awhile, but pretty much all his and Charlie's interaction took place outside, at the main house or at the market. So commenting on the way he hadn't changed much since Grandma had moved out wasn't all *that* weird.

Annoying, but not weird. "Suits me."

Charlie nodded, shoving his hands into his pockets. Again Dell was struck by how jumpy Charlie was acting. It wasn't like Charlie to be…unsure. About anything. Ever. "Everything okay?"

Charlie took a deep breath. "Yes. Well, I imagine not so much after the storm. Mom said it was bad."

"Worst I've ever seen."

"Worse than the blizzard when we missed school for two weeks?"

Dell found his mouth curving somewhat. "Shit, that was a good Christmas break."

"Aside from Mom wanting to strangle us by the third week."

Dell shrugged. Always the difference between him and Charlie, and what always put Charlie on top. Dell didn't really remember Mom being irritated. He remembered the fun.

"Look, Dell, I've been thinking a lot about a way to smooth things over. To make everyone happy."

Dell opened his mouth to tell Charlie that was his first problem. Not all of them were ever going to be *happy*, as far as he could see. Not when they were always at cross-purposes.

Why that made him think of Mia was neither welcome nor helpful right now.

"I think I have a plan. It's a compromise, really, but it would allow you to keep farming without Dad…making that difficult for you."

For a second, there was a little burst of hope. A compromise? A possibility? That was great!

Why couldn't *he* have thought of it? Why did it have to be genius, perfect Charlie? Dell blew out a breath. Knowing he was being childish didn't knock the feeling out of him.

"If you agree to let Dad sell to a developer,

I can invest in you as a company. You can buy a piece of land somewhere else. You still get to farm, and have the market, and do the CSA thing, it just wouldn't be here. And maybe with my investment, Dad would feel more secure."

Dell could only blink. "You're offering to…"

"It's a compromise. I have a decent nest egg. It won't hurt me to help you out."

"Help me out." Dell tried to work his way around this, because deep, deep in the center of this offer was a kindness he hadn't expected. Unfortunately, Charlie still didn't understand what he was fighting for.

This place. His heart. His bones. At least a little bit of his pride.

"Yes. If farming is that important—"

"It's not just farming." He tried to say it gently, tried to come off reasonable, but it was hard. Why couldn't he find the right combination of words to get through to the people who were his blood? Grandpa's blood?

Charlie sighed. "I'm trying to find a compromise here. To make everyone happy. Dad is losing out on having a son be something other than a farmer, and you're losing out on this particular piece of land, but in the end you both get what you want."

"No, Charlie, we don't." He shoved hands through his hair. It seemed so stupid to fight for this piece of land when it was currently emerging from hours underwater, but...

Mia understood. He couldn't be that off base.

"How can you not love it? How is it not..." He almost used the in-his-bones line again, but he didn't want to expose himself like that to Charlie. Charlie would probably use it against him.

Funny, he hadn't been the least bit reticent to tell that to Mia. Sitting curled up on that very couch, understanding. Sympathizing. Empathizing. Offering something that had felt like... like...

He didn't even have words for the way it had lightened the band around his lungs that he'd started to believe was permanent.

"I know. Maybe I don't feel it as deeply as you, but I understand not wanting to give up this piece of land because of family attachment. You've built a steady business here."

That the rain had all but destroyed.

"But Dad has a point about letting love and things like that cloud reason. It's better to leave now, to build a foundation with what I'm offering, than to overextend yourself trying to buy Dad out and losing in the future."

"Because that's such an inevitability?"

"The chances are high. Not because of *you*, but because of how the area is changing. You don't want to be the idiot throwing away money because of sentiment. Think about Mr. Egred. If he'd sold the first million times someone had offered, he'd be sitting pretty in a high-dollar house with a private nurse instead of having Casey live with him in that falling-down shack. Everyone in that family losing hand over fist."

"But he's still there. You don't think that means something to him?"

Charlie rubbed a palm to his head. "I'm trying so hard here, Dell."

"For what? Why does any of this matter to you?"

Charlie passed his hand over his mouth, but he didn't stop. He didn't back down. "A family that isn't at odds matters to me. Doing what's right—"

"Then, that'll always be your—our—problem, because we don't agree on what's right, and that... it isn't going to change. You're so busy thinking about what Dad wants and Dad's points, did you ever stop and think about what Grandpa would have wanted?"

"Did you ever stop and think Dad's worried about you taking over because he watched his father keel over at seventy-two, and Grandma all but lose her mind trying to take care of him for those last few years?"

Dell turned away, looking out into the darkness outside his windows. "This place didn't do that to him."

"It didn't not." A loud sigh infiltrated the silence. "Think about it," he said, and then the door creaked open and closed with a click.

And Dell was alone, with a whole hell of a lot of things he didn't want to deal with swirling in his head.

CHAPTER THIRTEEN

MIA PACED HER living room, hoping if she played out every single scenario she wouldn't be prompted to say something stupid. It had kind of worked when she'd first started working at the market. Practicing what to say had allayed her nerves to a manageable point, and people who hadn't grown up with her never looked at her twice.

That first year at the market, growing into her confidence, her ability to be around people without the label "geek" weighing her words had been amazing. Liberating. Every year had gotten better. Maybe she'd never entered social-butterfly territory, but nobody looked at her funny when she answered a question or offered change. She wasn't making lifelong friends, but she wasn't a laughingstock, either. Mia nodded to herself. Yesterday had been a blip.

She glanced at the microwave clock. 5:59. Okay, it was very possible she was going to be sick. She pressed a hand to her stomach, took a deep breath. Not going to be sick. Not going to be nervous. She was calm, cool, collected.

Sure.

A knock sounded at the door and Mia jumped. Yeah, real calm, cool and collected. Deep breath in. Deep breath out. She opened the door. The sky behind Dell was black and he had his beat-up baseball cap pulled low over his eyes. She could see only his mouth, a grim, flat line.

And stubble. She really needed to get over his stubble.

"Morning," he offered in a gruff voice. "Ready?"

"Yeah." Mia grabbed her coat and slipped it on before locking the door behind her. She followed Dell to his truck and silently repeated as many self-affirming, keep-your-mouth-shut mantras as she could.

"You see your damage this morning?" Mia patted herself on the back. A normal question. She could do this. She could totally be normal.

"Not much. Still too dark. Cold frame intact. Major miracle right there. Pretty sure the corn is shot. Tomatoes. Greens probably hit or miss. Squash might come through. But I just planted a whole bunch of stuff. Can't imagine it survived."

She'd find the same once she inspected her fields, but she didn't have a cold frame. She could also afford to break even this year. She wouldn't like it, but she could handle it knowing the weather was to blame. She had contingencies like that built into her business plan, and a family to bail her out if she absolutely needed it.

Mia glanced at Dell from her peripheral vision as he pulled out of the parking space. She couldn't see his eyes, but his expression seemed resigned. He looked tired. He didn't have those things, those options, and she hated the way the sadness waved off him and into her and made her want to help.

So not her place.

"You get any sleep last night?" Was that too personal a question? She didn't know, but at least it might keep conversation in neutral territory.

"Not much." His mouth curved into a small smile. "Few things on my mind."

She couldn't imagine being in his position. Her dad supported every decision she made, encouraged her to take what she wanted from the farm, never made her feel bad about not wanting to deal with the dairy portion.

"In case you didn't catch that, you were one of the things on my mind. Possibly the only smile-worthy thing."

The sound that came out of her mouth couldn't be counted as a word. Something like a squeak and a gasp hidden under the guise of saying, "Oh."

"Can't say as I know what to do about you, Mia."

She clamped her teeth into her bottom lip. It was the only way to keep another inarticulate sound from escaping her. And she wasn't embarrassing herself this morning. She absolutely wasn't.

He chuckled softly. "You're going to have to speak at some point. Even if you blurt out something goofy."

She shook her head. He was very wrong. She didn't have to speak. She didn't have to utter another word ever again.

"Suit yourself. Just means I get to do all the talking. If you're not talking, that means you can't disagree with me. That suits me just fine. It'd be quite a change of pace, though I wouldn't mind your babbling. That'd take my mind off things, too."

What happened to confident and collected? What happened to "she could do this"? She unclenched her teeth and focused on saying each word precisely. "What would I disagree with you about?"

"Well, I was thinking we could do this share-a-ride thing more often. I did some math last night when I was trying not to think about what I'd like to do to you, and if we split gas costs, I could save a decent chunk of change."

Her stomach flipped as it did whenever Cara badgered her into riding a roller coaster at Six Flags. Mia had never cared for that feeling, but Dell's cocky grin gave it some appeal. That, and the spark of heat in a sorely overlooked part of her anatomy.

"It'd save you money, too, so I figure we're not undermining our whole competitors' stance."

Mia nodded. "Right. No. That sounds good." Spending *more* time with the guy who knew she was a virgin and kissed her and was her farmers' market competitor. Yeah, *great*.

He gave her a brief glance and winked before returning his eyes to the road.

"Cara once told me only douchebags wink."

Dell laughed, which made her smile. There was something nice about making him laugh. The way some of the heaviness left his expression, his fingers loosened on the wheel. Making him laugh made her feel effective, even more so with less of that sadness waving off him.

"Only douchebags wink. Huh. I'll have to keep that in mind. Are you under the impression I'm a douchebag?"

"No." Since he was driving, she didn't feel self-conscious about studying his profile. His face was all angles and planes. A masculine face. Right under the brim of his cap, lines fanned out at the corner of his eye, either from smiling too much or squinting at the sun too much. Even in May his skin was tan and golden, and she itched to touch it.

She had, a little bit, and…was there a possibility for more? There shouldn't be, but here he was saying he didn't know what to do about her, offering her rides. *Kissing you*.

There was no sane reason to pursue it, but… Well, she'd never gotten this far with a guy before.

Did it matter if he was the wrong guy if she got some experience under her belt? "So what are you going to do about me?"

He met her gaze as he stopped at the stoplight and she took in the black under his eyes and the couple days' growth of beard. Some of her bravado faded into concern. Her hand reached out to touch his cheek, but she caught herself.

Which was stupid, because her hand was now just there, in the air between them. Awkward.

Just as she got enough brainpower to snatch it back, Dell grabbed it. Then, in a move that made her heart beat so hard it felt as if her entire body was pulsing, he pressed the palm of her hand to his cheek. Then he scraped the edge of his whiskered jaw across her palm.

The fact she could imagine him rubbing those whiskers on other parts of her body was enough to make her squirm and turn really, really red.

A honk interrupted the moment. She cleared her throat. "Um, green light."

He shook his head, released her hand. "Right." He returned his focus to the road as the guy behind them lay on the horn.

Dell muttered something about jackasses and then turned the truck onto the gravel drive leading to the farm. "Where do you want me to go?"

Mia pointed to the vegetable barn, trying not to grin at the thought she'd affected him as much as he affected her. This wasn't one-sided. It might be stupid, but it wasn't one-sided.

Yahoo.

He pushed the truck into Park and, without another word, they both got out and he helped her carry her pallets of vegetables to his truck as the sun began to rise in the east, covering the farm with a pretty golden glow. Dell had kept one half of his truck bed empty, and her goods fit with only a bit of room to spare. He had a good idea with this ride sharing. Especially in light of the money she'd lose rebuying seeds.

"Well, that's it." Mia pulled her phone out of her pocket to check the time. "Timed it pretty well, really."

When she looked up, she realized he was standing in front of her. The rising sun haloed his hat and he smiled. Not the cocky grin, but something slow and sweet that had her insides doing that Jell-O thing again.

"What?" she demanded. "Dirt?" Why else would he be staring at her so intently? She wiped at her face.

He closed the distance between them so fast she didn't even notice until she looked up and her chest bumped into his stomach.

Mia cleared her throat, closed her hand around her phone and squeezed hard. "I'm not going to say anything stupid this time." She closed her eyes and let her head fall back. *Because announcing you weren't going to say something stupid isn't at all stupid.*

Where was an apocalypse when you needed one?

"Glad to hear it." There was humor in his voice and when she looked up, he was still smiling, but it was a smile that made her return it. His fingertip touched the tip of her ear, curved down. A light touch. Simple enough her mind shouldn't be galloping ahead to where he might touch next and what she would be supposed to do in return.

It was a dizzying mix of nerves and excitement and uncertainty and want.

"You look good at dawn," he said, his voice low, feathering across her forehead.

"Well, you do, too." Her heart leaped into her throat and she couldn't force another word out. Which was probably really good or she'd say something like, "Want to make out in the barn?" She'd really like to know what making out was like. Even if she did something stupid, because Dell seemed really good at ignoring or humoring her stupid.

Instead, Dell leaned his head down and—

A horn blasting cut him off. They both looked to see her dad's truck bouncing up the path from the cow barn.

Mia swallowed. Okay, this was probably going to get weird. Dad pulled his truck to a stop next to Dell's. Slowly, he lumbered over to them.

Dad was never in a hurry, and it had never made her nervous until this very minute.

"Morning," he offered.

"Morning," Dell replied, taking a very obvious step away from her. "I don't think we've met, Mr. Pruitt. I'm Dell Wainwright. I'm pretty sure you know my dad." He held out a hand, and it hovered there. In the air. Unreciprocated.

Dad stood, hands in his pockets, thoughtfully working the chew around in his mouth as he studied Dell's outstretched hand. Mia wished to God he would say something. Anything. Please, just *anything*.

"Yup." Finally Dad pulled one hand free of his pockets and shook Dell's hand.

She let out an audible sigh of relief. Her cheeks were on fire with embarrassment, so she turned to the truck.

"We should get going, Dad. Did you have a chance to look around? Hasn't been light for very long, but I've got to get to the market."

"Some damage. Might be a slow few weeks, but replanting will get you back on track. Money'll be tight."

Mia sneaked a glance at Dell. His jaw was set. Was he comparing that response with his own father's? She wondered if he was being too hard on his father, if Mr. Wainwright might understand. She wondered a lot of things, and they all uncomfortably had to do with Dell.

"Hey, guys." Anna walked around the corner of the barn. She had her milking boots on and her perfectly wavy blond hair pulled back in a ponytail. "You mind giving me a ride? Cara was going to pick me up, but if you're already here..."

"You're coming?"

"Face painting, remember?" Anna grinned. "Besides, everybody wants to see the battle of the sexes. Even the kids at school are talking about it."

Dad returned to his truck without a word or a goodbye. He'd never cared for words like *sexes*.

"Um, well—"

"You don't mind, do you, Dell?" Anna bull-dozed on. "Just give me a second to get my paints and shoes. Be right back." She didn't even wait for an answer, just jogged to the house.

"Sorry. I..." Mia shook her head. "My family's kind of weird."

Dell chuckled. "Join the club." His expression sobered. "Forgot about the battle-of-the-sexes thing."

"Yeah." Mia frowned down at her boots. Even without the kiss, she felt bad about going after Dell's business now. He needed the sales a lot more than she did.

Except, she was a businesswoman. She had a business to run, too, and the hail damage could hurt her. If she worried about every farmer who was worse off, helped every guy struggling to make ends meet at the expense of her own business, she'd be done. Even if Dad left her everything, she needed an income to keep that everything going.

Mia looked up at Dell's face, met his gaze. He seemed to be thinking the same thing. That this was a mistake. Too complicated. Getting involved put them at odds with their own lifeblood. Lifeblood they both loved more than just about anything else.

"Mia, maybe we should—"

"Anna's coming," Mia interrupted, cursing her sister's hurrying as Anna squelched through the mud a few yards away.

"Guess we'll talk about it later, huh?"

Mia nodded. "Guess so." Just what she needed. More time to think about it.

THE MINUTE DELL got to the farmers' market, Charlie was already there in bitch mode. Which shouldn't have been surprising after the way they'd left things last night, the fact he'd had to have driven all the way downtown and then back with only about six or seven hours in between.

"Getting too cheap to even give me a ride now, huh?" Charlie glanced at Mia briefly. "Hey, Mia." Then he did a double take. "You two ride together?"

Mia's cheeks turned that pretty shade of pink that somehow prompted Dell to think about what other things might make her blush.

So not the time. "Mia had that hail damage to her windshield, so I gave her a ride."

"Ooh." Charlie drew the word out as if it explained everything. Dell wanted to laugh because it didn't explain a damn thing.

What was he doing? He didn't have a clue. The reminder of the battle of the sexes brought it all home. All the things he'd kind of ignored the past twelve hours.

She was trying to steal his customers. Maybe that was harsh, but having these little competitions every week had been her idea in a way, and it was going to earn *her* customers. He shouldn't blame her, couldn't really when he caught her looking at him all cute and nervous.

He was so screwed. Screwed because the things he felt about Mia weren't the things he usually felt about a woman. He didn't just want to sleep with her—he wanted to hang out with her, because when he did, he didn't feel like the idiot Wainwright. Even as smart as he knew she was, she didn't act as if he was the pretty face incapable of "intellectually stimulating" anything, as Corrie had once accused him. When they talked about farm stuff, Mia treated him like an equal.

She had reached over to touch his face, as if she cared. With her, he didn't think about not being able to get through to his dad, about Charlie's proposal, about all the things up in the air he might lose. He just felt…comfortable. Good.

That was a really sticky place to be in right now. He pushed his cap up on his head, rubbed his forehead. It took him a few minutes to realize Charlie was staring at him expectantly.

"What?"

"This is usually about the time you start whipping off clothes and women line up to mindlessly buy your cabbage—which is not a euphemism. I hope."

"Right." Dell sneaked a look at Mia, who was chatting with an elderly woman over a bunch of beets.

Whether or not he pursued this thing with Mia, he couldn't change his business tactics. If she didn't like it, well, that would be the end of whatever weird thing they had going on.

Dell pulled off his shirt and put his salesman hat on. He wasn't going to be satisfied unless he sold every last turnip green. The storm had seriously tested his resolve, but in some weird way Charlie's offer only steeled it.

He was going to make this work. He was going to succeed.

An hour in and he hadn't let himself look at Mia once. Whenever he got the urge, he went and restocked a pallet or took a walk around his side of the aisle, chatting up customers.

Val approached. "Hey, Dell, honey, how's it going?" She unnecessarily patted his bare arm.

"That storm was a nasty one. You come through all right?"

"It was tough, but we'll be fine. Can't get rid of me that easy."

She swatted at him playfully. "You ready for our battle of the sexes? I put on our Facebook page we'd start at ten." Val gestured to encompass the entire market. "I can already tell we have more people than usual."

"Yeah. Sure. Push-ups again?"

"Actually, Farrah and I were talking about making the events more farm-y and maybe doing this every week? Mia agreed."

Dell glanced at Mia's booth. She was smiling at some guy in a chef's coat. A chef's coat. Where did the guy think he was, on one of those cooking-competition shows?

"Dell?"

"Yeah. Yeah, I'm ready. Whenever she is." He didn't care for the jealousy burning in his gut, but that didn't make it go away. Maybe he'd channel it and kick her nice little ass in this stupid battle.

"You're so screwed," Charlie said with a chuckle. "Whatever you do, don't beat her too badly. You'll never have another female customer again."

"Whatever. Watch the booth." He followed Val to a truck full of hay bales.

"Help me up, honey?"

Dell helped Val up into the bed of the truck,

where she pulled out a megaphone and began announcing the battle-of-the-sexes competition.

"Last week we had a push-up tie. This week, we wanted to see these two flex their farm muscles. They each have ten bales of hay. Whoever loads their ten bales into the appropriate truck in the parking lot first wins this week's battle of the sexes."

Mia pulled a pair of gloves out of her back pocket. "You know this isn't fair, right?" Though she didn't seem too bent out of shape about it. He liked that about her, and he tried to smile back, but the chef guy was standing by the Pruitt stand...watching.

"Don't you think men and women are equals, sugar?"

Her eyes narrowed. "If you recall, I told you not to call me that."

This time Dell grinned. Val stepped between them before he could offer another comment to get her back up. Val told them which truck to put their bales in, then made a big show about placing them on opposite sides of the full truck bed.

A crowd had indeed gathered, but Dell couldn't take his focus off the stupid white chef coat. Asshole. Surely Mia was smarter than to be impressed by that, except the whole no-experience thing and the awkward-high-school-reputation thing.

Dell bit back a curse.

Val announced the event one more time into

the bullhorn and then gave them an "On your marks, get set, go!"

Dell focused on the task at hand. It was no easy feat moving the bales. It didn't just require strength, but dexterity in maneuvering an awkward square of hay around cars and people.

His muscles were screaming and his breath coming in quick spurts when he hefted the last bale into the truck bed. He looked around for Mia. She was scowling a few yards behind him.

He'd won. Ha. Of course, that might not equal customers. Shit. Dell trudged back to the start of the race and sank onto the ground, wiping his forehead with his arm. Jesus, he was spent.

A few minutes later, Mia collapsed next to him and Val declared him the winner.

"I'm going to kick your ass next week," she huffed. The guy in the chef coat waved as he walked to his hybrid car.

A hybrid.

Mia waved in return, and the jealous burn was back. "Bet your chef friend can't do that, sweetheart."

Mia's eyebrows drew together, but after a few seconds she laughed between huffed breaths. "He's the chef at Edibles. I'm a supplier. He was on his way to work and wanted to make sure his produce was going to be okay after the storm." She stood and bent over, giving him an ample peek down her shirt. She patted his cheek. "But you don't know what a confidence booster a little jealousy is."

Then Mia sauntered back to the Pruitt booth as if she was something special.

Damn it, he was beginning to think she really was.

CHAPTER FOURTEEN

MIA SETTLED INTO Saturday night with approximately five loads of laundry that needed folding. Exciting evening indeed.

She poured herself a glass of wine first. No reason she couldn't have a little fanciness in her otherwise boring evening.

Since this was Cara's third date with Kevin, Mia didn't anticipate her sister coming home tonight. So it was just Mia and her laundry. Not all that unusual, really.

When someone knocked on the door, she jumped. It was so unexpected, some of the wine sloshed onto her hand. Her stomach jittered a bit at the prospect of an unannounced visitor.

Maybe it was Dell. Between Cara, Charlie and Val all vying for her attention after the market was over and Anna expecting a ride back to the farm, they hadn't managed to get two words alone. So now she didn't know where they stood.

Except that he'd been jealous over Sam. And she'd come up with the perfect exit line.

Ten points for Mia.

"Just a second," she called, running her fingers

through her hair, tucking her oversize T-shirt into her jeans so it looked less schlumpy. When she looked out the peephole, her excitement deflated.

She undid the lock and opened the door. "Hey, Mom. Dad." Since her dad never left the farm except for church and supplies he couldn't send one of the girls for, anxiety replaced disappointment. "Is everything okay?"

Her mom stepped into the apartment, giving her a warm hug. "Of course, dear, but your father got this wild hair you absolutely had to have your truck back tonight." Mom looked around the room. "See, Franklin, she's doing her laundry." She shook her head and clucked her tongue.

Dad stepped behind Mom but moved past her, poking around the apartment. Unusual for him. Normally he sat on the couch itching to get back to his cows and solitude.

"Are you sure everything is okay?"

"So you don't have any company tonight?"

"What company would I have?" Then it dawned on her. Dad had seen her with Dell this morning. Mia glanced at her mother, who was poking around the refrigerator. Surely he hadn't told her, or she'd be lecturing Mia about the evil dangers of men she and Dad hadn't approved.

Which was all of them.

"Where's Cara? Her car is outside. And are you drinking? Alone? Oh, my heavens!" Mom's hands fluttered to her throat.

"Cara's out on a date with Kevin. I am having one glass of wine. Neither is the end of the world." Why did she bother trying? Mom was already halfway to Anxietyville.

"Who is Kevin? I've never heard of him. What's his last name? Do I know his family? What church do they go to? Oh, I am calling your sister right this instant." Mom pulled her cell phone out of her purse. She barely knew how to use it, but enough to badger her daughters if she got a whiff of something she didn't approve of.

"Cara? This is your mother. You answer this phone immediately." Mom wandered down the hall, preferring privacy for her badgering.

Mia studied Dad, who looked at the floor scratching his bearded cheek. "Dad, what are you guys doing here? Really?"

"Brought your truck back."

"I'm not stupid. You know I could have picked it up tomorrow. I could have had it fixed myself."

Dad hunched his shoulders. "Can't I do a favor for my daughter?"

"Daddy."

"I don't like that boy," he grumbled.

"Who? Kevin?"

Dad scowled at her. "Dell Wainwright. I saw him bothering you at Orscheln, and then there was talk at church last week they call him the Naked Farmer. And this morning he was all… crowding you. You're a good girl. You shouldn't be…" Dad cleared his throat. His entire face was red from the roots of his hair to his beard.

Mia smiled. Well, at least she knew where she got that from. "You don't have to worry about me."

"I thought I didn't have to worry about you. Then I saw the way you were looking at him. Don't like it. Not one bit."

Had she been looking at Dell any special way? As if he was a gift she was dying to unwrap, probably. And she had probably lost any chance of unwrapping with one well-placed battle of the sexes.

She could tell Dad that, though maybe not in so many words but, honestly, she was twenty-*six*. Both of her parents needed to accept the inevitability of a guy showing interest in her.

Even if she sometimes doubted that inevitability.

"I'm an adult. I make my own choices." She reached over and squeezed his hand. "Trust me to make the right ones, okay? I can only stand one parent questioning my every move."

He made a huffing sound. "You got the biggest brains out of all our children, but you also…" He cleared his throat, fiddled with his beard. "You've got the softest heart. Always did. You named all the cows and cried for two weeks every time we lost one or sold one or killed one."

Mia wrinkled her nose. Okay, that was true. But her heart wasn't involved when it came to Dell.

She didn't think.

"I'll make the right choices. I promise."

"Well, you always do." He slapped her truck keys on the counter. "Don't let that boy change that."

"Your sister." Mom stomped up the hallway. "She's ignoring my calls! Do you know where they went? I want to know more about this Kevin boy. I—"

"Come on, Sarah. We did what we came to do. Let's go home."

"Are you joking? Your daughter is—"

"Grown. Come on, now."

Mom and Dad argued out the door, but before Dad closed it behind him he rolled his eyes. "Love you, pumpkin."

Mia smiled. He hadn't called her pumpkin since she'd lived at home. "Love you, too."

Once the door was closed, she sank into a kitchen chair and then took a long, deep drink of her wine.

It was weird—everyone seemed to think of Dell as this bad boy. Someone to be wary of. She didn't see it. Even when he'd been annoying her with the shirtless stuff at the beginning of the season, poking at her, putting up that stand. Irritating, for sure, and maybe bully territory, but she'd never considered him merciless or dangerous.

What was she getting so worked up about? At this point all she and Dell shared was one kiss, a few not-so-innocent touches and not much else. For all she knew he'd pretend none of it had ever happened next Saturday. It's not as if they'd made plans otherwise. Even for sharing a ride next market day.

She thunked her head on the table. For once she was grateful she'd never had a relationship. If this was what they were all like, she was due for an aneurism by her thirtieth birthday.

Another knock at the door. Mia groaned, then downed the rest of her wine. If she was going to handle Mom the rest of the night, she needed something moderately relaxing pumping through her veins.

She opened the door, stopping short when she realized it wasn't her parents.

It was Dell.

She coughed as her last swallow of wine went down the wrong way.

"Hey." He'd looked grim when she first opened the door, but his lips curved upward. "Okay?"

She nodded furiously, eyes still watering. "Wrong pipe." *Holy crap.* He was standing in her doorway, all impressive height and broad shoulders. He was dressed in nice jeans and had a leather coat on. No baseball hat to be seen, just wavy blond hair looking golden under the porch light.

And she was standing there in an old T-shirt and jeans. Well, at least the jeans were a pair of her new ones that actually fit. Possibly only because Cara had thrown out all the other ones for reasons like this, Mia imagined.

"So, um, you busy?" He looked over her head into the apartment.

Mia swallowed and pointed vaguely at the laundry baskets on the couch and living-room floor. "No. Unless laundry counts."

His smile widened. "It doesn't."

"Right." She looked down at her fuzzy purple socks. There was a hole showing off her big toe. Wow, she was a mess.

"You want to go to dinner?"

Her mouth dropped open a little when she looked up at him. Was he asking her on a…date? While she stood in her ratty clothes choking on wine and barely putting together sentences. "I'm…" She pointed to her clothes.

He took his time looking them over. Enough time that a blush started creeping up her neck. "You could change."

"Oh, right. Um. Okay."

"You could also let me in."

"Right." She moved out of the way and when he stepped in she closed the door behind him. *Weird* did not begin to describe having Dell stand in her entryway.

"I would have called, but I don't have your number." He made his way into her living room. Dell Wainwright standing in her living room, casual as could be next to laundry baskets that contained her underwear, among other things. "I thought we could go to that Edibles place, since you know the chef so well."

Mia blinked a few times, realized her mouth was open, snapped it shut. Then realized she had to open it again to respond.

Dell was asking her out. On a date. Which, of course, was the natural progression here. They'd kissed. He'd been jealous. Why wouldn't they go out?

Enemies. Battle of the sexes. Competitors.

Hot. Kissed you. Does not run in the opposite direction when you babble.

Mia took a deep breath, focused on saying something casual and normal. When she thought about Dell being jealous and wanting to go to Sam's restaurant, it wasn't such a hard thing to do. "Edibles sounds great. Make yourself comfortable and I'll go change."

She sounded like a reasonable, adult woman. Yay. When she turned for the hallway, though, she stumbled over her own boots.

Better start praying the reasonable adult woman made it *to* dinner.

DELL POKED AROUND Mia's living room. Family pictures, cow knickknacks, basketball trophies, which had to be Cara's. He couldn't see Mia being coordinated enough to play a team sport.

The place was kind of cluttered and girlie, but it suited them. He wandered through the kitchen, then couldn't contain his curiosity in moving down the hall.

Curiosity was what had gotten him here after all. Wondering what she'd be doing on a Saturday night. What she'd be wearing. How she would react to him showing up. Was there anything extra going on with her and that chef guy?

After the backbreaking afternoon he'd spent trying to clean up the mess of his fields, darkness had descended. He'd spent the entire day mulling over contingency plans and where he could scrounge up some extra money, thinking about Charlie's offer, about what would get them all some peace...but there were no answers. So he'd turned his mind to much more interesting thoughts.

Since there wasn't anything else to distract himself with at home, he figured he'd show up and find out the answers to all those curiosity-driven questions regarding Mia. Maybe soak up some of her...concern, care, whatever the hell it was that drew him to her like a magnet.

Dell peeked through the open door of the first room in the hall. It was kind of messy, but he immediately pinned it as Mia's from the stacks of seed catalogs all over and the barn paintings on the wall. Cowboy and work boots littered the bottom of her open closet, a few old beat-up pairs of tennis shoes spilling out, as well.

He took a few steps inside, wondering where she'd gotten to if she wasn't in her room. Like the living room, it was cluttered and feminine without being fussy. It wasn't lace and pink like Kenzie's room at home. This room was a perfect reflection of Mia.

"Oh." Mia stopped short in the doorway, swallowed. She obviously hadn't expected to see him there.

"I like your room," he offered.

"How did you know it was mine?"

"Well, I figured seed catalogs weren't what Cara would consider bedtime reading."

She'd changed out of her jeans and T-shirt into skintight black pants and a long V-neck sweater. She'd pulled her hair out of its ponytail, and it looked as if maybe she'd put on some makeup. Her eyes were darker, her lips redder.

She fidgeted in her own room's doorway and he put two and two together. She was wearing Cara's clothes—that was why she'd come from the other room.

She looked really good in Cara's clothes.

"I, um, just need to get my shoes." She moved past him, and if he was reading things right, made every effort to keep a little physical distance as she did.

She bent over, pawing through the shoes at

the bottom of her closet, and Dell sent up a little prayer of thanks for Cara. The pants did amazing things for Mia's ass. Enough that he couldn't help thinking about what it would be like to slide his hands over the curve, move his hands under her shirt, grazing bare skin.

Dell let out a long breath. He was definitely jumping the gun. He wasn't even sure she'd want to sleep with him, let alone sure if he was up for such a...sensitive task. But that didn't mean he couldn't think about it. Only that he shouldn't.

She turned, a determined smile on her face. "Ready?" She looked more like someone about to go into battle than someone about to go on a date.

He wasn't sure if it was his pride or something else bothered by that. He wanted her to be excited or flattered or at least relaxed. He wanted to be able to offer her something, the way she offered him...something.

When she tried to walk past him, he took her hand in his. He wanted to say something reassuring, give her an out. Maybe she didn't want to go, and as much as he wanted the distraction, wanted *her*, he wasn't interested in this not being mutual.

She turned her hand in his so their fingers entwined. When he met her gaze, she smiled a little.

Holding hands in the middle of her bedroom. It was all...a little close for comfort. Something strange flopped in his gut. Something like nerves.

Frowning at himself, he curled his fingers around her shoulder, the fabric of her sweater soft against his palm. Her head tilted back, lips pursed and expression uncertain.

"You look really hot." He winced. Apparently Mia's uncontrollable blurting was contagious. "I mean, you look good. You usually do."

"Thanks." She smiled, pleased and not at all shy. Apparently his being an idiot was a good old ego booster. She actually stepped closer.

His brain knew it wasn't a great idea to touch her hair, but when she reciprocated by putting a hand on his forearm, his brain shut the hell up.

He lowered his mouth to hers. He made sure to be slow, careful. The last thing he wanted to do was scare her off.

He tasted whatever was on her lips. Something vaguely fruity. Her hand grasped his forearm tighter and then, hesitantly, her other hand moved to his cheek and her fingers rifled through his hair.

Though the desire to press against her was a beating, growing urge, he held himself back. He kept the kiss light, until the tip of her tongue grazed his bottom lip.

The kiss deepened. So lost in it, he wasn't sure who initiated it, but Mia met him move for move. She opened her mouth, granting him entrance, and as his hands smoothed down her back, she returned the favor.

The distance between them was gone, maybe by mutual decision, and as his hands cupped over her ass, he had the buzzing, disorienting realization things were moving too fast. Mia was not the sex-before-you-even-had-a-date kind of girl.

When he pulled away, he was surprised to find his own breathing as ragged as hers. She looked a little shell-shocked. Had he been too aggressive? "You just tell me if I need to back off, okay?"

"I will." Her eyes held his, and though her breath hitched a little, she looked absolutely sure. "I might be inexperienced, but I'm not Amish. Or about to let you or anyone push me into something I don't want." She tentatively slid her palm down his chest until it rested at his abdomen. Something about the mix of nerves and determination about did him in.

Dell smiled, tracing his finger over the edge of her collarbone. Mia might be a lot of things, but she was no pushover. It was comforting to think she wouldn't let him be an ass.

"So maybe we shouldn't be doing this in my bedroom." She pulled her bottom lip between her teeth, then took her hand from him, creating some distance.

He let out a breath. "Yeah. Good idea." He tried

to adjust himself before he followed Mia out of her bedroom. It was going to be a long night.

MIA RETRIEVED HER purse and keys. Her hand shook a little. Both from that kiss and from pride. She hadn't freaked out. She hadn't backed down. She'd kissed him back. She'd caused him to get aroused.

Her.

She wanted to do a little tap dance right there in the kitchen. *This* was the next step she'd been after, and it was *everything* she'd hoped. Everything.

It didn't eradicate the nerves or the what-nexts swirling in her mind, but it managed them in some weird way. Cataloged them away behind the giddy feeling of power and attraction.

Dell Wainwright had a thing for her. It validated something inside her she hadn't realized needed validating.

When she turned, she found him studying the papers spread out on the table. They outlined her plan of action for the next months. What seeds she'd need to rebuy. Cost sheets and current inventory. Field designs. A couple of printouts about cold frames.

In an instant her excitement fizzled, because they were right back to where they'd been this afternoon. A glaring reminder they were each other's biggest competition and there was a lot at stake.

Kissing and dates didn't fit in, and in a fight between farm and *finally* reaching some point in adulthood, Dell couldn't stand a chance.

CHAPTER FIFTEEN

MIA'S PLANS SCATTERED across her table were more organized and neater than his, but they both outlined the same problem.

Now they weren't just competing for customers, they were competing on growth times and who could offer what and when. The storm had knocked them both back, which meant they both had to fight harder to survive. To succeed.

And he was asking her to dinner and kissing her in her bedroom and enjoying her way too much. Getting all wrapped up in her. He couldn't remember someone getting to him this way, so quickly. Not since high school at the very least, and he was pretty sure that had been more the new prospect of sex than anything else.

Maybe his dad was right to think Dell was foolish. Being here reeked of exactly that. Having these unfamiliar feelings whirling around inside him had to be foolish and downright stupid. Thinking there was something he and Mia could do together that didn't boil them down to the fact they were always going to be at odds.

"You can back out, Dell."

He frowned at her. In this instance, he wasn't at all comfortable with how well she read or understood him.

She smiled sheepishly, putting her purse down on the counter and walking to the opposite side of the table. "It was nice of you to offer, but—" she gestured toward the papers "—this is more complicated than we seem to want to give it credit for. I mean, you don't see the head of McDonald's and the head of Burger King making out, do you?"

Dell snorted out a laugh. "Probably for other reasons. Not to mention we're not exactly at a McDonald's level of business here."

"Not monetarily, but doesn't it mean enough to you to think of it that way?"

Her expression was too naked, too full of emotions and things he didn't know how to handle. He had to look away because those things echoed inside him, deep and powerful. Completely unwelcome.

He touched the expense sheet with all Mia's meticulously written figures. It wasn't millions, but it meant more than money, that was for sure. She had a point. It was their blood and bones broken down to figures and plans, but it didn't change what it meant.

This week kept getting worse. Which didn't seem fair. Dell looked up from the papers, studied Mia. Her mouth was curved into a rueful smile, but she seemed disappointed, too.

She had to feel some…spark of what he did between them. Whatever nonsense it was, the depth of understanding they could offer each other, she felt it, too. Seemed reluctant to give it up.

He'd never seen much sense in self-sacrifice unless it was directly tied to the farm, and this was tied to the farm, but it didn't feel direct. Screwing with Mia was definitely wrong, but she had said she wasn't exactly saving herself for some white knight.

"You said you wouldn't mind a few Mr. Wrongs, right?" Because there was no way Dell Wainwright could ever manage Mr. Right. Fighting for his farm was all the good he had in him, and where all his intelligence and effort had to go.

But it couldn't be totally off base to offer a little wrong for both of them.

"Well, yes, but—"

"Well, I'm not looking for Mrs. Right." Wouldn't have the time for her if she plopped right into his lap, or across from him at the farmers' market. "So maybe we enjoy each other no matter how wrong until this stuff gets in the way." Didn't he deserve something that was fun and not stressful? That little drop of comfort she offered, that made him feel more capable, more sure of what he felt for the farm. He *needed* that.

"You're suggesting we…" She blinked, her cheeks faintly pink.

He grinned. How could he do anything but at

her barely contained shock? "I'm suggesting we have fun. Till it's not."

"Oh." Her eyes rounded as she cleared her throat from the squeak in her *oh*.

Yeah, he deserved something fun. Something good. Mia was definitely both of those things. "So, what do you say? I'm starving."

She blinked a few more times, then smiled brightly. "Yeah. Let's do that." Slipping her purse onto her shoulder, she shuffled the papers into a pile.

She walked toward the door and Dell followed. When she stopped abruptly, he almost ran into her.

She looked up at him, eyebrows drawn together. "Is this one of those keep-your-enemies-closer things?"

He wanted to laugh, but she seemed so serious. "Not a lot of farmer espionage that I know of. What am I going to find out? You're planting beefsteak tomatoes instead of Snow Fairy?" She looked so uncertain, Dell was compelled to wipe it off her face. He'd love to do it with a kiss, but he figured Mia Pruitt needed words. "I just like you, Mia." A simple truth he probably shouldn't have admitted, but she brought it out in him.

Her mouth curved even as the pink in her cheeks deepened. Something about her response made him feel less like a pansy ass for vocalizing it. Less as if he'd exposed some chink in his armor. An armor he was undoubtedly going to need.

Fun. Till it's not. He was an idiot.

She fiddled with her purse strap, opened her mouth silently, then closed it. It was baffling he found that attractive. Probably made him some kind of weirdo.

Well, so be it. "Going to say something embarrassing, sugar?"

Her nervous fidgeting stopped abruptly and she narrowed her eyes at him. "Watch it, buddy. You're not half as charming as you seem to think you are."

Dell chuckled. "I charmed you right out of doing your laundry on a Saturday night. My powers are endless."

She rolled her eyes, but there was humor in her curved mouth. "You're ridiculous." She turned to the door, then opened it before stepping outside. Dell followed, not sure what he was doing. Not sure what his end game was.

Maybe there was no end game. But what did that mean? He usually had a pretty clear idea what he wanted out of a relationship. Mia and her blushing and her one-liners complicated everything.

She locked her door. "For what it's worth," she began, her face angled toward the doorknob, her expression obscured by the dark, "I just like you, too."

Dell scratched his fingers through his hair. Maybe it was the fact he'd spent more time on the farm the past year than on his social life. That had meant spending a lot of time with a family who might love him, but didn't always like him. Certainly didn't understand or see him.

Mia's simple statement meant a lot. A lot more than he was comfortable with, but it didn't lessen that pull. Even in his discomfort, he wanted to be close to her.

So once she straightened, he held out his hand. She pressed her lips together, but if she'd been trying to suppress a smile, she failed.

She slid her hand into his, slender and strong. Mia was a tiny thing, but she was a solid presence next to him as they walked to his truck. "We don't have to go to Edibles. Really, Sam and I... There's nothing there." She clambered into the passenger side of his truck, and when Dell slid into the driver's seat, she looked at him earnestly. "He just got divorced and the restaurant is definitely his focus."

He raised an eyebrow. "And you know this because...?"

She opened her mouth, that flustered-fish look that lifted all the nagging discomfort right out of him.

"Well, he told me."

Dell shifted the car into gear. "And why did he mention that to you, I wonder."

"Friendly conversation?"

"I don't think people bring up divorce in friendly conversation. They do bring it up to let people know they're single."

"How do you know that? You're not divorced."

"No, but I have been flirted with by more than one divorced woman." He stopped at a red light, glancing at her.

Her expression was furrowed concentration. "You think Sam was hitting on me?"

"With his whole arsenal, sugar."

She blinked a few times, before a smile bloomed wide and pretty on her face. "Huh."

"You're on a date with one guy, and figuring out another guy is flirting with you makes you smile?"

"Uh, *yeah*!" She laughed, her smile infectious for some reason. "There has not been a lot of flirting in my life. I'll be pleased with any of it no matter who I'm on a date with."

The light went green so he had to tear his gaze away from her smile and the way her laugh made the whole air around them seem brighter. He was seriously losing it, and he had to concentrate on driving toward Millertown besides.

"So you want to go to Edibles to, what? Rub it in his face that you outflirted him and got me out on a date first?"

"I didn't even have to flirt to outflirt him. You

didn't know he was flirting, and I haven't been telling you how single I am."

"I think, in some weird way, all our…bickering is kind of flirting." She paused. "Isn't it?"

He hadn't thought about it, but he supposed she was right. Fighting with her was usually born of frustration or irritation, but it rarely ended that way. How many times had it ended with him smiling, baffled, after her?

"I guess, maybe."

"So we're the adult version of pigtail pulling on the playground, or whatever. Of course, when people pulled my hair in elementary school they were actually just being mean. It very obviously had nothing to do with liking me."

He slanted her a look. She was staring straight ahead, and she'd said it so matter-of-factly, as if it was the way of the world that people had been asshats to her. Including him. He'd been a total, undeniable asshat.

"Don't look at me all pityingly," she said on a disgusted huff. "I'm not that girl anymore." She straightened in her seat. "I built a life I'm proud of. A life I *love*," she said fiercely. "Nothing to pity me over."

He thought about that, about the way her dad had looked at him as if he was some invasive fungus at her farm that morning. The way Anna and Cara always seemed to rally around her. The way she smiled and talked and didn't act as though there were a cloud hanging over her head all the damn time, so unlike him it shamed him a bit.

He thought about the way she fought, the insults she hurled at him without being mean. It was self-defense, and she was a hell of a champion at it.

So, no, he didn't pity her. Not in the least.

CHAPTER SIXTEEN

DELL PARKED IN the Edibles parking lot. Despite all her assurances this was unnecessary, he'd never once wavered in his decision that this would be where they went.

In truth, she'd been dying to go. See what Sam did with the ingredients she provided him. But Edibles was a tiny place for people way cooler than her. And that wasn't self-pity talking, that was just fact. Give her an affordable chain restaurant where she knew what was expected of her any day of the week.

This was new. On every level, she realized, as Dell's hand took hers.

"Come on, sugar, can't stand gaping in the parking lot all night."

"Why do you keep calling me that?"

"What? Sugar?" He cocked his head, pulling her toward the entrance. "Because you're sweet?"

She made a finger-down-the-throat gagging motion, realizing halfway through that might not be the thing seductions and good first dates were made of.

But he laughed, and she could not ignore she

liked to make him do that. For a guy with a care-free party-lover image, to her Dell always seemed weighed down by, well, life. She liked when he wasn't.

They stepped into the door. The restaurant was small with various-shaped wood tables seemingly haphazardly placed. Everything was brown and green and white. The woman behind a small, mostly empty display case of desserts smiled pleasantly.

"Welcome to Edibles," she said in a soft, sooth-ing voice, pushing thick black frames up her nose. "Table for two?"

Dell nodded and they were led to a kind of un-comfortable diamond-shaped table. Which was really a square, but the bench chairs were set up at two opposite corners. Yeah, this place was *so* out of her league.

"Your server will be with you momentarily. Our menu, made completely from locally sourced ingredients, changes daily and can be viewed right here." The hostess tapped a mini chalkboard easel in the center of the table. "Enjoy."

They both leaned forward and squinted at the loopy script.

Dell looked around the room then back at her. "I don't understand a word of this."

Mia tried to stifle a giggle. "Me, neither."

"Well, as long as we're in this together. What the hell is a…" He squinted again. "Carpaccio?"

They talked over the menu, helping each other find suitable choices. She talked about the ingredients Sam bought from her and how she'd met him at an agricultural conference.

It was not...hard. Maybe because she'd almost forgotten it was a date. It was just talking with someone. Someone who cared about farming, which in her world wasn't very many people. Sure, Dad lived and breathed it, but talking wasn't his strong point.

Dell had the added benefit of being hot, besides.

They worked through their dinners, lingered over dessert. When the bill came, Dell paid even though she tried to argue. Edibles did not come cheap, and he had a farm to save and—

"Shut up," he said pleasantly when she tried to hand him some cash in the cab of his truck.

"I just—"

"This ain't a pity date, so don't give me your pity cash." With probably more force than necessary, he shoved the truck into Reverse and backed out of the parking spot. Then he grinned over at her. "Sugar."

She wrinkled her nose, but it was hard to keep a scowl in place. Something about the way he took such joy in riling her, without any of it being mean-spirited, felt like the kind of adulthood she'd been missing out on.

He wasn't being extracareful with her because

she'd once been made fun of, and while Anna and Cara didn't as a rule, there were times they pulled back.

And, once again, coming from a hot guy made it slightly more appealing.

Dell drove from the streetlight-lit suburb of Millertown into the dark of a highway, taking them back home. Though it had been a good evening, there was a tension in her shoulders that relaxed the closer they got to New Benton.

Home.

And then what?

Mia shifted, fidgeted, foot tapped, then mentally scolded herself for wiggling like a dog waiting for a treat.

She'd made it through the date portion without saying anything too embarrassing. The whole thing had been nice and fun and so damn good, thank God. But now...

What would Dell expect? A kiss? More? She was definitely interested in a kiss, but she was also definitely bound to say something really dumb. To ruin all the good of the evening with something foolishly blurted.

Get hold of yourself. You've handled this like a pro. One more hurdle and then first first date gets checked off the list, just like first kiss.

Both with Dell freaking Wainwright.

And then? Well, who knew what other firsts might crop up.

He pulled his truck up in front of her apartment and Mia couldn't possibly keep herself still. How was she supposed to act? How was she supposed to send the right signals to say she was open for a good-night kiss, perhaps a little more than a good-night kiss, but not too much more than that?

So, of course, she started babbling. "Um, well, that was nice. Fun. I mean, good food and conversation and—" Mia took a breath, noticing his bemused expression. "And shut up, Mia," she said, shoulders hunching.

"Relax. For some strange reason I find the babbling insanely cute."

"Ew. Cute?" Cute wasn't good. Cute was puppies and babies, not women you wanted to have not-quite sex with.

"I'm sorry. The babbling is sexy. So sexy."

How he managed to keep a straight face she didn't know, but then he leaned over and kissed her and she didn't care. It was hard to care about much with his lips pressing to hers, the smell of his deodorant or shampoo or whatever overpowering the more familiar smell of well-used farm truck.

She rested her hands on his forearms, more than a little bummed his coat was covering them. When he pulled away, she wanted to hold on. She wanted the moment to last, to go longer, to move forward. Not all the way forward, but at least a little bit. Waiting twenty-six years to have any decent interaction with a guy, let alone a hot guy, made her want to make sure she got as much out of the deal as possible.

"Um, you could come in. Not to, you know, but um, we could…" Oh, she was an idiot.

Dell squeezed her hand. "Come on." He got out of his truck and she scurried after him.

"How do you do it? The confidence stuff. I mean, is it all centered on being good-looking, or is there some trick to it?"

"To being confident?"

"Yeah! I'm all awkwardly inviting you into my apartment to not…"

"You can say it." His mouth curved in that stupidly sexy way that made her not want to be offended by anything he said. Ever. "It won't kill you to say it. Promise."

Mia took a deep breath. She opened her mouth, but no. Nope. She could not say it. It really might kill her. "The point is you're walking up to my door without a care in the world, and I'm sitting here obsessing like a crazy person over whether or not I used the right inflection on the words *you know*."

"You're not crazy. You're quirky. I've had a little more practice at walking up to girls' doors. Both with and without the result being sex. You said you like me. I can tell you like it when I kiss you. What would I have to not be confident about?"

"What if I'm lying?"

"Why would you?"

She stood on her porch trying to work through his logic. There were plenty of reasons why people lied. Why people pretended. The fact Dell didn't think them possible made her wonder if he ever lied or pretended.

At least when it came to this, what would he possibly get out of lying or pretending? He routinely had a line of women ogling him. Surely if he was here with her it was because he legitimately wanted to be.

She wasn't sure how to make out what that meant. Wasn't sure what to do with the buzzing adrenaline in her chest, the floaty feeling in her limbs. He just liked her, as he'd said earlier.

How long had she been wishing for something like that to come along in a male package? Overall package, not...*that* package.

Oh, *God*, her brain was a mess of a place. At least she hadn't said it out loud.

"I know you said 'you know' is off the table." He made little air quotes with his fingers and she wrinkled her nose. Then he grinned and something in her stomach started doing cartwheels. "But I can kiss you, right?"

It was a question, but of course he knew the answer. He wouldn't have that cocky grin on his face if he didn't know the answer. Could he kiss her?

She couldn't think of a time the answer would be no.

He raised his eyebrows expectantly. Oh, right. She should probably say something instead of standing around like a dummy. "Um, yeah. You can kiss me."

He didn't waste time, and thank God for that. With her mouth occupied, she couldn't say anything, embarrassing or otherwise.

His fingers brushed her jaw, then traced down her neck while he nibbled at her mouth until she was pretty sure her bones were dissolving.

He was really, *really* good at that.

The kiss deepened, and she pushed onto her tiptoes, but she didn't know what to do with her hands. Touch him, but where? How? Before she could run through the possible list of wheres, Dell's hands circled her wrists and pulled until her arms were around his neck.

That worked. Even better when he nudged her against the door and there was nothing between them.

The nerves were still there, but excitement and anticipation jostled for space so she felt only a vague sense of nervousness while her brain remained blissfully quiet.

He tasted like the mints they'd gotten after dinner and something she couldn't identify. Maybe it was unique to him or maybe it was just what kissing was like.

His body was pressed to hers, her back against the door. He was hard, and she was totally giddy over the fact she'd given a guy an erection. Twice in one night!

His hand moved down her neck, following the neckline of her sweater. He was going to touch her breast. What was she supposed to do about that?

When his hand brushed over her, his thumb circling until her nipple was erect, she forgot all about what she was supposed to be doing and enjoyed. Because, wow, that was amazing.

"You just tell me when I need to stop, okay?"

It bolstered what little sprouts of confidence she felt hearing his breathing as uneven and unsteady as her own. This wasn't just excitement because she was such a novice. This was actually really good kissing or he wouldn't feel it, too. She nodded, and then his mouth was on hers again and she couldn't imagine ever wanting to stop.

He pulled away again. "Maybe I should go."

"I thought you were going to come in." She felt the heat move to her face, but then decided she wasn't embarrassed. He was kissing her and liking it, and wanting to go home couldn't mean she'd done anything wrong. He was into this as much as she. It was too obvious to doubt.

"I want to come in. I do. Maybe…a little too much."

"Oh." Mia licked her lips. She really, really didn't want this to be over. "Come in anyway?"

In his pause, a million insecurities tried to take hold of her brain, but he kissed her again and they shut right up.

"Open the door."

Hands not quite steady, a fact she'd blame on nerves *and* giddiness, Mia dug out her keys out and unlocked the door. His hands wrapped around her waist as she opened it, and he propelled her forward, his mouth on her neck.

"Couch?"

Mia nodded, scurrying to move her laundry out of the way. Then they were sitting on the couch. Side by side.

If he didn't kiss her soon she was going to say something stupid. She could feel it bubbling up, so she shoved her palms under her thighs as if it might stem the tide of idiotic rumblings.

"You okay?"

Mia nodded emphatically, realizing too late it was way too emphatically and now she looked like a crazed bobblehead doll.

But he looked at her and smiled. "You look really good tonight."

She suddenly understood why women got stupid over men. A good chunk of her brain melted away at the compliment. His statue-sculpted face, missing the faint stubble of beard he'd had this morning, the brown eyes crinkled with amusement, with *interest*.

Yeah, stupid over a guy made a ton of sense

now, and she was totally okay with being its next victim.

He leaned toward her, his fingertips circling a design on the inside of her wrist. It took every ounce of willpower not to whimper or squirm.

"You're fun, too," he said, his mouth close to her ear, his breath warm against her skin. "Easy to talk to. Who would have thought?"

"I probably could have told you that. You just wouldn't have believed me. I might be awkward, but I've always been easy to talk to."

He laughed against her temple, then kissed her there, her cheek, her mouth. It was awkward on the couch with their height difference, and her neck would probably have a crick in it by the end of the night. But, jeez, who cared? His hand was venturing toward breast territory again.

Eek. Yay.

He shifted. She shifted. The ancient couch squeaked beneath them. It was hard to find a comfortable spot. But Mia wasn't about to complain when Dell's lips were on hers.

Dell broke the kiss, frowning. "Why don't you sit on my lap?"

She pulled back, nose wrinkled. "Isn't that weird?"

"How is that weird?"

"I don't know. I associate lap sitting with Santa, and in this context...weird."

He shook his head, and then pulled her to him

so she had to straddle his lap. Her knees pressed on either side of his thighs and, oh, holy moly, if she scooted an inch or two forward she could press herself against him, very, very intimately.

His hands slid down her back, then slowly pulled her forward those last few inches. The jittery nerves in her stomach were no match for the fizzling heat of excitement. She planted her hands on his shoulders to keep herself from wiggling against him. Was that appropriate? Was that crazy? She just wanted to know what it might feel like. The friction of him against her. With their clothes on, it didn't seem scary at all.

One of his hands toyed with the ends of her hair, the other resting to the side of her breast.

He grinned. "Still thinking of Santa?"

"Oh. No. Nope." She couldn't pick out Santa in a lineup at this point.

He kissed her again, his hands roaming down her back. She let her own glide over his shoulders to his chest. He was all hard muscle, and when she moved a little against him he groaned.

She had made Dell Wainwright groan. She was beginning to think this was all a very realistic dream. Then he moved against her, and the friction between them was a breath-stopping, thought-stopping pull of excitement and arousal.

Up to this point she hadn't considered having sex with him tonight. Not on the first date. There was so much other stuff hanging over them, and she wasn't prepared. How could she handle this without some kind of mental preparation?

Even knowing she shouldn't, she was tempted. And she was never tempted. But…this was… It was…

Really, really hot.

Maybe it would be best to do it without the mental preparation. To get it over with. Like ripping off a bandage. No time to think of all the consequences, all the ways she could screw it up.

His hands slid inside her shirt, his calloused palms rasping against the smooth skin of her back. She wanted to do the same. To know what his skin would feel like. To test this theory that—

The door flew open. "I hate you, you stupid jerk!" Cara stumbled in, almost landing on her butt before kicking the door closed.

Mia tried to scurry off Dell's lap but they got tangled in the process. Hopefully Cara was too drunk or too sad to notice.

Cara glanced over. "He broke up with me for his stupid not-so-ex-fiancée." The words were slurred as she stepped toward the couch. She squinted at them before her face went comically shocked.

"Oh, my God." Cara stumbled toward them. "You were finally going to have sex and I totally ruined it. I'm the worst." She dropped on the sofa next to Dell, who promptly stood up. "No wonder Kevin dumped me. I totally suck."

"I'm gonna go."

"Oh, God." She smacked a hand over her mouth and made a run for it down the hallway. Mia covered her face with her hands.

This was almost as embarrassing as blurting out she was a virgin.

"Now that I have your number, I'll call you, okay?"

The sound of Cara puking echoed down the hallway. "Yeah. I'll hold my breath."

Dell squeezed her arm, leaned far enough to kiss her cheek. "I'll call you tomorrow." And then he left.

She was going to kill Cara. *D-E-A-D*.

But Dell had said he would call her, and while she might not have had a lot of dating experience, she had been on the receiving end of more than her share of brush-offs, all those times she'd tried to insinuate herself into a group and been denied. This didn't feel like one.

Still, if Cara hadn't come home, maybe things would have progressed. Maybe...

Well, maybe didn't matter. It hadn't happened tonight, but the next time he asked her out, it *was* going to happen. Nerves or no nerves, she was going to take that final step, and it was going to be damn good one way or another.

CHAPTER SEVENTEEN

USUALLY DELL TOOK it easy on Sundays, but not only was he still recovering from the hailstorm, if he didn't throw every last muscle into work he was going to think about Mia and last night and need to take another cold shower.

Or five.

He could kill Cara. Or Kevin, for dumping her at the completely wrong moment. Or himself for going into the apartment at all.

Mia was a virgin. They should be taking things slowly. Not that she seemed all that interested in going slow. She was twenty-six, after all, and—

Dell pushed the tiller with more force than necessary. He could not let himself keep going in this idiotic circle.

But he'd started this circle. How many outs had he had? How many times could he have backed away from pursuing Mia in any way, shape or form? Too many to count. But something kept bringing him back for more.

There was no denying he wanted more, and that she did, and that they *shouldn't*. He should be pouring every last ounce of time and energy into farming.

Damn it.

The rumble of a truck down the main drive from the house caused Dell to pause. The sign on the side of the car caused him to freeze.

Ed Stevens Real Estate.

Fuck.

There were two real estate companies in New Benton, and Ed's was notorious for selling farmland to developers.

Then Dell noticed Charlie walking from the main house toward him.

Double fuck.

Dad sent Charlie to do his dirty work only when thing were really bad. Dell couldn't believe Dad would outright sell without his agreement, but there it was on a white truck door. Undeniable.

Too many emotions swirled in his gut to name. They all hurt like hell.

"How's it going?"

Dell ignored his brother's greeting. He didn't feel much like dancing around the issue or pretending Charlie wasn't the middleman.

"He's feeling things out," Charlie said in a low voice, kicking at a clump of overturned dirt. "Nothing's a done deal. You can take the pissed off and dial it down a notch. Come up to the house. Be an adult. We can all have a conversation. Maybe talk about my idea."

Dell bit back the angry retort, clenched his hands harder around the handle of the machine to keep from acting it out, too.

"Mom's almost got lunch ready. Come on up to the house."

Dell returned to pushing the tiller. "You don't want me to do that right now." Feeling things out. Talking to real estate agents. With months left of the market, of the CSA, with people depending on him and expecting things from him.

Swept away because he couldn't prove himself.

"Don't be a baby about this." Charlie was all put-upon sighs and eye rolls. "Dad's doing what he thinks is best. You can be frustrated, but you can't be ang—"

"You can both take that *best* and fuck off." Dell let go of the throttle, considered throttling Charlie, but where would that get him?

While Dad was "feeling" selling out and Charlie was telling him to be an adult, Dell was working his ass off. No one cared. No one gave a rotten damn.

"You can go back there and tell Dad I'm done. I'm not playing nice and I'm not pleading my case for the millionth time. He wants to sell? Fine. They'll be prying me off this land with a gun to my head."

Another long-suffering sigh. "You're being unreasonable."

"Yeah, well, you're being a selfish prick. This isn't your fight."

"What do I have to do with this? I'm trying to mediate some peace here."

"Yes, Charlie. Mediating peace. Selling a line. It's your job, and you're good at it, but this is my job. I'm good at it, too."

"This isn't about me. It isn't even about you."

Dell started the tiller up again even though he was finished. He'd till the patch over and over until Charlie went away. He knew it wasn't about Charlie. He wasn't even mad at Charlie, except for the bouts of unbridled condescension.

This was about *him*. His failure. Again. It was about not being able to show the people he loved who he was. So, no, he wasn't pissed at Charlie. Maybe he wasn't even pissed at Dad. He was just *pissed*. And awfully alone for a guy who'd once been the life of the party.

It took all of two minutes for Charlie to give up. Once his brother was out of punching range, Dell turned off the machine. Then he gave in to the childish desire to kick the shit out of something and stomped his boot through a big pile of dirt.

He didn't feel any better. Oddly enough, his mind turned to Mia. He had a few ideas of what could make him feel better.

Somewhere in the back of his mind he knew he should back off until the frustration and sadness and hurt wore off, but he ignored it. She was light, and he needed it as he needed this dirt. He pulled up her number, hit Call, and when she answered, didn't take a second to beat around the bush.

"Hey, you busy tonight?"

"Um." She paused. "Not after dark."

"Come over." He winced at the urgency he felt. This was stupid. But Mia either made him forget or made him not feel like the biggest loser on the planet, so screw it. It was urgent.

"Come...over?"

"Yeah. Over. To my house." He wouldn't read too much into finding himself smiling already.

"Oh." In the long pause, he had time enough to berate himself for being an idiot and an ass-hole. Then she let out an audible breath. "Okay."

Thank God. "Good. See you then." He hit End before the surprise and uncertainty in her voice could bother him. Then he ignored his grumbling stomach and threw himself into work.

When he was finally done for the day, all machinery cleaned and put in its place, his usual satisfaction at the end of a long, hard day was muted by the niggling worry that this would be the end. His last time tilling this earth, planting seeds where his great-great-grandfather had planted seeds.

It was a physical, searing pain in his chest, as

if someone had punctured his lung. The fact that his own family was doing this to him twisted it deeper.

Dell walked out of the barn and came face-to-face with Mom. He hated lumping her in with Charlie and Dad, but he could tell by the look on her face she wasn't here to throw her hat into the ring with him. "Sorry, Mom, I'm busy."

"Honey, don't be—"

"I've had enough of people telling me what not to be." He attempted to gentle his voice, but it was too much. He needed time to cool off. He needed Mia. So maybe he was being a baby about it, but at least he was trying to spare them all a meltdown.

"I know you're upset. I understand why you're upset. I want us to talk this through. Charlie told me he had a compromise."

Now he was going to be the idiot for not taking the compromise? He couldn't...

"I love you," he said, because sometimes it felt as if they didn't know that, they didn't reciprocate. Maybe that was on him, but he wanted it out there before he said the rest.

"But Dad, Charlie, you... None of you are going to convince me I'm wrong. I haven't given a shit about much in my life, I get it, but I give a shit about this and I'm not letting anyone try to tell me I'm wrong about that."

So he'd spend his time with someone who didn't.

PULLING UP TO Dell's cabin, it was hard to take in a full breath. Nerves squeezed and squeezed her lungs, birds with giant wings flapping around in her stomach.

"He invited you here. It doesn't mean anything special. You're fine. It's fine. Having sex will be fine, too…if that's even on the table." She kind of thought a house invite was code for sex, but she also didn't want to assume and then be embarrassed.

So she was just here, because he'd called her up out of the blue and asked if she wanted to come over.

Please be for sex. She'd prepared *so* much for it to be sex. She wanted it crossed off the list. Done. And, whether it was smart or not, she wanted it to be Dell.

So she'd go about it the same way she'd gone about building her business and her confidence. Prepare. One step in front of the other. Stand tall.

She hopped out of the truck. As she crossed the yard, she suddenly felt stupid for going home and showering and putting on a skirt. She should have come over dirty and in work clothes and—

Mia paused and squeezed her eyes shut for a second. *You are an adult. You are confident. You are in charge.*

With a firm nod, she finished the walk up to his porch and forced herself to knock on the door before she had a chance to let any negative thoughts creep in.

Dell opened the door, and she was only a little disappointed he was actually wearing a shirt. "Hey."

She smiled. "Hi." Silence descended. It was impossible to battle nerves in silence. Silence was always her downfall.

He stepped away so she could move inside. The lame greeting hung in the air like its own entity. Mia clasped her hands together. What was she doing? "So..."

Dell scratched a hand through his hair, the faded short-sleeve button-up he wore stretching across his chest. She had the distinct impression she would not be seeing what lay underneath that shirt tonight.

Pity. When she looked at his face, though, Mia frowned. There was a hard edge to him today, and that was weird. Even when they were fighting at the market he never looked so...gloomy. So tense. "Are you okay?"

His forehead crinkled with creases and his brows drew together. Some of the weird, agitated energy dissipated. "I'm sorry. I shouldn't have asked you to come."

She tried not to show the little prick of hurt, the slight heat of embarrassment. She didn't know what could have changed between his phone call and now, but she was not going to blame herself for it. Obviously something was wrong with *him*, not her. She straightened her shoulders. "I can go."

"No." He crossed to her, then cupped her face with his hands. "I just meant I've had a shit day and I shouldn't have dragged you into it, not that I don't want you here." Then he kissed her.

And people said women didn't make sense.

He pulled back, grinned. "Shit day getting better."

Mia smiled in return. He had the easiest way of being...sweet. That was probably dangerous, but she'd worry about it later. Or never. Maybe she'd end up with a broken heart, and maybe that was a life experience everyone needed to go through. Another check off her list.

"So what made the day so bad?"

His grin dissolved. "I saw Ed Stevens leaving the house today."

Her heart sank for him. "Oh, Dell."

"Charlie says they're just feeling things out, but...he didn't even tell me or warn me. Dad didn't say a damn thing to me. He's not even giving me a chance. He's..." Dell plopped himself on the couch. "I shouldn't have called you. I'm sure you didn't come here to listen to me bitch and moan."

Tentatively, Mia took a seat next to him. "You really think he'd sell out from under you?"

He leaned forward, rested his elbows on his knees. "More every day."

He stared at the haphazard stacks of papers on the coffee table. Seed lists and prices. Sloppy and in an almost illegible chicken scratch, but so like what she had on her kitchen table at home it was a jolt.

So often she thought of Dell as some mythical creature. Confident and gorgeous and perfect. But he had problems and paperwork and ground to till just like her.

She picked up one of the papers, scanned the to-buy list, barely making out the writing but finding the contents almost identical to her own. She picked up another paper with figures scribbled all over it.

"I know what I'm doing. You may be a genius and everything but you don't need to double-check my work. Doesn't matter what I do anyway. Dad looks at me and sees a screwup. I've been fighting so hard, and I can't change his mind. I don't know what else to do."

He sounded sad and lost, and she wished she had some power to help, some power to soothe. It was tentative, awkward probably, but she reached up and slid her arm around his shoulders.

"Maybe I should sell to developers," he said, voice low. As if he'd cracked open his heart and left it bleeding on the floor.

The pain of commiseration hurt her heart, but something else tinged with it. Irritation. She knew how hard it was to fight against an image of yourself that wasn't real, but she'd only ever had to fight strangers. Not her family. That seemed all too harsh. All too unfair.

"I'm not a genius and I'm not checking your work. I was noticing we're ordering the same seeds."

"Not surprising."

"No, it's not. But if we buy in bulk we get a better price, right?"

"Right, but I prefer buying what I need season to season. I'm not organized enough to save seeds, and I don't have the cash flow to—"

"We could go in together. Split the costs. I know it doesn't save us hundreds of dollars or anything, but at this point, doesn't every bit help?"

He stared at her for a while, forehead creased and mouth pressed into a line. "Mia…" He took the papers from her hands and put them back on the coffee table. "You don't need to split costs. You'll be fine."

"Fine, yes, but I don't want to be fine. I want to be good. Saving money, cutting the corners I can without compromising product, that's good business sense." She hesitantly touched his hand. "It doesn't make sense not to help you if it's helping me, too."

"Yes it does. It makes total sense not to help me. Business sense. Helping your competition is…"

Mia wrinkled her nose. "Softhearted?" She

pushed off the couch. She was good at math and growing and plans. She was not good at turning her back on someone who needed help, regardless of how in competition they were. But it wasn't the worst thing in the world. She'd rather be a little softhearted than be ruthless.

"It's my one weakness. I let myself have it as long as I'm getting something out of the deal." She faced him, pointed a finger at his chest. "This would save me money, too. So it's not terrible business sense. I'm helping you and me, and that is not the worst thing in the world. They say competition is good for business."

"Who says that?"

"You know…them." Lame. She was lame. "Just let me help you."

His mouth went firm again and he pushed off the couch and strode away from her. "I don't want your pity."

Without thinking, she followed. "I don't pity you. I…commiserate with you."

"That's not the same thing?"

"No. Pity is 'Oh, boo hoo, poor Dell.' Commiserate is… 'Oh, that sucks. I haven't been in this exact place, but I know what it's like to fight.' To feel like it's pointless to fight what other people think—and in a way it is. But I don't want anyone to feel the way that suffocates. So I commiserate, and I think maybe I can help in this mutually beneficial way."

He leaned against his kitchen counter, arms folded across his chest. "Splitting hairs."

"Well, so be it. Don't be silly about taking help."

His expression darkened immediately. "I'm not silly and I don't need help."

Mia rolled her eyes. Dell might be hot, confident and smart, but he was not without his faults or insecurities. That was actually a relief. He wasn't perfect. He wasn't a god. He was a man. The same way she was a woman.

They weren't on a different plane. They were on the same even, solid ground. "You really have a hang-up about that, you know?"

"About what?"

"You get all prickly when you think anyone even remotely insults your intelligence."

"Maybe my intelligence gets insulted a lot. You weren't the only one who had a rep in high school. One that's been hard to shake."

"Please. You were popular."

"I was a pretty face. You remember Corrie Washington?"

"Why yes, I do believe you two were wearing your King and Queen of the World tiaras when you called me names."

"Did you know she broke up with me?"

"Well…" No, she hadn't known that. She hadn't been privy to all the gossip in those days. She'd figured they'd gone their separate ways because of college if she'd thought of it at all.

"'Dell,'" he began in a high-pitched voice, "'you're hot and a really great kisser, but I need someone who will stimulate me, you know, intellectually.'" He rolled his eyes. "Apparently that meant dating some twenty-one-year-old philosophy major that summer."

"Ew. You were, like, seventeen."

"You're missing the point. The point is, I've had enough of being treated like an idiot, and I thought you were one of the few people who wouldn't."

Really, Dell getting dumped by one girl because he wasn't a college student wasn't anything compared with eighteen years of doing embarrassing things, but she liked that he thought she understood him. That she treated him better than a lot of other people had.

Yeah, she liked that a lot. Maybe too much.

"Well, we both know you're not stupid, so you should stop being such a baby about it." The second *baby* came out of her mouth, she realized she was sticking her nose where it didn't belong, being kind of pushy and maybe even a little harsh. Which probably wasn't the way to endear herself to someone she was hoping would help her with the whole virginity thing.

He glared at her, and Mia tried to go for a self-deprecating smile.

"Maybe there isn't a point to it anymore," he said.

His defeat broke her heart a little. Insult forgotten, she crossed to him and touched his face, thinking so much about offering comfort she didn't even feel self-conscious about it until it was too late.

"There's always a point if it's something you love this much. Why don't you show me around while you think about the seed thing? Maybe my genius can come up with a few more ideas for your pea-size brain." It was a joke she prayed would go over well.

Her breath whooshed out in relief when he cracked a smile. "Well, Mia, you're a lot tougher than I gave you credit for."

"Guess I'll take that as a compliment. So going to show me around or what?"

"Can't muck around in those shoes." He pointed at her ballet flats. "I'll scrounge you up a pair of boots." He gave her a brief peck, then disappeared.

Mia gripped the counter. What was she doing? What on earth was she doing? Last night and dinner and making out on the couch had been one thing. One very fun thing, and that was what she'd expected—and wanted—more of.

But this was serious, and she was in too deep. Invested in him and his farm and his insecurities, forgetting about herself. That was stupid. Stupid and dangerous and—

He reappeared with a pair of rubber boots and a grin. Thoughts of stupid and dangerous things faded away.

She put on the boots, he took her hand. He walked her around his portion of things, and they talked crops, CSA logistics, cold frames, weather. Everything under the sun and moon. He took her up to the pigpen on top of the hill. It overlooked his cabin and his fields, and the little piglets slept next to their mother in the pale moonlight.

"Oh, aren't they sweet? I love their little tails." She leaned over the fence to get a better look. "Do they have names?"

"Sure. Bacon, Pork Chop, Sausage."

Mia thumped his chest. "Stop!" He was grinning and she couldn't stop herself from smiling back. He was handsome all the time, but something about the dark and the starlight made him seem like something she'd conjured out of a dream.

He moved his gaze out across the fields below. All shadows and edges in the evening dark. "Have you ever…" He trailed off, shaking his head. "Crazy."

"What?"

He kept shaking his head. "It's just sometimes… it feels like more."

"More?"

"More than me." His throat moved as he swallowed, his eyes intense on the land in front of them. "The people who came before. Not, like, ghosts or anything, just…more than dirt and me and crops."

It struck a chord, a deep one. Not just because his love for this place was admirable, but because she'd felt exactly that. It had been a salvation growing up. She hadn't fit in at school or anywhere, really, but she'd fit in at home and knew she belonged to it.

"Crazy shit," Dell muttered. "That's what Dad and Charlie said when I brought it up once."

Mia scowled. "It is not crazy and it is not shit. I've felt the same thing."

He smiled, a little ruefully. "You don't have to humor me, sugar."

She elbowed him for the *sugar*, but then put her hand on his forearm and squeezed. "The back portion of my parents' house isn't used. It's kind of falling apart and there hasn't been the time or money to fix it with the rest of the house. You know, that house was built in 1897. My grandfather was born there and… Anyway, I used to sneak into the room. The ceiling was falling down, dust everywhere. A total mess, but…"

Mia swallowed, uncomfortable emotion closing her throat. She cleared it, took a little step away from Dell because she felt too close, and not just physically. "I felt that. Like you said, more than me. More than this time. Not in a mystical way exactly. But as if it was big and part of me. As if it was in my bones, my blood, my heart. It somehow made everything…more important. The house. The farm. I didn't belong everywhere, but I could belong there. I *did* belong there."

Uncomfortable with the depth of emotion, the words and feelings that had poured out of her without a second thought, Mia tried to laugh it off. "Well, who knew I'd have so much in common with the Naked Farmer."

He put his arm around her shoulder, pulled her close to him. Her head nestled right to his chest. It was a moment, crystalized in feeling, starlight and him. She'd never forget it. No matter what.

"Thanks, Mia." He kissed her hair, and it was hard to push words out of her constricted throat.

"For what?"

"For reminding me it's worth fighting for."

Mia swallowed at the lump in her throat. Her heart was busy doing cartwheels and other acrobatics. She could live in this moment forever.

She was in so much trouble, and she didn't even care.

CHAPTER EIGHTEEN

DELL DIDN'T KNOW how Mia had managed to flip the shit day on its head. He'd felt screwed six ways to Sunday before talking to her, but she'd reminded him what he was fighting for. And why. Maybe he would have gotten there on his own, but right now, walking down the hill hand in hand with her, he owed her some debt of gratitude.

Scared the bejesus out of him.

"Thought any more about it?"

He studied her profile in the dim light. He didn't want her pity. He didn't want Dad to know he'd had help to keep afloat, if he did in fact keep afloat, if Dad didn't sell before he could...

But Mia's offer would help, and could he turn that down? It was just a little help. A little mutual help. Like sharing a ride and splitting gas money. It didn't make him look incapable. It wasn't Charlie's compromise. It was...partnership-ish. Nothing like being bailed out by the infinitely more capable Mia.

Or so he'd have to keep telling himself.

The marvel was *she* didn't think he was incapable. She really didn't. Even when he'd doubted himself, even after all the ways he'd been a jerk to her, she held his hand as they walked to his cabin.

It was a gift, and no matter how many sharp edges it had, he wouldn't return it.

"Guess if we're buying the same seeds, wouldn't be a terrible idea." Dell let go of her hand, stepped onto the porch. It didn't sit right. It just didn't, but common sense overruled the shame of accepting her offer.

A little help, just a little, to get where he needed to be to finally, *finally* prove himself to Dad. There had to be a way to get where he needed to be, and maybe it was this.

"Great! Do you want to make a list and figure out how we're going to do it?" She babbled on about her ideas as they stepped inside, but he tuned it out. One step at a time. Accepting the help was one step, details and specifics would be another. For another time and place. A time and place when Mia wasn't wearing a skirt. In his house. Alone.

"We can figure all that out later. Let's change the subject."

She blinked, cocked her head. "To what?"

"How about we pick up where we left off last night?" He plopped himself on the couch, then folded his arms behind his head and sent her a cocky grin.

She shook her head, clucked her tongue, but in

the end she took a few steps toward him, pausing just within reach.

"And where did we leave off?"

"Hmm. I think we were about…" Dell pulled her to the couch, onto his lap, until they were in about the same position as last night. Except she was wearing a skirt, which rode up on her thighs but didn't allow the same flexibility. Since she was wearing something on her legs under the skirt, tights or leggings or whatever nonsense, he edged the skirt up farther until her legs were free to press on each side of his. Even better, it allowed her to press against him. "Seems about right."

Light and good and fun and Mia. The farm stress could take a break.

"Actually, it was more like this." She took his hands and put them on her waist, then with just a hint of pink to her cheeks and a moment of hesitation, she edged her shirt up a little so his fingers brushed the bare skin of her back.

Yeah, that was exactly where they'd been. It was exactly where he wanted to be. He smoothed his hands up her back. Soft, delicate. She was both those things, but underneath was lean muscle and a core of something he couldn't identify. He'd think it was confidence, but she was nervous, unsure.

Maybe it was just a clear sense of self, and acceptance of that. Whatever it was, it impressed him. Struck a chord with him. Something akin to affection and care and all the complicated things that went along with something more than fun.

But this was supposed to be fun. Fun until it wasn't, because they weren't right for each other. Eventually they were going to trip over the fact they were competitors. They could ignore it for a while, help each other here and there, but not forever.

Mia pressed a fingertip to his forehead, smoothing across the line there. "Thinking awfully hard for a man with a woman on his lap."

Truer words had never been spoken. Dell forced himself to smile. "Trying not to press my luck."

Her fingertip moved down the side of his face, across his jaw, and because he was kind of a screwed-up moron, he wanted to lean into the touch like a cat, nuzzle against her so she'd keep touching him like that.

"I think your luck is just fine."

"You know, for someone who blurted out she was a virgin the first time I tried to kiss her, you sure have figured out the right things to say tonight."

Her finger trailed down his neck. One damn finger making him just about crazy. "You caught me off guard that night. I prepared for tonight."

He rubbed his palms across her back, down her sides, wondering just what her preparation had entailed. He had a half mind to ask her, but he was busy fighting the urge to move his hands farther, to touch cotton or lace or whatever fabric her bra would be made of. He wanted her to make the first move. Maybe it was a safeguard to make sure she was ready, willing…or maybe he needed someone to show him they wanted him.

That thought bothered him enough to act instead of waiting for her. He traced a finger over the outline of the back band of her bra, then worked to unclasp it. She didn't say anything, just pulled her bottom lip between her teeth.

"You know, I read once biting your lip is a sign of sexual frustration."

She laughed and rolled her eyes. "If that were true, I'd have a permanent bite mark there at this point." She toyed with the top button of his shirt, then unbuttoned it. Just one button.

Her hands rested there, at the small space one undone button created, and Dell rubbed a palm up and down her spine, enjoying the feel of soft skin and the warmth of her body on his.

What was he doing? Usually it was jump ahead as quickly as his partner let him, but…he couldn't. He didn't want to. And he didn't know what to do about that.

"Sometimes it's surreal to stop and think, here I am," she said, her voice low as she toyed with another button, released it. "Sitting in Dell Wainwright's lap." She smiled shyly, her fingers slowly, hesitantly making their way down the column of buttons.

Because this moment was strange and intense and foreign, he felt the need to make a joke. "The Santa thing again?"

"No! I just… This, you, wasn't exactly something I'd considered for myself. It's a strange feeling to be so far from what I thought was possible."

He wasn't sure what to make of that. She kept her eyes fixed on his mouth, unmoving, then she lifted a finger and traced it across his bottom lip, a slow, exploratory journey that was way sexier than it should have been.

Then she kissed him. Screw good, bad, whatever. Didn't matter with her mouth on his. Her hands traveled his chest, pushing apart his shirt. She was all bold moves followed by hesitation.

There was something irresistible about that mix of nerves on top of a drive and determination that didn't seem to falter.

He trailed his fingertips over her skin, smoothed his palms around to her abdomen and then up to move her bra out of the way. He cupped her breasts, took his time exploring the curves, the weight, then brushed his thumbs across each nipple.

Her breath caught against his mouth, her hands slowly traveling down his stomach. The slow path of her fingers was both agonizing and amazing. He broke the kiss enough to pull off her shirt, exposing pale, gorgeous skin. Some flowery scent filled the room, her soap or perfume, whatever. It would stick with him long beyond this minute.

She moved against him and he pulled her closer, using his mouth to travel the column of her neck, down until he found her nipple with his tongue. She made a squeaking sound, but not of the embarrassed kind.

So he lingered, tasting her, teasing her until her fingers moved through his hair and held him there.

He tried to keep the desperation out of his movements, but the more she rubbed against him, the farther down her fingers inched, the less control he had over the need to push up against her, to dig fingers into her hips and move her at his rhythm.

There were a million ways she could undo him. One more touch, one more kiss, and it'd all be over. "Want to go to the bedroom?" His breathing wasn't remotely even. He wanted her to say yes, even while a little part of him wanted her to say no and stop this irresistible fall.

She swiped her tongue across her bottom lip, eyes focused straight on him. After a moment, she nodded. "Yeah. Let's do that."

"Are you su—"

"Don't ask me if I'm sure. I said yes. I'm sure."

Best damn answer he'd ever heard.

OH, GOD. SHE was really going to do this. She was going to have sex. With Dell. She was going to have sex with Dell.

She hadn't been lying when she said she'd pre-pared. She'd spent the day going over and over in her head how this might happen. What she should say. How she should act. Of course, it wasn't quite following the script, but that was okay.

She was shirtless and so was he. His hand was in hers and he was leading her to his bedroom. Everything wasn't just okay, it was fantastic.

They stepped into his bedroom and Dell flipped on the light. Mia got the overall impression it was messy and cluttered, but mainly she looked at his big, unmade bed and crossed her arms over her chest.

"Jeez, it's freezing in here."

"I can fix that." He pointed to the bed, crooked an eyebrow.

She chuckled, and instead of taking the hint, she crawled under the covers, pulling them up to her chin.

He stood at the end of the bed, his mouth twitching into a smile. "Not quite what I meant."

"Oh?" She had to swallow back a nervous gig-gle. She was in Dell Wainwright's bed. His *bed*. Half-naked. He was standing at the end of it, half-naked. She really had to stop letting that make her giddy.

Sex couldn't be all that different from the idea in her mind. It wasn't as if she'd never seen a sex scene in a movie or read one in a book. An or-gasm with somebody couldn't be that different from doing it herself. She knew a lot about sex. She just hadn't done it yet.

He unbuttoned and unzipped his jeans. All confidence and swagger, he pushed them down and stepped out of them. All that was left was boxer shorts.

He was...just gorgeous. She had no other word for it. The strong, broad shoulders, those stupid six-pack abs that weren't fair, the way his waist dipped in where the elastic of his boxers held on.

His legs were new, and she should probably play it cool and not ogle, but his thighs were like pieces of artwork worthy of praise. The strong, pronounced curve of muscle that led to his knee...

She wanted to run her hands over his legs the way she'd run them down his chest. She wanted to follow the curve of every muscle.

And she really wanted him to lose the boxers, but he moved onto the bed with them still on, pulling the covers off her before he covered her with his body.

Oh. Wow.

"Better?" he asked, his voice husky in her ear.

Cold was no longer an option. She was heated inside and out. Her breasts pressed against the bare skin of his chest, his breath was on her neck and she had to bite her lip to keep from squeaking out something silly.

Focus. She wanted this to happen. Oh, God, she wanted this to happen. So she needed to focus on what would get her there. "I should probably take off my skirt."

"You read my mind." But instead of moving out of the way so she could, he unbuttoned and unzipped it for her, his fingers brushing the hem of her leggings. "Can I take these off, too?"

Mia swallowed. She still didn't trust her voice, so she nodded and Dell pulled her leggings off her. His hand traveled the length of her leg, ending at her hip. Now on their sides facing one another, they were both naked except for their underwear.

Holy moly.

Okay. She could do this. She could totally do this. She knew what to expect, mostly, and it wasn't as if she'd never pleasured herself before. This couldn't be *that* different. You know, aside from the human being next to her. The really hot human being next to her who had certain equipment she'd never been anywhere near.

Mia took a deep breath, squeezed her eyes shut. Wouldn't help to think about that. One step at a time.

"We can stop anytime. I mean it. If you're uncomfortable, you just tell me, okay?"

It was sweet. Really sweet. But it wasn't necessary. She'd waited twenty-six years to do this. It wasn't as if she was some teenage girl being talked into it by her hormone-crazed boyfriend. "I'm nervous, but that doesn't mean I don't want to. Nerves and not sure are two separate things. I'm sure."

He smiled, cupped her chin and rubbed his thumb across her bottom lip. There was something affectionate about the gesture, something that wasn't just about sex. That was nice. Oh, scary as hell, but nice.

"Um, do you have a condom?" Look at her sounding all adult and normal. Of course, she'd practiced the line about eight million times.

He nodded.

"Okay. Good. That's good. I mean—" He cut off her babbling with a kiss. Thank God for that.

His hands slid into her underwear, cupping her butt and pulling her against him. She could feel the hard length of him through the cotton of his boxers. Different from when it had been covered by both their pants.

This was more intimate, and she could get an idea of the length and shape of him. She tried to keep her imagination from galloping ahead because then she would lose all the good parts of this moment.

Like him slowly pushing her panties farther and farther down until she was completely naked. He caressed her inner thigh, inching up as his mouth explored her neck, and everything inside her vibrated with nerves and desperate excitement.

She wasn't tentative about touching him, or holding on to him. It felt like the exact right thing to do. In the moment, he was hers as much as she was his.

When his fingertips brushed her sex, she almost jumped. His finger stroked her, and the butterflies in her stomach slowed, overrun by a warm cascade of need.

"D-Dell."

"Want me to stop?"

"Not on your life."

His smiling mouth hovered just an inch from hers and he kept his eyes steady on her face as he slid his finger inside. The only sound that came out of her mouth was a kind of squeaky sigh. He kissed her, soft and languid, and it matched the slow rhythm of his caress.

He was so close to bringing her to the brink, some of her hesitation and worry evaporated enough that she grew bolder. She moved against him, letting her own hands explore him. Ridges and dips, soft skin and coarse hair.

His mouth grew more demanding on hers and she whimpered against it, so close to orgasm she couldn't even think about being nervous as her hand dipped into his boxers.

She closed her hand around him. Hard, hot to the touch, and when she stroked him, he groaned. That was just as exciting as what he was doing to her—knowing she was giving pleasure to him, too.

It wasn't all that different from bringing herself

to orgasm, except it was Dell's hand inside her and his mouth on her and him in her hands, and that somehow made everything way more fantastic.

Yeah, way better than taking care of herself.

"Ready?"

"Yeah." It came out breathless and not totally confident, but she was. Confident she wanted to do this with him. Now.

Mia watched as he rolled the condom on. She pressed her legs together, completely excited and also a little bit freaked out.

He moved on top of her again and rested himself between her legs, but didn't get right to it. Instead, he touched her, gently stroking. When he entered her, it was with his finger. She hitched in a breath as he rubbed her closer and closer to climax again.

When she was close, the thick tip of him replaced his finger. Mia bit her lip, ordered herself to relax as he entered her slowly. He continued to touch her, even as he inched deeper inside. It wasn't a comfortable feeling. Not quite painful, but not really all that enjoyable, either.

His thumb brushed her. Oh, well, that felt good. Really good. She sighed against his neck, holding on. His strokes were slow, each one easier than the last. He said her name in a hushed whisper that made her heart turn to absolute jelly.

It was strange. Both physical and emotional. Both perfect and uncomfortable. She wondered if she was doing it right, if it was okay, but then his thumb found the exact right spot and she was able to forget about nerves and concentrate on arousal.

His breathing quickened, and so did his hand moving against her. Mia closed her eyes, let the sensation of him bringing her to climax by hand wash over her until the orgasm built again, falling over the edge with an intensity different from any she'd ever felt before.

Dell pushed inside her one last time, teasing out those last jolts of pleasure, then stilled and kissed her jaw. He buried his head in her neck.

Was he done? He had to be, right? And she wasn't a virgin anymore! She had half a mind to get up and do a little dance.

His hand smoothed up the curve of her hip, and his mouth nibbled kisses against her throat.

Silly to think it was perfect, but it so was. This was what she'd hoped a first time would be. Waiting twenty-six years to get it didn't seem so bad here in the moment.

He pulled up, resting his weight on his elbows, then chuckled. "You're grinning."

"Of course I am. I just had sex. Finally. What else would I be doing?"

He laughed, pulling out of her. It was such a strange sensation. Being filled and then not. He kissed her forehead. "Good point. Be right back." He disappeared into the bathroom.

Was she supposed to go? Weird, in all her

prep, she hadn't really thought about the after part. Crap. Mia searched the room, remembered her shirt had been discarded in the living room. So had his.

She took a break from worrying to do a little booty shake. Awesome sex *required* a little post-orgasmic dancing.

Once she got that out of her system, she sat up, holding the sheet up to her chest. Maybe she could take it with her to the other room. Put on her skirt, which was somewhere at the end of the bed, grab her tights, shirt. Give him a kiss and say, "See you later" like a mature, adult woman.

That was what they did, right? Why hadn't she asked Cara about this part?

"Going somewhere?"

Mia practically jumped, one leg off the bed and one still on. "Oh, well, I wasn't sure what the protocol was in this kind of situation." Probably didn't include using words like *protocol*. She pulled her leg back onto the bed, feeling weirdly self-conscious. He'd already seen her naked. He had quite expertly taken her virginity. What was there to be self-conscious about?

He frowned, studying her, and she felt heat rush into her cheeks. How did he not look ridiculous standing next to the bed completely naked with a thoughtful frown? So not fair.

"The protocol is you're supposed to stay. If you want." He said it with a nod, then returned to bed, his arm sliding under her neck in one fluid, easy movement.

Her cheek was pressed to his arm, and going home seemed silly. Why would she leave when he wanted her to stay and she wanted to stay? What was the point in safeguarding her heart when it had never been broken before?

"That...sounds good." She snuggled in, closed her eyes and reminded herself to live in the moment rather than dwell on something that couldn't be changed.

Falling for Dell was as inevitable as things ending between them, but, well, that was life. She really liked living if it meant even a little more of this.

CHAPTER NINETEEN

DELL SLAMMED A palm to his alarm clock without bothering to open his eyes. Why was he so tired?

Oh, right. He opened his eyes and found no sign of Mia in the dark shadows of his room. He frowned and scraped a hand over the few days' worth of growth on his chin.

Maybe it was for the best she was gone. No attempts at awkward morning-after conversation suited him fine.

So why did he feel...disappointed?

Not something he wanted to think about. He got out of bed, found a T-shirt and pulled it on. He needed a drink of water and about five gallons of coffee, and then he needed to get himself to work.

His head was full of jumbled to-dos when he stepped into the kitchen. And there she was. The sun hadn't come out yet, but the faint glow of dawn infiltrated the room from the sliding-glass door next to the counter. She stood in front of it in the dim swath of light.

Why that made his chest constrict wasn't something he wanted to think about, either.

She turned to face him, offering a shy smile.

"I, um, needed a drink of water." She held up the ancient blue glass, then pointed out the window. "Foggy."

He crossed to her, words failing him. What was he supposed to say? *Good morning. How'd you sleep? Want to get naked again?*

Since the third was a little too tempting, he didn't say anything, just stood next to her taking in the misty gray clouds that covered the outside world. He couldn't see the house over the hill or the fields or even the shed a few yards away from the door. All he saw was the wood of the back porch that connected to his house, then mists of floating, eerie gray.

"Kind of pretty," she said in a soft voice.

"I was thinking more along the lines of creepy."

She shook her head, drawing his attention back to her. She'd pulled her hair back into a ponytail, and though she'd put on her shirt and skirt from the night before, her legs and feet were bare.

A few weeks ago popped into his head, when Charlie had called her cute and he'd basically agreed. She was cute, but she had a beauty about her, too. It probably made him a tool that he hadn't noticed it then.

He tucked a stray strand of hair behind her ear, and when she turned her head, he kissed her, because why shouldn't he? Why shouldn't he kiss her and keep kissing her while he had the chance?

Take what he could from this, and give what he could in return.

She leaned into him and the kiss, and he couldn't remember the last time he'd wanted to blow off work so badly. He pulled back, because deepening the kiss would be too dangerous when he didn't have the luxury of being dangerous.

Her eyes fluttered open and she smiled, and Dell wanted nothing more than to take her back to bed and stay there all day long.

Which unfortunately wasn't an option. He had a hell of a lot of work to do, and she probably did, too.

"Stick around for breakfast. At least until the fog lifts." No sense in her risking her neck or her truck driving on foggy roads just because he had things to do. If he enjoyed himself over some peanut butter on toast, what was the harm?

She glanced around his kitchen. Since the week had been a little hectic, it was a little messier than he usually liked to let it get. Dirty dishes, soda and beer cans, a few crumpled paper towels.

"Housekeeping may not be my strong suit."

She chuckled. "Lucky for you I lived in the same house as Anna for many years. She's the dirtiest person on the face of the planet. I once found a bowl of old cereal under her sink in the bathroom. This is spotless compared to her."

"Thank you, Anna." He rubbed his thumb across Mia's bottom lip because he wasn't ready to step away, to completely give up the fantasy of a day of just them. No dirt. No seeds. No farmers' markets or families. Nothing but what they'd had last night in his bedroom.

And that scared him enough that he moved away to make breakfast.

"We still have to talk about the seed thing. If we're really going to split, we need to get on that. I'd planned to get my order in by Wednesday."

Dell's muscles stiffened as he slid two pieces of bread into the toaster. "Right." She was right. They needed to talk about that.

Damn, he didn't want to. *Suck it up, Wainwright.* "What do you want on your toast? I've got peanut butter, grape jelly, honey."

"Butter?"

"You want just butter on your toast?"

"I grew up on a dairy farm. I could eat butter plain. No toast needed."

Dell chuckled. "Fair enough. Juice?"

"Sure." He glanced at her over his shoulder. She took a seat at his little kitchen table. Kind of strange, but he'd never had a woman over for breakfast. Some women had stayed the night, but he'd never sat at the table his grandfather had built, had once sat at every morning with his grandmother, and eaten anything.

Well. There was a first time for everything. The toaster popped and he focused on slathering each piece. In silence he handed her a plate, then went about pouring them both orange juice.

When he finally sat, she was watching him. "You know, you don't have to do the seed thing," she said.

He looked at his toast. "I know."

"Because I get the feeling you don't want to. So if you don't want to—don't."

"It's a good idea. Solid business decision." He bit into the toast. Those things were true. But it didn't make him *want* to do it.

Was it too much to want to be able to do this on his own? To have Dad and Charlie and everyone realize he was capable? Mia's help threatened that, and as much as he needed it and as much as it was nice of her to offer, he didn't want to be in the position to take it.

But he was. *So man up, dude.* "How about we skip the seed talk for this morning? We can talk about it over dinner. We can meet at Moonrise. Be very business official."

She cocked her head as if she was trying to work something out but didn't quite have all the pieces. "Why isn't this official?"

Dell grinned, reached under the table until his hand found her knee and squeezed. "I'm a little distracted."

Though her cheeks went pink, she did manage a completely ineffective scowl.

"All right. We'll discuss it at Moonrise, but you

need to bring your paperwork and we're not leaving until we've come to an agreement. No more evasions or excuses. Got it?"

He grinned and slid his hand up to the hem of her skirt. "I bet I could talk you out of that."

She leaned forward with what he was going to call her farmers' market glare. It was no-nonsense and all about work. Which meant he probably shouldn't find it such a turn-on.

"I bet you can't. That is not some kind of perverted challenge, Dell. It's a fact. This has to be done. And quickly. You can save your distractions for another time." She jerked her leg so his hand slid off.

"Okay." Dell took a bite of toast, chewed thoughtfully. "But just to be clear, after business is settled, we can go back to those distractions." He'd need them, and what was the harm in having them if he was giving her something in return? All these firsts to get out of the way.

He ignored the acid in his stomach, like the day at the market when Sam *the chef* had been standing there, *smiling*.

Firsts meant someone was waiting to be a second, and he didn't know who the jackass would be, but he hated him anyway. *Get a grip, dude.* "You enjoy those distractions," he said, mustering all the cockiness he could manage.

She bit her lip, but her mouth curved upward anyway. "I guess."

"You'll come home with me, too." Bossy, but jealousy made him incapable of reining that in.

All the reward he needed was in her widening smile. "I guess."

"Oh, don't guess, sugar. I'd say you better be sure."

She shook her head. "You're impossible." But she was smiling, and so was he.

MIA PULLED THE truck into the parking space in front of her apartment. Her cheeks hurt from smiling the whole way home, an inner chorus of, *Not a virgin, not a virgin, woo-hoo, not a virgin!* looping through her mind.

And, okay, she might have sung it out loud to her own melody once or twice on the way home. Nothing wrong with that.

The fog had lifted, and sunrise turned the sky a blazing orange. She was a little behind schedule after breakfast with Dell, but she just had to run through the shower real quick and change. Hopefully she'd be in and out before Cara even woke up to realize she'd never come home.

Mia hummed to herself as she practically skipped up the walk. Still grinning, she opened the door, then froze when she saw Cara in the kitchen, frowning.

"Morning," Mia offered carefully, trying not to sound as cheerful as she felt. "Not like you to be up so early."

"I got called in to work the morning shift and I didn't have any work clothes clean, so I had to get up to do laundry." Cara folded her arms across her chest. "Do you know why I had to get up early to do my laundry? Because my sister, who would normally be helpful and do it for me before she headed off to the farm, never came home last night. At all."

Mia tried very hard not to grin. Damn right she hadn't come home last night. Go, her. "Sorry." Except she wasn't. Not even a little bit.

Cara clucked her tongue. "The walk of shame after the second date. I'm not sure whether to be impressed or concerned."

"Don't be concerned."

Cara crossed over to her. "Okay. So…you're okay?"

"Of course I am." It was stupid to be irritated. Sure, Cara was younger, but she'd been doing this whole thing a lot longer than Mia.

"Dell was okay? I mean, was he not a jerk, not how was he in the sack. Although…"

"I have to get in the shower. Dell was great. I mean, nice, not…" She gave Cara a little shove when her sister dissolved into a fit of giggles. "Oh, grow up. I have to get in the shower."

Mia ran through the shower, arrived at the farm only fifteen minutes later than usual. Luckily Dad was with his milk guy loading up the day's offering, so he would be too busy to notice.

Mia worked through the morning, still assessing hail damage, retilling, determining what seeds were lost as best she could. When she took a break for lunch, she sat on the porch with Anna sharing a bag of pretzels and eating out of packets of tuna.

Mia took a forkful of tuna out of the packet. If she could cut lunch down to ten minutes, she could still get everything on her to-do list done and have time to go home, shower, get ready and be at Moonrise by six to meet Dell.

Just the thought had butterflies flitting through her stomach. They weren't the debilitating ones she was used to when it came to social situations—especially guy social situations. No, these were more like how she felt before the market. Nervous, yes, but excited. Ready to take on whatever challenges it offered.

She was *so* ready to take on the challenges of Dell and distractions. Those were awesome challenges to be facing.

"So Kenzie said she saw your truck at Dell's last night."

Mia practically choked on the bite of tuna.

Anna smiled sweetly. "And this morning."

She coughed a few times. "Oh. Well." It was totally pathetic for an adult to ask, but she had to know. "You didn't tell Mom and Dad, did you?"

"Oh, was I not supposed to?"

Mia was fairly sure her heart had stopped before Anna laughed.

"Calm down. Of course I didn't tell them. I'd be locked in my room for twenty years if Mom caught wind of it. They've given up on Cara, but you're the last paragon of virtue I have as an example, apparently." Anna laughed again. "Not such a paragon of virtue anymore, though."

"Yeah, yeah, yeah." Mia tossed the packet of tuna half-uneaten. It was just teasing, and silly teasing at that, and she was *twenty-six*, for goodness' sakes. She couldn't stomach it—the thought of Mom and Dad finding out that she'd... Oh, that would not be good. "I have to get back to work."

"Just don't get knocked up. I'll be totally screwed."

"Jeez." Well, she finally understood why some people didn't want to live in a small town and work with their family. Absolutely zero privacy about anything, ever. That had never been a problem before.

Now she finally had something to be private about. Thoughts of Mom and Dad finding out faded.

Mia Pruitt had a sex life. She couldn't help but smile. Shoot. It was too awesome for her to care who was poking into it.

CHAPTER TWENTY

DELL WASN'T SURE what it said about him, or what it said about what was going on with Mia, but after this morning with Mia and hard work in the fields before lunch, he was feeling much more in control. Less as if he'd snap a stray family member's head off.

Well, as long as that family member wasn't Dad. He hadn't quite worked through all his anger there, but he was feeling centered enough that he wanted to smooth things over with the rest of them.

Maybe once he got through to Mom and Charlie, he'd find a way to work up the same interest in smoothing things over with Dad.

Maybe.

Regardless, in order to ever make any progress, he needed to start going about this differently. Accepting a little offer of help—just a small one, and not just beating his hard head against Dad's. He needed Mom and Charlie not just feeling sorry for him, but behind him.

Kenzie already was, for all she cared about the

farm, but that care wasn't much, and he doubt it'd have much weight with Dad.

All the weight was with Mom and Charlie, so he'd start with the hard one first. Since Charlie had as much difficulty swallowing his pride as Dell did, Dell knew that was what he had to do.

Swallow his pride. He grimaced at the phone in his hand and put it facedown on the counter. He needed to finish lunch and do this on a full stomach. He polished off his sandwich, dawdled over potato chips and then finally picked up the phone and pulled up Charlie's number.

This was like taking Mia's seed-sharing offer. It rankled, it *sucked*, but it was a necessity to keep this place. So he'd do it.

"Dell, everything all right?"

He couldn't blame Charlie for opening with that. He couldn't remember the last time he'd called his brother. Usually it was texts.

"Hey. Um, yeah, everything is fine. I just needed…" He had to take a deep breath, picture the fields outside to get the words out. "Your help."

"My…help?"

"Advice, more like. I guess."

"Oh, well, sure, I can give that."

Was it his imagination Charlie seemed more disappointed at being asked for advice than for help? Had to be.

"I, um, was talking to…" For some reason he

hedged. "Another farmer today." After all, why did Charlie need to know it was Mia? "Her— His— Their farm had the same kind of damage and they offered to buy seeds in bulk together. It doesn't save a huge amount, but enough to make a difference with the time delay I'll be working with now."

"Oookay."

He had to force himself to do the deep-breath thing again, picture the fields, remember what this was for. "I just wanted to know if you thought that sounded like a good idea," he said through gritted teeth.

"You want to know if *I* think that sounds good?"

"Yes," Dell ground out, hoping the phone hid some of his impatience and irritation.

Charlie's silence stretched out, but Dell was not going to be the one who broke it. He'd sit here in silence the rest of the day before he was the one to speak next.

"Does this have to do with Mia?"

"Huh?"

"Kenzie said… She said she spent the night at your place."

Damn it, Kenzie. "So?"

"So is Mia the 'them' offering to split seed costs with you?"

"Does it matter?"

Charlie sighed, that long-suffering sigh that

never failed to make Dell want to punch something. On more than one occasion as kids, that something had been Charlie. He pictured one such time—the first time he'd managed to knock his brother off his feet.

Ah, good memories.

"I suppose it doesn't really matter," Charlie said at last. "And since you know Mia, and I know her a bit, it helps. She's smart. I doubt she'd offer if it hurt her, and I can't see any way it'd harm you."

She's smart. All the pride he'd swallowed, and for what? Not even real advice. Just "Mia's smart." *And you're not.*

"Dell?"

"What would it take…" His voice was rough, and he wished it was only anger or irritation in it. But there was more. A whole lot more. "What would it take for you guys to see that I'm smart, too? That I know what I'm doing."

Something beeped on Charlie's end and he swore. "You had twenty-some years to prove it, Dell." Charlie sighed. "I don't mean this to sound harsh, but I have to get this call. Maybe…you're too late to prove anything."

The line went dead. Dell stared at his phone, blinked. Too late. Maybe it was too late to prove anything.

He stood, fingers clutching the phone so tight it was a wonder it didn't crack.

Because too late? Screw that.

MIA RUSHED THROUGH her chores, offered Dad an even more cursory goodbye than he usually offered. Back at home, she zoomed through the shower and pawed through Cara's closet. Even though she'd bought a bunch of new jeans that fit, her wardrobe was still woefully void of date clothes.

Then again, they were going to Moonrise. A restaurant in New Benton where plenty of lifelong residents liked to linger over coffee. People would see them. People would talk. If she looked as if she was going on a date, people would *really* talk.

She was used to being the butt of a joke, but she wasn't used to being the source of gossip. She had a feeling this would be some juicy gossip.

She crossed the hall back to her room and looked in her own closet. Not exactly sexy. But, since she'd agreed to go home with Dell, she could pack a little overnight bag. Maybe she had some sexy pajamas.

She laughed out loud. Right. She'd never had a reason for sexy pajamas. She'd never had a reason for sexy anything. She glanced at the clock, cursed. Without paying too much attention, she pulled on a pair of jeans and a long-sleeved T-shirt. She shoved a couple of extra clothes, a toothbrush and her glasses into a bag. Grabbing a few other essentials and her seed notes, she slipped on her tennis shoes and hurried out the door.

During the short drive, she tried to practice what to say. Focus on business first. That was the most important thing. He was being weirdly evasive about it, and she didn't have time for that. Either he accepted her offer or he didn't.

She would not be swayed or distracted by sex. Business first. Because farm stuff always had to be the most important thing.

Then he was free to distract her in any way he saw fit.

Giggling to herself, she pulled the truck into the parking lot of Moonrise Diner. On the outside, the place looked a little worse for wear, but for Mia's entire life it had looked that way. A sagging, slightly outdated facade, but the food was good.

Dell's truck was already in the parking lot. Mia took a deep breath. This was somehow both exhilarating and 100 percent frightening. What was she supposed to say to the guy she'd had sex with last night?

Probably the same thing she'd said to him this morning. Sometimes it was hard to remember because she'd been overanalyzing social situations for so long, but she'd pretty much only been herself with Dell, and he'd never balked at a thing.

So when it came to him, she needed to let the anxiety go. She grabbed her purse and seed notebook.

Dell sat in a booth with his back to her. He had his usual baseball cap on, blond waves sticking out the bottom. He wore a faded black T-shirt that somehow emphasized his broad shoulders. God, he was hot.

Mia bit her lip to keep from grinning and forced her feet to move forward. She slid into the booth, hoping it came off cool and confident instead of giddy and way too excited. "Hey."

He closed the menu he'd been looking at and smiled. "Hey." He glanced at her notebook and there was that weird...tightness about his expression. That thing she couldn't figure out. He didn't want to do this. So why the hell was he?

"So." If he wasn't going to start, she was. This was important. She couldn't wait on him to figure out what he wanted just because he was good in bed.

Mia smiled to herself. Using terms such as *good in bed* and actually having some kind of idea what that meant was too new not to enjoy.

She smoothed open the notebook. "I have a couple ideas based on what I saw of your notes, but obviously you'll need to see if they match up with what you were thinking."

When she looked up from the pages, he wasn't there. Instead, he was sliding into her side of the booth. "Let's see." He took the notebook from her as his shoulder bumped hers.

Mia scooted over a little to give him more room, but they were still pressed shoulder to shoulder, hip to hip, as he went over the pages of her notebook.

"I got you a Coke, Mia." Mallory pushed a glass toward her. "Usual?"

"Oh, yeah."

"Dell?"

"Cheeseburger. Fries. Coke."

Mallory hovered for a minute. So unlike her.

"You guys…working?" She peered at the notebook.

"Um, yeah."

Mallory chuckled. "That makes a lot more sense. Get those orders in for you." She disappeared.

Dell didn't say anything, so Mia looked around the diner. More than one set of eyes were glued to them. The heat spread up her neck into her face.

"What do you think she meant by that?"

"By what?" Dell took the pen she'd placed on the table, started writing down a few things next to her notes.

"The whole that-makes-a-lot-more-sense thing?"

Dell shrugged. "Dunno."

"Dell."

He shoved the notebook at her. "Most of what you had should work. I added a few things. You want to place the order and then give me a figure, I'll write you a check." For the first time, Dell turned his head so she could see his eyes under the brim of his cap. "Now. No more business."

Mia frowned down at the paper. He hadn't changed much. Why couldn't they have done that this morning? She looked back at him. "People are watching us."

"You embarrassed to be seen with me, sugar?"

She scowled at the nickname, hated herself a little for starting to like it and the drawl he said it with. "No. I just..." Mia looked around again. Mallory was talking with Ed and Margaret, and all three of them looked her way. Mia looked back at the table. "People will speculate. Why you're with me."

"Maybe they'll speculate why you're with me."

Mia snorted. "Right."

"Trust me. They will. Smart and dumb, remember? 'Is that nice, smart Pruitt girl falling for the not-so-bright Wainwright boy? Why, I guess a pretty face *can* make a smart girl do a dumb thing.' But what's it matter? So they speculate. Doesn't change anything, does it?"

He had a point, as mixed up in his insecurity as it was. Hadn't Cara and her dad already insinuated Dell was some kind of bad influence? "No, it doesn't change anything." That was the lesson she'd been teaching herself for years, right? It didn't matter what other people thought if she was happy, and this thing with Dell made her happy when it didn't make her a little bit crazy.

Anything and everything she'd chalk up to life experience. Sure, let people wonder. Why the hell not?

DELL HAD NO APPETITE, but he forced himself to work through most of the burger and fries. He had a feeling Mia would have noticed otherwise.

There were a lot of things he wanted her to notice. A lot of things he wanted her to understand.

What the conversation with Charlie this afternoon had done to him was not one of them. He liked the sense of purpose being pissed off and angry gave him, but he didn't like the reason for the anger. Didn't particularly want to share that with Mia.

For all the ways he'd poked at Charlie for doing everything for Mom and Dad's approval, he wasn't any better. He was twenty-eight and desperate for a morsel of it. Just a glimmer.

Parents wasn't even fair. Mom was a glimmer. Dad was an impenetrable dark.

He barely resisted the urge to thunk his head against the table, but Mia would probably figure that one out, too.

He was still seated next to her, rather than moving back to the other side. He hadn't felt like being looked into all through dinner. Side by side, he could feel her warmth, smell her shampoo, occasionally graze her thigh with his hand under the table.

She jolted every time, followed by pressing her lips together, trying not to smile. And failing. It made him smile, and he wanted to feel like smiling.

People did watch. He had no doubt they puzzled over it. Questioned what they saw, and who could blame them? He couldn't help but wonder himself.

What was Mia doing, smiling at him as if he was something special? He could chalk it up to the virgin thing, but *she* had been the one who'd only been looking for Mr. Wrong.

You are supposed to be looking for Mrs. Wrong. Scratch that. Looking for nothing. You don't have time for this.

But being with her was like a nice long nap after a rough day weeding.

And, bottom line, there wasn't an inch of anything wrong with Mia Pruitt.

"You ready to go?" she asked, her smile pressed together, that mix of shyness and determination he wanted to roll around in like a dog in fresh hay.

He was seriously losing it. "Yeah." He slid out of the booth. She followed suit, scooping up her neat little notebook. She plucked the bill out of his hand so fast and out of the blue, he didn't have time to react.

"Business expense," she said in a singsongy

voice, handing it and a credit card to Mallory before he had a chance to get a word in edgewise.

"You two were sitting awfully close for business," Mallory muttered.

Mia didn't respond, so neither did he. He fished out his wallet and as she was signing her name to the receipt, tossed a tip onto the counter.

"I don't like you paying my way."

"You don't like anything that might insult your mighty masculinity, but I figure at some point you're going to have to suck it up and deal with it. Might as well be today."

He stopped midstride for about a second before he worked up the brainpower to follow her outside the diner.

"You sure get some charge out of putting me in my place, don't you?"

"I do." She laughed loudly, clearly pleased with herself as she turned to face him outside the diner. "But something about you brings it out in me. And it's awesome. I never have the right thing to say at the right time!"

So pleased with herself, grin wide, he couldn't stop himself from smiling back, but it didn't change the facts. He leaned closer. "You still should have let me pay."

She got up to her tiptoes, fingers curling around his arm, as if she was going to kiss him to shut him up. He even leaned down farther to let her do it, because it would shut up the stupid voices in his head, too.

But she stopped halfway, glancing at the windows.

Frustration and hurt and all manner of ugly things bloomed. Festering in the ugliness of the Charlie phone call, Ed Stevens's truck, everything that had been bursting to near overflowing this season. The words spewed out before he had a chance to stuff them back. "I know you said you like me, but, hell, what do you see in me?"

She blinked at him, falling back to her heels. Her fingers dropped from his arm and she pulled her bottom lip between her teeth. "You mean aside from the pretty face?"

"Yes, that is what I mean," he ground out.

"And apart from the abs, I assume."

It was stupid. So long ago, but all those old voices. Teachers who'd insinuated it wasn't applying himself that was the problem, it was a simple lack of brainpower. Corrie and her "I need someone who will stimulate me, you know, intellectually." Charlie. Dad. Even Kenzie razzed him about what everyone saw as some lack in him.

"Dell." She cocked her head at him and he had to bring himself back to the present. If he was really going to let all that old stuff get under his skin, he was in a bad way.

She put her hand back on his arm. Gently. The

kind of gentle that pissed him off because it was a pitying kind of gentle.

"You...get me, in a way that even my family doesn't. The farm stuff. And you're not scared off by my blabbing or blurting out craziness." Her hand rubbed his arm, and that still felt a little pitying, but her words smoothed over it. Made it warm and welcome.

"Being hot helps, though."

He rolled his eyes, but he knew she was messing with him. "Ha-ha."

"I like your face." The hand not on his arm touched his cheek, then his temple. "I like your brain. I like your heart." She pressed her palm there, right over his too-hard-beating heart. "There are probably other parts I could say, but I won't because we're in public and because I'll blush even more."

It was hard to breathe past all that...honesty and sweetness and her seeing something he sometimes doubted existed. Brain. Heart. No one else saw it. He'd never figured out how to make them see it.

But she did. "You're something else, you know that?"

"You mean it in a good way, right?"

He touched his mouth to hers. Probably stupid in the middle of a parking lot, but *good way* was an understatement. She was a miracle.

When he released her, her mouth was curved

and pretty, still pleased with herself, and happy besides. "I'll take that as a yes." Her smile faded and she looked at the windows of the diner. People had undoubtedly seen, and she didn't like that.

Now, that was a familiar pain, wasn't it?

Or it was, until she reached out and slid her hand into his. "It's weird for me. To have people..." She closed her eyes and shook her head. "I don't know how to explain it. I spent a lot of years trying to figure out what people thought of me, why I couldn't...be like them, and I spent a lot of years shutting that off. So having people look and talk and wonder, it's... I need to refigure how to deal."

She dropped her gaze to their entwined hands. "It's not about this. It's about...recalibrating."

"Recalibrating?" he asked, surprised his voice sounded so rusty.

"Like, getting used to this new set of...stuff. Having people look at me, probably talk about me, and maybe in a bad way. Maybe not. Not caring, but also not working so hard to stay invisible so they won't talk at all. It's a new step in the new Mia, Queen of Farming, not geekery."

"Queen of Farming, huh?"

She nodded determinedly, walking hand in hand with him to their trucks. "Yes, and if you're very good I'll let you be a duke or earl or something."

"Sugar, I'm not settling for anything less than

king." *I can't.* But he didn't say it out loud. He let it echo in his head, then drowned it out by caging her against her truck.

She looked up at him, tapping her chin. "Hmm. Then, you'll have to be very good."

He leaned closer, his mouth right next to his ear. "Oh, I'm very, *very* good."

When she kind of shivered in response, every last bad voice in his head disappeared. "You going to follow me home, Queen Farmer?"

"Uh-huh." Her assent was little more than a squeak.

Yup, bad thoughts officially vanquished.

CHAPTER TWENTY-ONE

DELL WASN'T SURE how it had happened. Somehow, five out of the past six nights had found him with a houseguest, and he wasn't the least bit tired of her.

She was sitting on his couch, going on about the cold frame she wanted to build, and kept having to push her glasses up her nose. It had taken all of two nights for her to bust those out, saying she couldn't keep wearing her contacts or they were going to end up in the back of her eyes and lodged into her brain.

He didn't know why her weird little anxieties were so endearing. Why they made him want to cozy her up in bed and never leave. He didn't know what to do with that impulse, so he ignored it.

"I love your glasses."

She gave his shoulder a shove. "Shut up."

"I do. They're so nerdy. It's like a fetish I didn't know I had."

"I hate you." She wrinkled her nose. "Unfortunately, I have to bring out the big nerd guns tonight."

"And that is?"

She pulled her overnight bag off the floor and retrieved a little plastic case out of her bag and opened it.

He looked at the bizarre instrument inside. "What the hell is that?"

"My retainer."

"I'm sorry. We're not sixteen. You cannot have a retainer."

She flung her head back onto the couch. "I have a migrating tooth," she mumbled, staring up at the ceiling.

"A what?"

"My tooth moves if I don't wear my retainer. It will slowly inch its way back to the roof of my mouth, and I can't believe I just told you that. I'm never going to have sex again, am I?"

"You have a tooth in the roof of your mouth."

"I *had* a tooth in the roof of my mouth." She covered her face with her hands. "I have to go home now."

"Not on your life." He laughed, couldn't help himself, wrapping his arms around her and pulling her to him. "My little freak of nature."

"Yeah, that's not what you were saying in high school."

Ouch. When he'd apologized to her at the bar that night, he'd meant it. In high school he hadn't thought about how she might feel being the butt of a joke. He'd just thought about how she was one of those people he'd never be. Good at school, tests. Charlie stuff his parents had praised to high heaven and wondered why it'd skipped a kid.

"Hey." She poked his chest. "Don't get all frowny. I'll have to start reminding you I deserved at least a little of it. Remember the talent show?"

"Oh, God. The cow-milking play?"

She nodded. "It was awful."

"Please tell me your parents videotaped it. I need to see that again."

She shoved at his chest. "No." But she was laughing, and everything about this felt right.

He was in trouble, but he couldn't resist her. He cupped her cheek, thumb brushing across her earlobe, and looked at her, right in the eye, refusing to let himself chicken out. "I wasn't very nice to you then." It was uncomfortable, but it needed to be said.

"No one was."

Christ, she killed him. All matter-of-fact, not all screwed up over it as he was. Infinitely stronger and wiser than him, and he didn't even care, because her being here made him feel worthy of her. She'd chosen him, and she hadn't had to. She liked him, face, brain, heart. Words she'd uttered a week ago and he'd yet to stop turning over in his head.

His fingertips touched her hair, his thumb grazing her cheekbone. She squirmed, but he didn't let go. He didn't ever want to let go.

"I was jealous, you know."

"Jealous?" She scoffed. "Of what?"

"You were so smart…and I wasn't very."

She let out a shaky breath, meeting his gaze. "I think we both did okay." Her voice wasn't much more than a whisper.

The words hovered, weighted with importance. He didn't let his eyes leave her face. "Yeah, I'd say we both did pretty damn good."

She smiled and he managed one in return, leaning in to kiss her, to lose himself in her. But her phone went off.

"Ignore it."

"I can't. I can't not answer a ringing phone. What if it's important?"

He slid his hands up her sides, bringing her tank top with them. "What if it's not?"

She shook her head and pushed him away. "Can't. Can't do it." She hopped up, found her phone and flipped it open. Even from a few feet away he could hear the immediate onslaught of a woman's voice.

"Mom. Mom. Jeez. Mom." Mia held up a finger and disappeared down the hall. Dell scrubbed his hands over his face. What on God's green earth was he doing? He was two bizarre idiosyncrasies away from falling for her completely and about ten bricks short of a load.

He looked up at the ceiling. What exactly was the harm in falling for Mia?

She's your direct competition, moron.

Right. Right.

Why didn't that feel right at all?

Probably because they hadn't been to market yet. How was he going to feel tomorrow when customers lined up at her booth instead of his? Was it really going to be that easy to forget she'd been the one to start the battle of the sexes? That every customer at her booth meant one less sale for him, and each lost sale put him on increasingly crumbling ground?

If she tried to help him again, he was pretty sure his man card would be revoked along with thoroughly imploding any chance he might have to earn his father's respect. As much as he needed her help, as much as it seemed harmless on the surface, if Dad found out he'd be even more fucked than he already was.

Any success he managed would be undermined by Dad finding out about Mia's help. Dad would think it was because of her and sell the farm away anyway.

No matter how many times he thought it, Mia came into view and he forgot it all. She stood with the phone off her ear and a tight smile. His depressing thoughts stopped. When she slid onto the couch next to him, any of her humor and ease from earlier was gone.

"Something wrong?"

"I guess word got to Mom that you and I…" She rubbed her tongue over her bottom lip, so he let his hand travel from calf to thigh. It was only fair.

"You and I?"

"Had dinner at Moonrise the other night. And you know someone saw us kissing in the parking lot."

"That was hardly a kiss." He stroked his index finger up and down her leg from her kneecap to the hem of her shorts. He wanted a lot more than pressing his lips to hers right now.

"Well, enough of a kiss for my mother." She pushed off the couch and began to pace. Dell folded his arms behind his head and enjoyed the view.

Despite being short, she had long, pretty legs. She wasn't wearing a bra under her tank top. A very nice view indeed.

"She wants me to bring you to dinner."

Dell stilled, wrenching his gaze from his chest. "Whoa. What?"

"I didn't say *I* want you to come to dinner. I said that's what my mother wants."

He straightened, the offhanded comment pricking at his pride. "You don't want me to come to dinner?"

She blinked at him. "You want to?"

This conversation had gotten weird quick. "I… Let's rewind for a second. Why does your mother want me to come to dinner?"

"Because if I'm seeing 'that boy'—that boy

being you—'he'd better be willing to come visit with your family.'"

Her imitation of her mother made him smile.

She shook her head, looking grave. "Yeah, you definitely cannot come to dinner."

"Why not?"

"Because everything about that smile screams 'bad boy' and my mother will flip."

Dell upped the wattage of his grin. "I love to make mothers flip."

"Dell, be serious. You don't want to come to dinner with my family. They're nuts." She looked down again, eyebrows all furrowed. "Besides, this is supposed to be a fun thing. I'll admit my knowledge of flings is as nil as my knowledge of relationships, but I don't think family factors into...fun till it's not."

Which was true. He hadn't met a woman's parents since high school, and dinner with Mia's was probably a bad idea. But...

He leaned forward, grabbing Mia's hand and pulling her toward him. "Do *you* want me to?"

She looked down at their joined hands, her expression pained. "No. Yes. Yes and no? Can my answer be both?"

Dell shook his head, then tugged until she was on his lap. She framed his face with her hands, and he had the uncomfortable realization he'd do just about anything she asked him to. Including go to dinner with her crazy family. If it meant more of this…what was the harm?

He ignored the little voice that whispered, *profits, money, farm*.

"I'll go."

"Are you sure?"

His hands smoothed down her back. Not even a little bit, but apparently that wasn't going to stop him. "Now can we stop talking about your parents?" He curled his fingers around her hips, pulling her closer.

"Please." She rifled her hands through his hair, a smile curving her mouth. Looking straight at him with green eyes he'd begun to notice had the tiniest flecks of an almost blue in them. He liked finding that, thinking he'd been the only one to see it, appreciate it.

But lately when he would find it, a heavy weight would band around his lungs, making it hard to take a full breath. Usually that prompted him to jump right along, whip off her shirt, haul her off to the bedroom.

But her fingers were toying with the hem of his shirt, and there was no galloping forward when she worked up the courage to take the reins. No, he couldn't bring himself to do much more than sit back and soak it in.

She pushed his shirt up and over his stomach and chest, and then she tugged until he held his arms out so she could lift it completely off.

Her appreciative sigh didn't rankle, not when her fingers trailed over his shoulders and she leaned in to kiss him. Mia put everything into every kiss, as if it was the last and only thing they'd ever do.

Sometimes she made him think that it was all he needed. Which was insane. So he grabbed her shirt and pulled it off her, just as she'd done to him.

It didn't help. In fact, the more he had of Mia, the less it seemed to help this chest-crushing feeling. But he didn't do the sensible thing like get away from her or suggest she shouldn't stay.

No, he kissed her, drowned in her, worked to get all of her clothes off her, then flipped her underneath him.

"I can't get over you. Everything about you." He hated when words like that spilled out of him, but she liked it. He'd do just about anything she liked. To make her smile. To make her sigh.

"Bedroom?" she breathed.

"How about right here?"

"But con—"

"Just sit tight." He needed a second, a breather, some solid ground. Get his head on right so he wouldn't drown.

As if you haven't already.

MIA WAS LYING on Dell's couch staring at the ceiling. Naked. Though they had managed to have plenty of sex in the past week, there were moments when she still had to sit and try to wrap her mind around it.

She was in some sort of pseudorelationship with Dell. Spending the night at his house more nights than not, getting all wrapped up in him and the way he made her feel. She was soaked in it. She could barely remember the parts of the week she'd worked, because those days she'd had her mind more on Dell than if the strawberries were going to come through.

When Dell returned, condom in hand, the fierce look about him had subsided, only to spark back to blazing when she smiled at him.

She didn't know what that was, what it meant, and as far as she was concerned, when he pulled the condom out of the wrapper and rolled it on, she didn't need to know. Not right now.

Not when he moved on top of her, or slid inside her, or kissed her neck, her shoulder. Not when his hands trailed over her, resting on her hips, anchoring her as she answered each thrust.

She said his name on a sigh, because he always held on a little tighter when she did. Bringing her closer and closer until she arched into orgasm, and he quickly followed suit.

Holy moly, sex was awesome. Or was it just sex with Dell that was awesome?

None of that, brain.

With Dell's weight pressing her into the couch,

she couldn't manage a full breath, but it was too nice a feeling to complain about. She felt close to him, all satisfied and warm and…

Maybe words for emotions she shouldn't let herself think about. Not yet. *You mean not ever.* Right. Right. This was her first adult fling.

He moved to take care of the condom, but then he slid next to her on the couch again. "Mmm. I'm going to sleep right here."

"'Kay." She started moving to get out of the couch. "Be right back."

He opened one eye as she scooted down and slid off. "Where are you going?"

"I have to, uh…get something."

He moved onto his elbows, frowning. "Get what?"

She sighed. "My retainer."

He flopped back onto the couch pillow and laughed and laughed. But it wasn't a mean laugh. She couldn't help but join in for a second. It *was* ridiculous.

"Oh, sugar, you are one of a kind."

She liked that he thought so, and that he seemed to *like* that. It would be foolish to think this would last, dinner with her parents or no, but maybe she could console herself with the fact Dell would always remember the girl with the retainer.

Funny, that didn't offer much solace at all if it meant there'd be a girl after her with *no* retainer. Nope, no solace at all.

CHAPTER TWENTY-TWO

MIA SCARFED DOWN a bagel with one hand while Dell helped load his truck with her market produce. They were running about ten minutes late, due to activities this morning, and she couldn't keep the smile off her face.

"How do you have so much?"

"I had some canned stuff left over from winter, some garlic, onion. I kept them up in case of emergency. Good potato crop."

He frowned, finished shoving the last pallet into the bed of the truck. "Quite the planner."

Mia's stomach turned as she climbed into the passenger seat. The past week it had been easy to pretend this stuff didn't matter.

But it did. Suddenly. Harshly. Her having more than him *mattered*, and he was frowning.

All her smiling and giddy happiness faded. More varieties in crop to sell meant more people would buy from her stand, where they could get different things all at one place.

It irked her that she felt guilty. She shouldn't feel guilty for doing her job. It wasn't her fault he didn't have an emergency crop. She *was* a planner, and a businesswoman.

But the guilt didn't desist, and the stomach-turning edged deeper. And deeper still when silence lingered as Dell drove toward Millertown.

Silence wasn't something that happened much between them. They'd spent so much time together the past week and they'd yet to run out of things to talk about.

But then, they hadn't talked much in specifics. Not when it came to the market. Not when it came to competition. It was all seeds and people they knew and how hard it was going to be to ever get certified organic.

Now the market loomed, and with it competition and her being better off. *Which is not your fault. Don't let him make you feel like the asshole here.* No. No amount of sex or company or… feeling was going to make her feel as if she'd done something wrong.

"The Cardinals won last night," she offered into the silence. Baseball had to be a safe topic.

"I know. We watched the game together."

"Oh. Right."

She glanced at him out of the corner of her eye. His hands were tight on the steering wheel and his expression was…hard. Unreadable. Not pleasant.

"Oh. Here." Mia pulled a twenty out of her purse. "Here's my share for gas."

He glanced at the twenty in her hand, then

nodded to his wallet in the center console. Somehow, though she didn't think it possible, his expression hardened further.

She'd screwed up somehow, but…how? What had she done? Just having more stuff to sell? Well, that wasn't fair. And it was kind of petty of him to get upset over that.

"Supposed to rain tomorrow."

Mia looked over at him. There was nothing relaxed or easy about the way he said it, but he was trying, so she would, too.

"Yeah. Can't say as we need it."

"Nope. Sure don't."

Silence again. The only thing that punctuated the silence on the thirty-minute drive was stupid, inane conversation like that.

When Dell pulled into a parking space at the market, they both sat for a second, staring at the windshield. Then he patted her knee.

"Good luck today, sugar."

Mia blinked, but he was out of the truck before she could respond. Her throat felt tight, a lump lodged there. But why was she upset? He'd wished her luck. This was…nothing to be worried or upset over.

So why did it feel like the end of the road?

Cara and Charlie descended, yapping and complaining a mile a minute while they unloaded the truck bed. They went their separate ways, and the throat-clogged feeling didn't go away, it grew, a tension in her stomach tightening right along with it.

"Isn't it going to bother you when he takes his shirt off?" Cara asked, placing onions in a neat row.

Mia hadn't given it any thought. Which, considering as much thought as she gave everything, was kind of strange. But she hadn't thought about Dell and his shirtlessness at the market. Because they didn't talk about the market. They didn't talk about all that this meant, and what idiots they had been.

Mia sneaked a glance at him. Was him taking off his shirt and flirting with customers going to bother her? He still had his T-shirt on and he was talking to Charlie about something as he set up their booth.

"Mia?"

"What? No. No, it won't bother me. He can do what he wants." Which was true. As much as she wanted to read into him inviting her over every night but one this week, agreeing to go to dinner with her family, the bottom line was they'd always agreed what was between them was going to just be fun until things got too complicated.

Was this too complicated? The ride here seemed to point to yes.

Mia spent the morning on considerable edge. She kept glancing at Dell. Trying to discern what every little thing meant. Such as, for starters, why it took him nearly an hour to take his shirt off when he normally whipped it off before customers even started arriving. Or why he didn't seem to be smiling quite so much as usual. Or…

For the billionth time, Mia closed her eyes and reminded herself she needed to focus on herself. On Pruitt Farms. On what was really important.

Of course, that just made her glance over at Dell again. She hadn't caught him looking at her once.

"All right, Mia. Ready for BOTS?"

Mia frowned over at Val. "BOTS?"

"Battle of the sexes. Today it's who can hull the most strawberries in a minute. We're going to try to balance out the events each week. I hate to come off sexist, but I think it's pretty obvious Dell would win just about every physical event. And we want there to be *some* suspense. I tell you what, this battle-of-the-sexes thing was genius. Just genius. We've had an increase in customers and earnings each week."

Val led Mia over to the little tent, where they'd set up two chairs and two cartons of strawberries. Mia squinted over at Dell's booth, but didn't see him.

"You know, I heard a funny little rumor." Val's voice was low, conspiratorial.

"Yeah?"

"Someone said they saw you and Dell kissing."

"That is a funny little rumor." Mia took her

seat and clamped her mouth shut. What she really wanted to do was tell Val that, yes, she and Dell had been kissing and doing a hell of a lot more than that and it was great.

But that would be weird.

Dell finally appeared and sat down on the chair next to her. He didn't smile. His gaze didn't meet hers. "Got quite a line over at your booth."

She glanced at her booth, then at his. Yeah, she was winning. It didn't feel good at all. "It's one week, Dell."

"For you."

Mia leaned closer so she could whisper while Farrah and Val set up. "So you're pissed I'm earning more money than you?"

He scratched a hand through his hair. "No. I'm not pissed." He leaned back in the chair. "I'm not pissed at *you*. I'm just…pissed. What am I supposed to be doing, cartwheels?"

"I'm sorry." And she was. She didn't want him to lose his farm. But she'd done all the helping she could afford to do. Had to remember that.

He glanced at her then. "Me, too."

She got the uncomfortable feeling he didn't just mean about the farm stuff. That it had only taken showing up at the market to realize anything between them was a fantasy.

Val started talking to the crowd in her bullhorn. Farrah handed them knives. When Val shouted

"Go," Mia methodically hulled the strawberries without much thought.

Val and Farrah counted, then pronounced Mia the winner, and the crowd that had gathered clapped enthusiastically.

Not one second of it gave her any pleasure. She didn't know whom to blame for that. Herself? Dell?

"Of course you're going to win the girlie activities." Dell didn't say it with any humor, and it grated.

"Don't be a sore loser." Maybe she was overreacting, but she hadn't done anything wrong. She hadn't. He didn't get to make her feel as if she had.

His brows drew together, his mouth turning in to a hard-edged line. "I'm not losing anything."

Because she was irritated and apparently stupid, she kept going. "For what it's worth, you could probably keep your shirt on at least one damn week." Her cheeks heated because, hello, that was jealousy talking, and she'd never known jealousy to be an attractive trait.

"Yeah, well, you could have not made this guys against girls, because I'm losing customers right and left. So thanks a lot for that."

She opened her mouth to apologize. She knew how much each customer mattered to him this year. She knew he hadn't talked to his dad all week, that it was squeezing any enjoyment out of his work, and of course she knew he could be in serious trouble.

But she could *not* give up her farm for his. Maybe she wasn't in as much danger, but what kind of person did it make her if she rolled over just because some guy had had sex with her?

"I thought you understood I wasn't the girl desperate for attention anymore. Sleeping with me wasn't going to get me to give up on my lifeblood."

He stood a little too quickly, knocking his chair back. She was sure they were earning at least a glance from Val if not a few customers.

"You really think that's why I was…" He looked around, stepped closer so he could lower his voice, his eyes blazing into hers. "You think that's why I was with you?"

Her face heated, because she didn't really. She'd wanted to make him feel bad the way he'd made her feel bad. It didn't help. Hurting each other didn't help. "No, I just…"

"This is…" He shook his head, and then without another word he walked away.

So she walked back to her booth because what other option was there? Go after him? Argue in front of everyone? No, and while she regretted insinuating his motivations had been mercenary, she couldn't feel bad for the rest of it.

Pruitt Farms was not going to roll over and die just so Morning Sun Farms could stay in existence.

If there was anything she prided herself on when it came to the whole waiting-for-sex thing, it was that she'd learned how to be her own person. She'd stopped trying to fit in, and she hadn't sacrificed that for male attention. Ever.

"You okay?"

"Fine." Mia pushed past Cara to get behind the table. She took a long drink out of her water bottle and purposefully did not look at Dell or anywhere near the vicinity of the Morning Sun Farms stand.

Yup. This was too complicated. *Fun till it's not.* Well, this wasn't fun. Watching him flirt with other women wasn't fun, and arguing with him over customers wasn't fun, and feeling as if her stomach was tied into a thousand knots was not fun.

Mia blinked. She was not going to cry. She'd had a quickie affair. Good for her. No sense crying over it.

Cara squeezed her shoulder and it took everything Mia had not to give in to those tears. She didn't want it to be over. She didn't want it to be complicated. She took a deep breath and let it out.

She couldn't change the fact that Dell's farm was in trouble any more than she could change the fact that she felt horribly sorry for him. She couldn't change her jealousy any more than she could change the fact that they were competing for the same customers and apparently couldn't do it without arguing.

Another breath and she felt a little more in control of the tears. She'd had her fun; now it was time to move on. Dell loved his farm, yes, but she loved hers just as much. Helping a little hadn't hurt her any, but if she kept things going with him she'd be tempted to help him and hurt herself.

She couldn't let her soft heart get in the way of her life.

Why couldn't she have realized that before her heart got involved?

DELL SLOWLY CLIMBED into his truck. Mia was already sitting in the passenger seat, staring at the windshield, hands clasped in her lap.

Way to go, asshole.

He wasn't pissed at her. Nothing that had happened today was her fault. Not even the stupid battle-of-the-sexes thing, because if he hadn't egged her on at every turn in the beginning of the season it would have never escalated this far.

He couldn't even blame her for saying he was sleeping with her to get her off his back here. He'd been too big of a dick for her not to deserve a dig, no matter how unfounded.

So he had no idea why not being pissed at her had him acting as he was.

"Just to clarify, I'm not expecting you to come to dinner tomorrow night or anything. I think I get the picture."

"Mia—"

"No, look, we agreed. Fun till it's not, and this isn't fun." She kept staring at her hands, twisting her fingers together in some intricate pattern.

No. It wasn't fun. Being irritated with her over something that wasn't her fault wasn't fun. Her having more customers than him today wasn't fun. Him acting like an ass wasn't fun. And thinking this might be the end of whatever thing they had going was really, really not fun.

"I mean, it wasn't a relationship anyway, right?"

He stared at the spot on his steering wheel where the leather had worn away. It had been short, but it sure as hell had felt like a relationship. "I don't know. Maybe it was." He gave a passing thought to bashing his head into the steering wheel because he had not meant to say that out loud.

"Well, anyway." She gave him a small smile. "Whatever it was, was nice. Really nice. Better than nice." Her brows drew together. "What I'm trying to say is thank you."

"Don't thank me." Dell scrubbed a hand over his face, then looked over at her. *You know what, we had a bad day.* Not even a bad day. A bad morning. One bad morning. He could fix this. He didn't have to walk away like some pansy-ass piece of shit.

He'd walked away from a lot of things in his life, but he didn't walk away from the things that mattered. Mia mattered.

As much as Morning Sun?

It didn't have to be an either-or. It didn't. He knew he couldn't have everything he wanted, but he'd at least try to have the two things that made him feel...capable.

He took her hand because...well, because. "What if I said I was sorry?"

She looked at his hand on hers, then back at his face. "What?"

"What if I said I was sorry? Sorry for being a dick this morning. I meant what I said. I wasn't pissed at you, but I know it came off that way. I don't do pissed well." Hell, maybe he didn't do anything well. "The thing is...I don't want whatever's going on here to be over."

There. Laid it on the line. That would damn well fix it. But then all she said was, "Oh," and he wasn't sure.

"Do you want it to be over?"

After a pause, she shook her head.

His slow exhale sounded a little too relieved, but screw it. Screw all of it. "Good. So we just gotta figure something out. Some way to make this farm stuff not be the source of being shitty to each other."

"I wasn't shitty to you."

"The crack about keeping my shirt on? Acting as if I was sleeping with you to get something out of you wasn't sweet talk, sugar."

She huffed out a breath. "Well, it's not exactly fun watching women paw all over you."

"No one was pawing over me."

"Val practically shoved her hands down your pants."

"If you're jealous of a woman a good forty years older than me, you need your head examined."

Mia laughed, and just like that she was smiling at him, and just like that it softened into less than a smile. She sat back in her seat.

"Dell, maybe we're not right for each other." Before he could argue, she kept going. "I don't...I don't think I can do this." She visibly swallowed and looked down at her lap. "I'm a soft touch, and if we keep this up and you need something to keep your farm, I'd do just about anything to help. Even if it meant doing something stupid to myself. I can't trust myself."

"You think I'd want that? I don't want that." Because her giving something up for him would mean he'd be even more indebted to her. It would mean he'd lost and everyone was right about him not being able to do this. Help, no matter how much he might *need* it, undermined everything he was trying to accomplish. "How about you trust me not to let you do something stupid?" Why did he feel so desperate? Why couldn't he let this go?

Because no one got him like Mia did. No one

looked at him like Mia did. And nothing made him feel like Mia did.

He took a deep breath. "I like…being with you. I don't want that to stop because we had one bad morning. Just because we've got this one little thing complicating it."

"Is it really that little? I mean, what happens next week if I have more customers again? Don't you think this is going to repeat itself every Saturday?"

He shrugged. He didn't want to think about that. "Every couple fights. What's once a week?"

"Dell."

"We'll figure something out. We're grown adults with two brains between us. Yours being far superior and all, but we'll figure it out."

She was silent, a silence that grew so big Dell began to fidget in his seat. Christ, he never fidgeted.

"But…why figure it out?"

"Huh?"

Lines formed in her forehead as she looked at him so seriously that, in another situation, he might smile.

"You have a line of women at your disposal every Saturday. Probably more than just Saturdays. What's so special about me that we'd spend all this time trying to avoid the fact we're competing?"

Dell frowned and stared out the windshield.

Blue sky and a nursery boasting tomato-plant sales. The problem wasn't the answer to her question, the problem was voicing it. But she was waiting expectantly, so he had to.

"I don't know, Mia. You just…are." He swallowed the uncomfortable emotion behind the words. Normally he'd swallow the words down, too, but he figured he owed her. If he wanted this, he owed her the truth. "All that stuff you said at the diner. Face. Brain. Heart." *Tenfold*. "That's never happened to me before," he grumbled. *Not like this*.

When he worked up the courage to look at her, she was staring at the windshield with a baffled kind of smile on her face. Good or bad? He wasn't sure.

"That's sweet." She met his stare. "You really think we could work something out?"

"Sure. How hard could it be?" Really damn hard, but he'd find a way. One of these days, something would give for the farm, and one of these days something would give when it came to her. He couldn't get there if he gave up.

"Okay."

"Good. So we're on the same page, then."

"I guess so."

"And I'm coming to dinner tomorrow."

"Okay."

"And you're spending the night tonight."

"Oh, am I?" She squinted her disapproval.

Dell grinned. "Don't worry, sugar. I'll talk you into it." When she grinned back, he felt as if he'd won the lottery.

A really complicated and not at all smart lottery.

CHAPTER TWENTY-THREE

"DON'T MENTION ALCOHOL. Or fertilizer. No mention of reality TV or bowling alleys." Mia ticked off all Mom's hot buttons. All the while her inner freakout sounded a lot like *What are you doing? What the hell are you doing? Whyyy?*

"Bowling alleys?"

"Yes. They attract bad people and they're dirty. If she asks if you have a gun you can say yes, but make sure you tell her you lock it up and hide the key even if you don't. And—"

Dell leaned over the console and cut her off with a kiss.

"Definitely don't do that in front of her." Mia looked at her parents' house from the inside of Dell's truck cab. Oh, this was stupid. Worst idea ever. Worse even than falling for Dell in the first place and letting him talk her into continuing to do so.

As if it was falling anymore. She'd fallen. She'd been felled. And while obviously he felt at least *somewhat* similarly to want to keep...doing this, it didn't fix any of their problems. Problems that were always going to be there.

Their farms were at odds. Really, the only hope was Dell's dad *did* sell out from under him, but she couldn't hope for that at all. Even selfishly.

So this was stupid and pointless and she should call the whole thing off.

Dell patted her leg before shoving his door open. "Relax. What's the worst that could happen if she doesn't like me?"

She sank deeper into the passenger seat. "I could hear about it for the rest of my life."

"That seems a bit dramatic."

"Welcome to life with my mother." Mia could already hear it. Twenty years down the line. *Remember when you let yourself be deflowered by that Wainwright boy, who is now married and has a pack of beautiful children with some nice girl who didn't give the milk away for free.*

Okay, possibly not all Mom's voice there. The deflowering and giving the milk away for free, yes. The pack of beautiful children, though, that was her own brain being ridiculous. He'd have beautiful children someday, of course, but there was no way she was ever going to believe or fantasize they'd be with her.

She was not *that* big of a weirdo.

"Don't be a wuss. Get out of the car, young lady." He got out, but Mia didn't. She was rooted to the seat, and nothing could get her to move. He skirted the hood to her side, opened the door and jerked a thumb over his shoulder. "Out."

"You can't make me."

He grinned. "Wanna bet?"

"This is stupid." They had no future. *Except how he wants to work it out.* When did the prospect of actually working it out become scarier than the alternative?

Probably when she'd realized she'd bend over backward to help him.

"You're telling me. A grown-ass woman pouting about going to dinner with her family. Really stupid."

She glared at him. "I am not pouting."

"Come on. Let's go or I'll call you 'sugar' in front of your mother."

"I hate when you call me that." She hopped down onto the gravel of her parents' driveway. He could so not call her that in front of Mom. Or Dad. Or Cara. Or Anna. Her sisters would never let her hear the end of it, and her parents would probably spontaneously combust.

He closed the door, his mouth brushing next to her ear. "Liar."

Mia almost smiled. Okay, yes. She did like it *now*, but the dread over the evening beat out any happy feelings that someone had a term of endearment for her. "Just be on your best behavior, okay? No grinning or flirting or—"

"What about stripping naked and going at it right there on the table? I thought that might be a good idea."

She squeezed her eyes shut. Okay, she was being crazy. Point taken. "I'm sorry. It's… This is a first. Bear with me."

"Oh, I'm bearing. Wait till you have to have dinner with my family."

Jeez. What were they doing? Going to dinner with families and spending every night together. It was the makings of something real and big and lasting.

But they'd yet to find any solution for what every Saturday morning would bring. Jealousy. Guilt. Hurt. Doubt. And so on and so on.

Mia pushed open the front door. She couldn't figure out the whys of what she was doing with Dell. The only thing she had a handle on when she was with him was that she kept wanting to be.

What was the harm in thinking he was right? That they could figure out some way to get around this little sticking point? It was just a farmers' market after all. She could almost believe it when she didn't think about all that it symbolized for each of them.

"Mia." Mom wrung her hands. "Dell. So nice of you to come to dinner."

"Thanks for having me, Mrs. Pruitt."

Mom's smile looked pained. "Well, we're all at the table. Come on in." Mom began walking into the dining room.

"Are we late?" Dell whispered behind her.

"No. Dad tries to eliminate any chance for

small talk with strangers, so they're always seated when people get here."

"Seriously?"

Mia nodded, stepping into the dining room. The table was set, everyone was sitting except her and Dell, and Dad was scowling even more than usual.

The pit of dread in her stomach knotted itself together and grew heavier. Mia forced a smile and slid into her normal seat next to her father.

With no preamble, Mom said prayer and then began to pass around dishes of food. Silence reigned.

Well, shoot.

Mia looked at Cara, who shrugged. Finally, Anna started talking cows. Dad grunted a few times before Cara tried with a story about yesterday's battle of the sexes. Mom's shocked gasp wasn't exactly scintillating conversation, but it was fairly normal.

Dell tried, and failed, to start conversations, to tell a joke that would get a laugh out of someone besides her.

He charmed approximately no one, but he tried. He was so sweet for trying. Oh, who cared about the rest of it? This sweet, hot, good guy wanted her. He wanted to be with *her*. Screw the rest.

Mia took his hand under the table, squeezed. He smiled at her and squeezed back. Yeah, they could definitely figure out some way to make the farm stuff not get in the way of this.

"All right...I can't hold my tongue." Dad tossed his napkin on his plate, his face red and his voice full of...anger? "What in the hell are you two thinking?"

"Dad!"

"Well, it's dumb. All there is to it. What possible sense does it make to see a boy who is your direct competition? Mia, you're smarter than this."

In her entire life, she couldn't remember her father ever expressing disapproval with her. Not once. How often had Cara or Anna complained she was Dad's favorite and got whatever she wanted from him?

Now he wasn't just expressing disapproval, there was utter disgust mixed in with the admonition. An admonition voiced in front of everyone.

She hadn't felt so embarrassed in...years. This was more than just being sorry Dell had to see it. Her father, the one who had understood her and gave her a place to belong, who said nothing to anyone, was telling her she was wrong in front of *everyone*.

She had to bite the inside of her cheek to keep tears from forming.

"I think it's time to go," Mia said softly to Dell, hoping if she was quiet enough the hurt wouldn't reverberate in her voice. If she stayed, she might cry, and the last thing she was going to do was sit here and cry in front of everyone. She had grown past *that* at the very least.

"You stay. I'll go." He squeezed her hand, but she couldn't bear to look at him. He sounded so sympathetic, and seeing that would only make the tears fall.

Mia shook her head, unable to look around the silent room. She stood on unsturdy legs. "I want to go."

"All right." Dell followed her out of the dining room.

Mia was a little surprised no one followed. Not Mom to worry over something, not Anna trying to smooth things over. No one tried to stop her from leaving. *Because they all agree with Dad.*

Mia stepped outside, swallowing down the lump in her throat.

Dell slid his arm over her shoulders. "You okay?"

Since she didn't trust her voice, she nodded. Even though it was a lie. They got into the truck and didn't say anything as Dell drove off Pruitt property.

Dell pulled onto the road, his finger tapping against his worn steering wheel. "So are you mad at him for saying it, or mad because he's right?"

Hit the nail on the head right there. This wasn't just about how Dad had voiced his opinion. It wasn't even about everyone agreeing with him, thinking she was wrong, foolish. Same. Old. Mia.

More than all those things, this was about him being 100 percent right. What was she doing?

"What if we go back to my place and talk this through till we have an answer for everything? No sleep, no breaks, just banging this out until we've got a solution."

"That's not a euphemism for sex, is it?" she said, wearily attempting a joke.

Dell chuckled. "No. I'll even go as far as to say no sex till we figure this out."

She blinked. "And if we can't?"

"Don't be such a pessimist."

Optimism wasn't going to help her any. What they both needed was a healthy dose of reality neither of them seemed to want to face.

Dell took her hand, brought it to his mouth even as he kept his eyes on the road. He pressed a kiss to her palm. "If we weren't giving up yesterday, we're not giving up today."

He had a point. The problem hadn't changed. She just...wasn't sure the problem *could* no matter how determined they were.

DELL DID HIS best to make dinner. Macaroni and cheese from a box. He usually subsisted off sandwiches and vegetables. But this...challenge required something a little heftier. Mac and cheese was all he had in his cooking arsenal.

Mia was quiet and still. Mia was never quiet and still. But this evening she stood in front of the sink, supposed to be pouring drinks, still and quiet, staring into the black outside the small window.

"Why don't you let me?"

She sighed and shook her head, taking the gallon of milk back from him. "No, it's fine. I've got it."

She poured two glasses, screwed the cap back on the jug. Then stood, quiet and still again.

Normally, he wasn't too great at reading why people were upset, but he'd been here too many times to count not to understand what was going on.

"You can always go back. Sit down. Talk with them."

Mia shook her head. "There's nothing to talk about. He thinks my choices are..." She slanted a glance back at him, and then blew out a breath "It doesn't matter."

"It does. Or you wouldn't be upset."

"He's never..." Her finger traced a drop of condensation on the milk jug. She cleared her throat. "Mom was always a constant barrage of the things we were doing wrong. She means well, she does. I... She and Dad had...a child before I was born, that died. Um, sudden infant death syndrome."

Christ. "Mia."

"I just mean, she has a reason to be overprotective. She lost a child for inexplicable reasons. And Dad has his reasons for being kind of shut off.

They don't talk about it. I don't think even Cara and Anna know. But it happened, and so they are the way they are for reasons, and I've learned to deal with both, but Dad has never…been that way to me before." He knew she was fighting tears, but she still didn't let them fall, even as she had to visibly swallow. "He's never told me I was wrong. Chastised me. It's a silly thing to be upset about, I know, but I wasn't prepared."

"You think I'd think it's a silly thing to be upset about?"

She lifted her gaze to his. "Well, maybe. It's only the one time and I know you've…been struggling with it for longer."

"It doesn't matter how long, I don't think." He finished mixing together all the ingredients and scooped portions into the bowls Mia had set out. "I don't want to care what he thinks, but I do. How do you not want your parents' respect? I mean, maybe if they were lousy, but our parents aren't. They're good people, so you want them to see you as good people, too."

She stepped toward him, always ready to soothe a hurt. "If Dad got to know you—"

He laughed a bit at that, nodding her toward the table, a bowl in each hand. "I'd never be good enough for you, Mia."

"You *are*." She was frowning, standing in his way, so emphatic.

"I'm just saying that, typically, if a guy cares

about his daughter, the guy who…" There were a lot of words that had wanted to come out of his mouth there, but they all left him with a vague feeling of dread. "You know, is involved with his daughter isn't ever going to be good enough."

"He's wrong."

"So is my dad about all this." He shrugged. "I haven't figured out how to convince him of that, so I'm not sure I've got any advice." He placed the bowls on the table and took a seat, pointing to his grandmother's old seat. Not that he should think of it that way. This was his table now.

Mia's spot.

Don't get crazy.

"What I do have is mac and cheese and commiseration. So sit, eat, commiserate."

She didn't sit. She still stood there, but the quiet brooding had left her face. In its place was that determination that must have gotten her here. Away from the girl she'd been to this…amazing, tiny little steamroller in front of him.

"They are wrong and we are going to prove them wrong."

He grinned. "That's my girl."

She finally sat down to her pasta. "Your. *Girl?*"

"Okay, what part are you taking offense to?"

"I'm not a *girl*."

"No, definitely not."

"So…" She swallowed a bite of food, her eyes staring hard at the table. Then her fork clattered against the bowl. "Oh! I have an idea. What about a merger?"

He blinked, having *no* idea where this was going. "A merger?"

"Yeah, I'll have to find the article, but I remember reading about these guys who were neighbors and ended up merging their farms because they each had different specialties. It adds cash flow and possibilities, and maybe if you have a partner your dad would feel more secure. Maybe someone your land butts up to?"

Dell rubbed his hand against his forehead. His knee-jerk response was a pretty emphatic no, but he tried to get past that. It was a compromise, and it was better than Charlie's because it would allow him to stay here.

But it undermined the second part of what he wanted. Approval. Acceptance. Belief.

He cleared his throat and tried to find a way to be rational about that. Not just fly off the handle as he tended to do with Dad, with Charlie. "Unfortunately, bringing someone else in… I'm not sure that's an option."

"What about Dean Coffey? He does pigs like your dad. If he sold—"

"I've suggested it. Dad's not interested in anything that isn't developing. He thinks a farm can't thrive. A partnership or merger isn't going to change that. And a partnership without me having my name on the deed to this land is too risky."

Mia nodded. "I guess you're right." She was quiet for a moment, and he noticed they both pushed the food in their bowls around a lot more than they ate.

Probably because they'd eaten dinner at her family's. He was an idiot. "Why'd you let me make this? We already ate."

She chuckled. "I don't know. It seemed like an idea at the time. Something to do in quiet."

"I can think of much better things to do in quiet."

"I believe you said sex was off the table until we figure this out. Remember?"

"Did I say that? I must have been having a stroke."

She snorted a laugh and he managed a smile. He wanted that. The easy, the comfort. The way things felt good. But he'd been the one to say they needed an answer.

As it was already well established, he was an idiot.

CHAPTER TWENTY-FOUR

"I'm ALL OUT of ideas," Dell said with a yawn. "All I have left is sleep."

Mia pushed her glasses up her nose, studying him over the mug of coffee she'd been sipping. Pulling an all-nighter was stupid when they both had jobs to do tomorrow, but Dell had been right.

They needed to figure this out. They needed to bang their heads against it until something gave. Which meant she had to man up and say the thing she'd been avoiding saying for days.

"There's one option we're ignoring."

He raised his eyebrows, apparently completely oblivious to it. "There is?"

She took a deep breath, part of her shrinking away from saying it. He wouldn't like it. She didn't want to say something he wouldn't like, deal with the negative reaction, not after Dad's, especially, but that was weak. She wasn't weak. "You need to sit down and have a talk with your father."

"Oh. That." Dell pushed away from the table and his barely touched mug of coffee. He scratched his hand through his hair.

"Yes. That."

"Do you think I haven't tried?" he asked quietly, standing with his back to her. "That I'm just over here stomping around not pleading my case?"

"No, that isn't what I think." There was a part of her that did not want to do this, that didn't think it was her business to do this.

But there was another part of her, a part she wasn't sure what to do with, that...well, that was in love with him. A feeling she wasn't quite sure he reciprocated, but she was sure there was a chance he could. If this obstacle was removed.

So they'd both have to do some uncomfortable things to remove it, if their being together was worth it. To her, it was. As long as she kept her business intact, just about anything else would be worth it.

"We've been down the talk-it-through road before, and thus far all it's ever done is get worse. What else can I say? How else can I prove myself?" He finally turned to face her, and her heart *ached* at the baffled resignation on his face, in his voice.

She wanted to wrap him up and hold on until he could see some of what she saw in him without it being tempered by what his family didn't. The way he put her at ease, the way he made her feel as if she wasn't some weird outlier in a world she didn't fit in. Like the farm, he'd become a safe place.

And it was because of him, the light in him, the sturdy love of this place, the fierce determination to succeed and the fact there was a part of him still looking for someone to see.

They understood each other; their hearts fit.

Maybe she couldn't make him see that, maybe he wasn't *ready* to see that, but she could cross the room and wrap her arms around him. Hold on and try to…get some of that through to him.

His cheek rested on the top of her head, though he had to bend over a bit to do so, and he held her as tightly as she did him.

"Isn't it worth a shot?" she said into the warmth of his chest. "To keep trying?"

He let out a sigh. "For you?" His fingers curled around her arm, and he slowly pulled her back so their gazes met. "I would do that for you."

Something about those words and the way he was looking so intently at her made her breath catch in her throat. Her heart thundering in her ears, she forced herself to speak. "It should be for you, and for your farm. And…"

He waited a few beats, but when she couldn't force herself to spit it out, he prompted, "And?"

"For…" It was two letters. They shouldn't be hard to say. She shouldn't feel as if she was a few short breaths away from a panic attack. "For us," she managed, not at all steadily.

"Us." His hands drifted up her back, then he pushed them through her hair.

She shook him off, feeling all weird and shaky and…vulnerable, which was the last thing she wanted to be feeling right now. "My neck is hurting from looking up at you so much."

He chuckled, but his hands didn't leave her hair, and he didn't pull away. Instead, he drew her back to his chest, where she could smell him, wallow in him.

"All right, my little genius. What am I supposed to say to Dad that I haven't said before?"

"Well," she said into the soft fabric of his worn T-shirt, "why don't you tell me what you've said before and we'll go from there."

Though he didn't move, she could feel the tension sneak into his muscles. "All right," he said eventually, sounding anything but all right. And he didn't release her; instead, his hands slid down her back, over her butt, and he pressed his lips to her neck.

She gave him an ineffective push, unable to stop the laugh from bubbling up. "None of that," she warned, sounding anything but stern.

"Just a little…break," he said, pulling her earlobe gently between his teeth. *Gah*. "Everyone needs a break."

She cleared her throat, mustered her best authoritative tone. "You're trying to distract me."

"Uh-huh." She could hear the grin in his voice. As much as she'd like that, the emotional toll of the past two days was a little harsh. "I don't want another market day like yesterday."

He stilled. "We won't." He pulled her back so she had to deal with the crick in her neck again, looking up at him. *So many times worth it.*

"Okay?" His hands curled around her shoulders and squeezed. "We won't." He pointed to her seat at the table. "Sit. I'll tell you what I've done and you can tell me what to do."

"Dell."

"No funny business, now," he said, tsking at her before grabbing his coffee and heading for the microwave. "Let's get this sorted."

She slid into the seat, pressing fingers to where a headache was starting to brew. Get it sorted. He was going to try to talk to his father again, for her.

She took a deep breath and let it out. For them. *For us.* Something they both wanted. So they'd find a way to get it.

DELL WOKE TO a stabbing pain in his neck, a foot that had fallen asleep and the weight of someone's head on his shoulder.

Weird to like it when he'd never been much of a cuddler before. He shifted, trying to find a little comfort without waking up Mia, but the minute he moved she stretched and sat up.

"What time is it?"

He glanced at the clock on the wall, then adjusted the hour for daylight savings, because months later he still hadn't fixed it to the right time. "Seven."

She groaned. "Late. Exhausted."

Yes, exhausted. They had been up until 4:00 a.m. going over what to say to his father. *You need to act instead of react.* Mia had said that sentence as if she'd solved all the universe's problems. As if acting over reacting would be magic.

He'd let her believe it. How could he not when she smiled at him as if... Hell if he knew. As if the sun and moon revolved around her.

Maybe they did.

She ran a finger down the slope of his nose, smiling again. "Don't worry. It'll work."

He crossed his arms behind his head, watched as she ran her fingers through her hair, yawned. Pain lodged in his chest at the thought of doing it, then having to break it to her that she was wrong.

So maybe he should ease her into the possibility. "And if it doesn't, maybe we accept the inevitable."

Her expression tightened and she was very careful to look at her hands instead of him. "The inevitable?"

He took one of her hands. Kissed it. "Yeah. Dad's going to sell this place out from under me. There will be no enemy farms anymore, because this won't be a farm."

"Dell." She intertwined her fingers with his. "Don't say that. He's your father and he isn't a bad guy. He'll see. He'll have to see. You can't keep circling each other like fighters. You have to sit down like father and son, farmer to farmer."

Dell shrugged.

"It's just an honest conversation."

"Yes, as you've mentioned three hundred times."

She smiled all overly bright, still sitting next to him on the couch. The most beautiful thing he'd ever seen. Worth all of this, a million times over, but that didn't mean he didn't have his doubts. And he wanted... He needed her to have some, too.

Doubt was so much better than disappointment, a good defense more handy than a solid offense.

"All you have to do is express your feelings."

Dell huffed out a sharp laugh. "I'm pretty sure the Wainwright motto is Show No Feelings That Might Get You Knocked Down a Peg."

She slid off the couch, stretching again, which distracted him enough to sit up and watch the thin fabric of her T-shirt stretch across her breasts.

"I imagine you're not unique. Being honest about hurt blows."

"Thank you for this invigorating pep talk."

"How about this?" She leaned over and brushed a kiss across his cheek before taking his face in her hands. "I know you'll find the right words. Just remember to be active, not reactive."

"Better," he muttered. Though he was still

dreading the whole thing, Mia's words did something to fortify all the niggles of worry in his stomach. *I know you'll find the right words.*

So absolutely sure. Someone sure he would succeed. He could get drunk on that feeling.

"I could come with you," she offered, still standing in front of him, chewing on her bottom lip.

He got off the couch, careful to make the move easy and not as tense and jerky as he felt. "Nope. It's fine." The point of all this was proving to Dad he was capable, mature. To be the one making the overture, instead of always reacting to one of Dad's proclamations.

He was taking the reins, and Mia being anywhere near that would reek of…weakness. As if he needed her to stand behind him and play puppeteer. He did not.

Maybe it had taken Mia pointing that out to him, that he was the reactor, not the decisive decision maker. That he needed to get Dad behind him, and maybe he wanted to ignore that she was right because it didn't come from him.

But he was not ignoring it. He was taking her advice and making this overture. *For us.* She'd said it softly, almost timidly, and the word *us* had made him ready and willing to do anything and everything to make that a reality.

Even swallow your pride?

Pride wasn't what he was worried about. It was this farm and running it as he saw fit. And…Mia.

If Dad said no… He stared out the window that faced his parents' house. If he went up there and acted instead of reacted, laid every feeling on the line, and Dad still said no?

He looked back at Mia, who was smiling so *hopefully*. As if this was a given. An inevitable yes. In her world, he supposed it would be. But it wasn't in his.

"I need you to believe there is at least a chance this won't go the way you want." Because if he had to disappoint her later today, it might kill him.

"No."

"If he says no, it won't be so bad. I'll be unemployed and homeless. You know, you can hire me so I can be a total useless joke." He was trying to make light of the situation, but all his junk was making it less of a joke and more pathetic than anything else.

"You make jokes like that and I don't think you have any idea how good of a man you really are."

The sentiment, the serious way she looked at him and said it, *meant* it, had something foreign clogging his throat. Because the tide of emotion was so overwhelming, he fought it away. "Come on, I'd make one hunky farmhand for you."

Mia's brows drew together, but she didn't argue with him. Instead, she looked…thoughtful. Dell's stomach jumped uncomfortably.

"What? What's that look about? It was a joke."

"No, I know, but I have an idea. I think. Maybe." She turned abruptly and began to gather her things.

"I'm not going to work for you."

She waved him off, slipping her purse onto her shoulder. "I know that." But she didn't elaborate.

"Well, what, then?"

She shook her head. "I'm not sure yet. I need to look over some things. Run some figures. But… it might be a viable backup plan."

"Wait. What?"

"It's just an…idea. I have to think it through." She pulled a sweater over her head, shoved her feet into her boots.

"Mia."

She walked back to him, kissed his chin. "You go have your talk. Be honest. Give it everything you have, and if for some insane your-father-is-a-total-jackass reason he says no, I may have a backup plan. But I have to make sure first, okay?"

"Make sure of what?" They were running in some circle he couldn't keep up with, and instead of hope he felt some faint sense of dread.

"That it'll work. That it'll help us both. That I'm not totally nuts."

"Just tell me and—"

She kissed him on the mouth, a quick peck. "Nope. Gotta go. I'll come back tonight."

"Mia. Just tell me."

"Trust me, sweetheart." She patted his cheek before she stepped out onto the porch.

Dell followed, frowning. He did not like being kept in the dark like this. Did not like the way she was running ahead of him. "Don't I have some say?"

"Be patient. It's a virtue and all."

"Screw virtue." He pressed his mouth to hers and let some of his frustration out in a kiss that left them both a little breathless.

She laughed, gave his chest a shove. "Not going to get me to talk that easily. Go talk to your dad. I'll see you tonight." Her smile was pretty and hopeful, her hair a tangled mess from a night on the couch.

His couch, with him, trying to work out some kind of future. The uncomfortable squeezing feeling in his chest that had bothered him all last night returned.

"Mia, I…" He raked his fingers through his hair. What was he trying to say? He had no idea. Or maybe he knew exactly what he wanted to say and the idea scared the hell out of him. "It'll drive me crazy all day."

Head cocked, she studied him. "I need to work a few things out first. Maybe it's crazy, maybe it's possible, but I need to know it's one or the other before I go yapping about it." She touched his cheek, rubbing her palm there. "I need to know it'll work for both of us. Not just you."

"You know I want that, too." He covered his hand with hers. "If this is about helping me again—"

"It's about us. I think." She smiled, pressed a kiss to his cheek, then paused with a thoughtful look on her face. She shook her head. "I have to go. I'll be back. Good luck." She took a few steps off the porch, then froze. So did he.

DAD WAS STANDING at the fence, an unreadable look on his face. Mia looked back at Dell briefly, then powered on. He heard her cursory "Good morning, Mr. Wainwright." Then she got in her truck and left.

Dell didn't move. This was ruining his plan already. To go up to Dad with his old business plan, to rationally and calmly ask Dad if he'd read it, if he understood what Dell was capable of.

Unfortunately, Dad didn't turn and go. He walked up to the porch. Occasionally he looked over his shoulder, watching Mia and then her truck's progress away from the cabin.

When he finally reached the porch, he gave one last look back, then studied Dell. "Mia Pruitt."

Dell didn't offer a response. He and Mia were none of Dad's business.

"Mia's a smart girl." Dad rubbed his chin,

leaning against the post of the porch. "Really smart girl."

It bristled, even though it shouldn't have. "I'm aware."

"She knows farming like nobody else."

Nobody else?

"Heard her give a speech once."

"Mia?" Dell couldn't imagine Mia getting in front of a group of people and speaking.

"Few years ago when she was at Truman. I was up for a conference. All the ag students presented papers. You know, actually, first time I seriously thought about selling this place was after her presentation."

"What?"

"Her paper was all about the changing face of farming. I didn't like what she had to say. She was right, too, but I didn't want that future for me. Not one bit. Knew I couldn't keep up with it, and you'd have a rough time doing the same. So, I thought selling would be the best option." He shrugged. "Then you got the wild hair you wanted this place, so I've held off."

"It's not a wild hair. I…" What the hell was going on?

"Smart girl."

"You said that already." He was gritting his teeth, trying to fight off that stupid need to *react*. This was messing everything up.

"You serious about her?"

Dell couldn't make out what was churning through him. Anger. Frustration. Downright confusion. "What?"

Dad shrugged. "If you got really serious about her, down the line, well… She'd keep you in line. Maybe I wouldn't have to sell."

Dell couldn't catch a breath. He must be dreaming. He'd fallen asleep after Mia left and this was some kind of twisted nightmare. "Are you joking right now?"

"Look, son, I know you want to make me out to be the bad guy here, but you don't know what you're getting yourself into. I'd rather sell the place now than have it get foreclosed on because you can't keep up or change your mind once you realize what this place means. But Mia'd keep you on the right track, and if you were serious about her I doubt you'd change your mind down the line. I'd keep her around if I were you. She'd be good for you." On that sentiment, he patted Dell on the shoulder and walked away.

Dell stood on the porch, frozen. Dad had finally given him a way to keep the farm. Keep Mia around. Which he wanted to do anyway, which was the whole point, but…

The lack of faith in him, the total disregard for what he brought to the farm burned. Mia was smart. Mia was capable. If he kept her around and got the farm, that was all Dell would ever hear. Mia would get all the credit.

He wasn't sure he'd ever be able to live with that.

CHAPTER TWENTY-FIVE

MIA DRAINED HER third cup of coffee, immediately regretting it. She was already amped enough. Caffeine just added to the jitters.

She sat on an overturned pail. The edges of it dug into her butt, but she barely noticed. She hadn't been able to concentrate on the work she was supposed to do with all the ideas swirling in her brain. So she'd given up and sat on the pail and scribbled down every last detail, working and reworking them until they made a coherent plan.

She read it through for the third time and knew it was risky. Possibly stupid. Dell said he didn't want to merge farms with anyone, but...wouldn't it be different if it was her? He could trust her implicitly, and he wouldn't have to worry about not having the deed to the Wainwright farm the way he might with someone who didn't understand.

She understood. And this wouldn't be hiring him, it would be partnering with him. Surely he would see that as different. If he...felt about her the way she felt about him. *Love. You love him.*

She pushed away that thought. They'd deal with that later. For now...for now she still had to get

Dad's approval. After last night. After him calling her dumb.

He wasn't going to give it.

Mia squinted up at the sky. Was she doing the right thing? She took a deep breath, frowned down at her notebook. She'd spent a lot of time in her life wondering if she was doing the right thing, the thing that wouldn't get her made fun of or would magically make her fit in.

She'd worried over every little step, and it had never gotten her anywhere. She'd finally started enjoying life and herself when she'd shoved that worrying away. When she'd been determined not to care what anyone else thought. When she'd learned to trust herself.

Now she'd finally taken that last step. Not just to keep true to herself and be happy with it, but to have relationships beyond her family. Wasn't worrying if she was doing the right thing, worrying if emotion was getting in the way of common sense, worrying if Dad thought she was an idiot the same thing she'd struggled with all those years?

Maybe she had to trust herself. Maybe she just had to jump in and deal with the consequences.

A little easier said than done.

Mia glanced at the sky. Well past noon. She hadn't eaten much, and the sensible thing to do would be eat her lunch, get some actual work done and then go talk to Dad.

Also the cowardly thing to do. Straightening her shoulders, she walked to the dairy barn. At this time of day, he'd probably be sitting at his desk with a magazine and lunch. He'd never seen much point in heading inside to eat.

She took a deep, steadying breath. She could do this. She could make her dad see the potential. She had asked Dell to do the same. *For us.* She could do this, and all she had to do was take her own advice.

Act, not react. Be honest about feelings no matter how hard or uncomfortable that was.

Dad sat hunched over his desk, scribbling something into an ancient notebook.

"I have to talk to you."

Dad held up a hand, cutting off anything she might have said after. "I'm sorry about last night. I was frustrated, and I shouldn't have said what I did. Let's forget about it." He put his head back down as if that was that.

Mia took a deep breath. "Let's not."

"Come on, now, Mia. I apologized." He sounded a bit like a whiny kid.

"I need to talk to you, and I need you to listen."

He groaned, but he pointed to the rusting folding chair in the corner. Mia pulled it over to his old, rotting desk. It was where he hid his chew and did his paperwork because it was the only place on the farm Mom wouldn't go.

"Not pregnant, are you?"

"Oh, my God, no!"

Dad shrugged, his face completely red. "Good."

Some of her bravery deflated. This was so not going to go well.

"Get on with it. I've got work to do." He tapped a pen against the desk, looked everywhere but at her.

"Dell is a good person."

"Aw, now, let's not talk about *him*."

"I need you to hear me out here. He's a good person and a good farmer, and his dad is talking about selling out from under him. To a developer."

Dad scowled. "Never did like that Wainwright fella. Lived beyond his means is what he did."

The highest sin in Dad's book. "I want to help Dell keep his farm."

"Now, Mia, it ain't your place. I don't want you giving anything up for that boy. You hear me? You look out for you. You let him look out for him. If he's asking—"

"Oh, he's not asking." She wasn't even sure he'd go for her idea, but she had to give it a shot. "A couple years ago I read about these friends who merged their farms so they could avoid losing them. They did this whole big thing. CSA, farmers' market and food supplier. In the end, they succeeded and did better because they worked together."

"I do not like where this is going, young lady."

"I don't have room to grow here. If Anna takes

over the dairy, there's nowhere for me to expand.
But if I merged with Dell, we could do more. I
could integrate into his CSA, he could help supply Edibles and maybe some other restaurants. We
could offer more variety at the farmers' market.
We could grow."

"No." Dad's face was still red. She doubted
it was from embarrassment anymore, but she
couldn't stop. Couldn't back down. She had to
keep going until he saw, until he understood. So
far, "keep going" was the only piece of advice
that had ever truly helped her.

"It would mean that little piece of land wouldn't
be developed. Not as long as Dell and I had it.
Now, it'd mean adjusting our deal. The five percent every year. I'd need to put that off a bit."

Dad stood, ran an agitated hand through his
thinning hair. "I don't like it. You can't go in there
and buy that fool's farm for him."

Mia stood, too. Desperation and nerves and a
million other emotions rattling through her. "No,
it's not like that. It'd be a partnership. A merger.
We'd work together. We…work well together."

"I don't like it."

Mia slumped back into her chair. Of course he
didn't. Why should he? It sounded idiotic when
she said it out loud. It sounded as if she was some
kind of mindless love-struck moron who was trying to buy someone's favor.

But that wasn't it at all. The merger would cut

away the need for competition, and that meant they could keep being together for however long that worked out no matter what Dell's dad said to him today.

It wouldn't mean Dell's dad couldn't sell the farm out from under him, but surely if there was a partnership involved he'd be less inclined to believe Dell couldn't hack it.

Even if Dell broke her heart, she wanted him to have his farm. She didn't want to see a developer ruin a piece of land that someone loved as much as Dell did. So she had to do whatever it took. No matter what.

Mia took a breath, straightened her shoulders. "Remember when I used to hide in the back room of the house?"

Dad grunted. "Well, sure."

"One time you and Grandpa came in and sat with me."

"Oh, those morons up at school'd been making fun of you." Dad slid back into his seat, scowling.

"Yeah, and you guys told stories about the house. About the farm. About how you'd grown up. And it felt like...it wasn't just us. Grandpa even said it. He felt it, too. That this place and that house were more than just us who are left. It means more. We belong to this place."

He fiddled with the brim of his hat. "Yeah, yeah, I remember."

"I never talked about that with anyone. But the

other day, Dell was talking about his farm and he said the same thing. He said it was in his bones. I think I maybe fell in love with him right there." Admitting out loud, to Dad, that she loved him was scary, but it was true, so...so what?

Dad's face was beet red and he stared hard at his desk. "I really need to hear this?"

Mia smiled a little. Good old Dad. Completely embarrassed by any male-female relationship topic. Even love. "I can help him, and in the same breath, help myself. Farming is changing, and this will help me keep up." She pushed the notebook toward him. "Look it over. I've figured it out. Gone over figures and cost and a million other things. I could grow what I have, and so could Dell." Mia took a deep breath. "No one should have to lose a part of themselves."

Dad leaned back in the ancient chair, rubbed a hand over his poorly kept beard. "It's a risk."

"Farming always is."

Dad almost, *almost* smiled at that. "Love, too."

"Be careful. I might start thinking you're poetic or something." But she knew the truth. Under all the gruff silence, he was a softie.

He waved a hand at her. "You have my permission or blessing or whatever damn thing it is you want. I trust you, Mia."

Mia swallowed at the lump in her throat, reached over the desk and squeezed his hand.

"That boy better treat you right."

"He does. If that changes, I'll sic Cara on him."

Dad laughed at that. "You sure this is the right thing?"

"I have to trust myself, and I really think it is."

"All right. Enough jabbering. Get on with you." Dad shooed her out of the little office. She held the notebook to her chest.

Nerves did a little tap dance on her lungs, making it hard to breathe right. This was such a risk, but it would give them what they both wanted. So maybe it wasn't a risk at all.

IT WAS NEARLY seven o'clock and Mia still hadn't shown up. Dell sat on his couch staring out the window.

He hadn't showered. Dirt still caked his hands. He hadn't even planned to stop working. He'd come inside to refill his water bottle and then had sat down and...not moved.

He'd worked his ass off today but had barely felt it. Because he hadn't had a talk with his father as he'd promised. He'd just let Dad walk away, and gone to work.

Ever since this morning everything felt off. For the first time, he didn't want to see Mia. He didn't want her to come. He didn't want her to have a backup solution. He wanted to go back to when things were simple and he didn't give a shit about anything.

Not her. Not this.

Because no matter how he worked it out in his mind, he was fairly certain he was going to lose both the things he cared so deeply about.

He hadn't done what he'd promised he'd do, and he didn't want to take the chance Dad had offered him. He wanted none of this.

A brief knock, followed by Mia barging in. "Jeez, it's dark in here. Why don't you turn on the lights?"

"Rather not." The weird fog around him thickened; he felt so separated from everything this didn't even seem real.

No one was ever going to see who he really was. No one was ever going to believe he was capable. Honest talks wouldn't change that. Backup plans and beautiful farmers who lit everything up couldn't erase what he was.

Keep Mia and he could keep the farm. It should be the perfect solution, and yet without trust or belief, the things he wanted were poisoned. He and Mia would always be on some weird quicksand of him not being good enough.

"It didn't go well," she said softly, sitting gently next to him on the couch and sliding her arm over his shoulders. All kindness and comfort and… and…

He wanted to bolt, but the fog kept him glued to his spot.

"I'm sorry. I am. But…we have my backup plan."

She gave his shoulders a squeeze before she started flipping through her notebook.

It didn't matter. Anything that might help him via her didn't matter. "Actually—"

She gave his shoulder a shove. "Stop being so weird. Look." She opened the notebook, pointed at a word it took him a few seconds to work out.

"Merger. Merge? But I said I didn't—"

"I know you said a merger with a neighbor wouldn't work, but…this is me. If we combine our farms, we can do a lot more than we're each doing individually now. I'm stuck where I'm at. Most of our land is for the dairy, and on the other side county property and behind us Curt Simmons, who won't sell anything, ever. His son is taking over, too. If I ever want to expand, I need more land. If we merge, I can infuse the money I have into Morning Sun so we can partially buy out your dad right now. No waiting and seeing what he does. Then we can do the CSA, the restaurant, the farmers' market together. We might even be able to expand beyond that."

Dell kept staring at the word. The excitement in her explanation did nothing to break through the fog. If anything, depression and futility pushed deeper and deeper.

"Your grand plan is to buy the farm for me."

"Not for *you*, Dell. For both of us. We work well together, and I ran the figures." She flipped through the pages. "I know you didn't like the idea with someone else, but you can trust me. You already know we work well together, and it wouldn't be striking up a deal with someone you barely know. It's me. Think of all we could do."

Think of all *she* could do. Because that was what everyone would think. They'd think Mia had saved his ass. They'd think Mia was the brains and he was nothing but glorified muscle. This wasn't partnership. No one would see it as that. They'd see it as Mia buying him out, and keeping him on through some kind of pity for the dumb, senseless Wainwright boy.

This was no better than Dad's solution. This was actually worse.

He didn't look at her, because he knew what he would see. A dancing excitement, an unshakable confidence. Except he was about to shake it. Kill it. So he wouldn't look.

He stood, letting the notebook fall. "Not interested."

Mia looked at him, the notebook, a confused line digging into her forehead. "But…you didn't even look."

"Don't have to. Not interested."

"What's wrong with you?" She retrieved the notebook and stood. "Why don't you tell me what your dad said when you—"

"I didn't."

"You…didn't."

"I didn't talk to him."

Her mouth dropped open. It was almost comical how shocked she looked. As if he'd pushed her.

Push me. Hit me. I deserve it.

"You…said you would."

He shrugged, holding on to all the don't-give-a-shit he had deep inside. "I changed my mind."

"You… Why?"

Something about the tremulous hurt in her voice pierced through the buffer he'd surrounded himself with, and for a few seconds apologies formed on his lips. For half a second, he thought about reaching out to her, fixing this.

Fix it? What a laugh. There was nothing to fix. He was always going to be the problem that only Mia could somehow make okay. Well, screw that.

"What happened after I left?" She still sounded hurt, and he used the way that hurt *him* to find some cruelty.

"Nothing happened. I changed my mind about talking to him. I'm not interested in your stupid plan because I don't need to be saved, Mia. I can do this on my own." *She'd be good for you.* As if he didn't know that? As if he was that stupid not to know Mia was everything to hold on to?

So why are you pushing her away?

Because how was he supposed to go through life with everyone thinking *she* was the only thing keeping them going? How was he supposed to accept that as long as she was around, he was the brainless muscle?

"It's not stupid." Hurt laced her words, but he didn't care. Couldn't care.

"Well, that's your opinion."

She studied him. "What's really going on here?"

"Nothing. I don't need you to save me, Mia. I'm not an idiot. If you think you have to swoop in and take everything over—"

"That's not what I'm doing. I'm getting rid of the competition and I'm helping us. And I'm helping you. If you would calm down and read what I've come up with—"

"No." If he read it, he'd be tempted. If he read it, he'd think more about her than living the rest of his life as the butt of a joke. More about her and the farm instead of all that would always be missing from it.

There would never be any hope of people looking at him as if he was something more than a pretty face. And what about when that was over? What would he be then?

She touched his arm, smoothing her palm from elbow to wrist. "Honey, what happened?"

He jerked his arm away from her touch because it felt like being scraped raw. He didn't want her warm, rough hands. He didn't want...

It was not easy to make the decision, but it was the only decision he had to make. He didn't want *her*. As much as he did.

"Nothing happened. I just think… It was a stupid idea. Us. There's no point to this."

Everything about her stilled. "Excuse me?"

"Should've cut our losses before."

Her mouth hung open for a minute before she slowly closed it and swallowed. "What are you saying?"

Dell shrugged. His throat closed up and he wasn't sure he could get the words out. "We should probably give up the ghost. There aren't any real solutions."

"I see." She looked at the notebook, her chin so close to her chest he couldn't see her expression, only the top of her head.

Her hair was a mess. Half her ponytail had fallen out and random chunks of hair curled out in weird patterns. A deep, scraping pain edged down his chest.

"Why isn't this a solution?"

"I have to do this on my own. I already get enough grief for being dumb and worthless."

She looked up at him, baffled and frustrated. "But you aren't either of those things. Haven't we gone over that enough?"

She was so certain, so earnest. He wanted to touch her, and then maybe some of that confidence would rub off. But it would burn and it would hurt and it would scatter his certainty.

He had to trust his certainty. His gut. "Well, only you and I seem to know that."

"No one else matters." She flung her arms into the air, trying to meet his gaze. "If someone doesn't see the real you, they don't matter. That's a lesson I learned the hard way. Believe me. It's one worth learning."

Dell shrugged. He didn't know how to explain she was wrong. Didn't know how to put in words that his father's opinion mattered. That every comment demeaning his ability poked deep and stayed there.

"Maybe you should go."

She made a weird sound, kind of a laugh, except there was no humor in any of this. When she looked at him, there were tears in her eyes and everything inside his chest ached.

"This is about your dad? About him not believing in you?"

Again, Dell shrugged. He couldn't find his voice and even if he could, he wouldn't know what to say.

"No, you know what, that's giving him too much credit. This is about you, Dell. About you being a childish, whiny baby. Thinking the only way this can be right is if it's perfect. Life isn't perfect. It's complicated and messy and sometimes there's compromise."

"Oh, please, continue with this riveting lecture. Obviously I have no idea what life is fucking like."

"Apparently not. Because you are so obsessed

with people seeing you some way you want to be seen that you are giving up and pushing *everything* away. All because your father doesn't pat you on the back and say, 'Good job, Junior.' You'll give up on this and…"

She trailed off, and never said whatever she'd meant.

But he knew. She'd meant to say *me*, and the lump in his throat grew, the pain in his chest went deeper than he thought possible.

"I don't give a shit what your dad thinks about you," she said, her voice growing raspy. "Or me. It shouldn't matter. If you loved this place half as much as you claim to, it wouldn't matter what he thought. Sure, it's not perfect and it sucks, but nothing is perfect. We don't get to make people see us the way we want."

"You did."

She snorted. "I worked my ass off for it, and you know what? People still whisper behind my damn back, Dell. But I don't care. I learned not to care about people who weren't going to see me for me."

"Lucky you."

"Yeah, I'm real lucky. The idiot who thought you were one of those people." She snatched up her purse. "Go to hell."

She stormed out of the house, leaving nothing but darkness behind.

She didn't get it. She didn't. How could she

doubt he loved this place after everything he'd told her? Just because he didn't want her swooping in and saving the day and getting the credit. Just because he didn't want to be seen as someone dumb and useless who had to be saved by some woman he'd been stupid enough to fall in love with.

It was about pride and family and his good name. It was about this place, too. Nothing wrong with wanting—needing—to do this on his own. Not a damn thing.

She was wrong. She had to be.

CHAPTER TWENTY-SIX

MIA DIDN'T CRY. She wouldn't let herself. She'd had a lot of practice holding back tears, and she used every last ounce of that skill to get her home, in bed and under the covers before she let the tears escape.

She wasn't sure what had happened. Obviously Dell's dad had said *something*. But what, Dell wasn't telling, and what had changed in his mind he *really* wasn't telling. Instead, he was throwing everything away with both hands.

She would not feel sorry for him. No way. He'd cast her off as if she didn't matter, so she hated him. She absolutely 100 percent did not feel sorry for him and did not want to make it better.

He couldn't talk to his father after everything she had done to try to make this right? He was a worthless asshole who deserved that "Go to hell" no matter how terrible she felt after saying it.

You shouldn't have let your soft heart get in the way.

She wished she could tell the obnoxious voice in her head to go to hell, too.

"Mia?"

Mia tried to wipe the tears from her cheeks as she heard Cara's footsteps approach. A few minutes and she could totally pretend she wasn't a sniveling mess over a stupid, stupid, stupid guy.

"I saw your car. I didn't think you lived here anymore." Cara entered her room, then stopped abruptly. "You're in bed. You've been crying. Well, shit." She turned around, disappeared.

Mia sat in bed, not sure what had just transpired. Until Cara returned with a bottle of wine. "Okay, what'd the jerk do? Do I need to kick him in the balls? 'Cause I'm up for that." She plopped next to Mia on the bed and jammed the corkscrew into the top of the wine bottle.

Mia tried to catch up to Cara's tirade. She probably would have been up for ball kicking a few minutes ago, but the tears and the bed had sucked some of the anger out of her and now she mainly just felt sad.

Broken.

Devastated.

You are pathetic.

"Mia, you better tell me what he did right now or I really will go over there and kick him in the balls."

"He broke up with me." Such a weird statement, and really one she should be celebrating. Life experience and all. First guy out of the way. Now she could start looking around for Mr. Right.

When had Dell started seeming like Mr. Right?

"Bastard. I'll key his truck. Or egg his house. Or both? Yeah, both."

"Cara."

Cara shook her head, popping the cork. "Lesson number one in breakups is we don't actually do any vandalizing. We just talk about doing it. It's cathartic."

She let out a breath, stared at the bottle Cara held out to her. She didn't feel like drinking. She didn't feel like talking about vandalizing anything. She wanted to curl up and sleep and pretend she hadn't wasted her whole day on a stupid, idiotic plan. And worse, gotten way too excited about it.

Dreamed about mergers and…love.

"So what happened?"

Mia took a deep breath. "I…I'm not even really sure. He was supposed to talk to his dad today about the farm, and then I had this backup plan where we could merge our farms, but something happened with his dad and…" She couldn't make it make sense, not when it didn't make any sense to her.

This was not how she'd pictured today. In all the scenarios she'd gone through in her head, this was not one of them. Not even close.

Last night he'd been so sweet and determined and…she'd been convinced he could love her. She had been utterly sure of it, and she was never sure of people's feelings unless they were family.

But obviously she'd been wrong. If he could cast her aside so easily all for his pride.

"I…came up with this whole idea. I even ran it by Dad. That we could merge our farms, because it's me. He could trust me. We could work well together, and we *do*."

Cara nodded, soothingly rubbing a hand back and forth over Mia's shoulder. "It was a surprise to all of us, but you did seem to complement each other."

"Right? Right! I'm not wrong. I wasn't wrong to think we could…" Make something lasting. Ugh, that hurt. Like slicing your skin right open. "Then he started going on about how people would think I'd saved him and how he would look stupid and… As if any of that matters."

"Ooh." Cara nodded as if she understood. As if she understood Dell's point of view.

"What does he care if it gets him what he wants?" Mia demanded.

"Well, there's something to be said for pride." Cara shrugged. "As the screwup of our family, I can tell you it's not really fun."

"You're not a screwup."

Cara shrugged. "I don't farm. I sleep around. I never went to college and I answer phones at a salon. I'm no Mia Pruitt." She patted Mia's hand. "That's okay. It's not who I am, but it's not always easy to be seen as the loser. To feel like…

in order to be anything, someone has to swoop in and save you."

"But *I* don't think he's a loser." Even as angry as she was at him, she knew he wasn't stupid. He was hurt, and there was no accounting for the things that made sense when you were hurt.

But turning her away had been cruel and unnecessary. When she only wanted…to be with him.

"Which is exactly why he is a loser for breaking your heart. You see the best in everybody, and his pride shouldn't get in the way of that." Cara pushed the bottle of wine into Mia's hands. "I get where he's coming from, but he didn't need to break up with you. You deserve better."

Mia went ahead and took a gulp straight from the bottle. Oh, she wanted to believe that. She did. But Dell got the farm stuff. When she was with him, she could be herself without questioning. When she was with him, she was happy. Was there really better out there?

FOR THREE DAYS Dell came home only after the dark made it impossible to do any more work, then sat on his couch and stared at the notebook Mia had left on the table.

The first night, he didn't touch it. Just stared. He'd also downed a six-pack and thought about Dad listening to Mia give some speech when she'd been in college. *That* being what had spurred Dad to talk about selling.

This was all Mia's fault, then. At least, that was what he'd decided after his sixth beer. In the light of the next day, he hadn't been able to hold on to that blame.

He knew whose fault this was.

The second night, he picked up the notebook, flipped through the pages and then hurled it across the room. He popped open a beer and couldn't stomach the thought of drinking it, so he poured it down the drain.

He went to bed and didn't sleep. He thought about Mia. Apologizing to him at Orscheln before he pissed her off again. The way she'd sauntered off at the market after telling him to watch out.

He should have listened, because he was pretty sure he was dying.

On the third night, he read her plan. Then he read it again. Then, despite every voice in his head telling him not to, he began to make notes over Mia's lists and calculations.

It was a pointless exercise. He had no idea why he was doing it, but every time he convinced himself to put the pen down, he caught something else he had an idea about.

He adjusted a few figures, did a little restructuring to how sharing the CSA and supplier gigs might be split between them, and then sat back and wondered what he was doing.

Just because her plan was a good one didn't mean it was the right choice. Just because his adjustments made it an even better plan didn't mean he should do it. Just because knowing he'd have to face Mia at the market tomorrow scraped at every inch of him didn't mean he should give in.

He flipped through the pages again. His brain could spout all the reasons he shouldn't do this, but his heart...his heart wasn't really having those reasons.

He hadn't held up his end of the bargain. He hadn't talked to Dad, not really. He'd been a coward, a child, all the things she'd accused him of. And worse, he'd let fear make his decision for him. Reacted instead of acted.

If he stripped it all away, the details and the hows and the whys, it was simple. He wanted the farm. He wanted Mia. This plan got him both of those things. If it meant he never got to be seen as the brains of an operation... Did it really matter?

Mia had tried to tell him it didn't, and a few days ago he'd convinced Mia what the town thought about their being together didn't matter. Was this really all that different?

His brain didn't want to answer that question, but his heart knew. The answer was no.

Dell stood. Glanced at the clock. Ten. A little late to try to talk to Dad, but he couldn't sit on this. He'd already sat on it too damn long. He'd wallowed in stupidity, so maybe it was only his fault if people thought he was an idiot.

He was sure as hell living up to that right now.

So time to act instead of react. Go after what he wanted instead of…letting everything happen to him. Fall on top of him. Crush him.

Clutching the notebook, Dell shoved on a pair of tennis shoes and marched his way across the hill to the main house. The living-room light was still on, so Dell pushed in the front door.

Kenzie and Anna sat in the living room, noses pressed to their phones until he walked in. He felt a little weird being in the same room as Mia's sister, but he decided to ignore it. Especially since she was sending him death stares.

"Dad still up?"

"In his office."

Dell nodded, then walked upstairs. Dad's office was a small corner bedroom that had been Charlie's before Charlie had gone off to school.

It looked about the same. Dad probably worshipped Charlie's debate trophies in candlelight.

No time for that. "I need to talk to you."

"Going to bed." Dad pushed up from his desk, but Dell blocked the exit. "We can talk tomorrow."

"No."

Dad sighed. "I'm not in the mood for a fight, Dell."

"Good. Now, I'd appreciate it if you sat down and listened to what I've got to say."

Dad sat, made a big production out of being bent out of shape. "Fine, but I'm not going to sit here and listen to another speech about how much you love the farm."

"That's fine. I just want to know something." He took a deep breath. The conversation he'd planned to have days ago ran through his mind. What he and Mia had planned.

There was a moment of hesitation, that little voice in the back of his head saying, *Oh, you really want to make an idiot out of yourself again?* giving him pause. But it was almost immediately eradicated by Mia's voice saying, *I know you'll find the right words.*

Why couldn't he have remembered that three nights ago? Well, it didn't matter. He hadn't, and now he had to be a man and deal with the consequences, instead of let the consequences happen to him.

"Do you remember the business plan I gave you a few years back?"

Dad sighed. "Yes."

"Did you read it?"

Dad's eyebrows drew together. "What do you mean?"

"I mean, did you read it? Did you look at it and really think about it, or had you already decided farming is what ruined Grandpa's life, and yours, and you weren't going to see any more lives ruined?"

In all the years he'd watched his father, in all the past few he'd tried to get through to him, he'd never once seen him look so unsure, so… uncomfortable. "You'll thank me some day. I've lived this life, and you aren't cut out for it. You're too much like…"

"Like what?" Dell settled in and waited for all the negatives. Built a wall against them. It didn't matter what Dad thought. Mia and the farm were his end goal, so all the negative characteristics his dad lobbed at him wouldn't hit.

"You're too much like me," Dad said quietly. "You think I ever loved this place?" He swung an arm that encapsulated everything Dell loved as though it was some kind of hell. "That I wanted this? But I couldn't go to college and I didn't have a choice. *My* father didn't give me a choice, and once he was gone, it was too late. I won't have the same for you. I'm giving you a choice. Take it."

Dell was shocked enough not to have a response for that. He stood there in his father's office and…

What the hell?

"And in all these years, you never thought to tell me that?"

"What good would it have done?" Dad asked testily, staring gloomily at some point beyond Dell.

"Well, it makes me feel a lot better than, 'You're too stupid and irresponsible.'"

"Wanting this and thinking it's your future *is* stupid, and you *have* been irresponsible," Dad huffed, but for the first time in his entire life, Dell saw what was behind it.

Fear.

He had to sit. He sank into the chair Dad kept in the corner for the rare times he had a meeting to conduct.

"Is that all, or can I go to bed?"

Dell studied his dad. So old, halfway miserable because he felt as if this farm hadn't been a choice, but he'd just dealt with it. Taken it as a burden and never done anything to...

And he thought Dell was just like him.

No, he wouldn't be. So he tossed the notebook on the desk. "I want to buy. Actually, we want to buy."

"We?"

"Yeah. Me and Mia."

Dad raised an eyebrow. "You and Mia?"

"She— We've got it all laid out. First two pages have a timetable, offer, everything."

Dad opened the notebook, began to read. "That your chicken scratch?"

"Yeah."

"Lowballing me." Dell had scratched out Mia's figure and written in a smaller one.

"Yup. I figured I deserve a discount for the years I put in."

Dad flipped through the pages a few more times. "If things go south in the relationship department?"

Dell opened his mouth to say something about being professional enough for that not to matter, but that was not what came out. "It won't go south. I won't let it."

This was his second screwup where Mia was concerned, and each time he'd found a way to make things up. Because she mattered. Because he couldn't walk away. Because Mia was what he wanted.

"And in ten years, when you decide this is more of a burden than a thing you love, what happens then?"

"You said Grandpa didn't give you a choice. That this is what you got saddled with until it was too late. Right?"

"Yes, Dell, and no matter how you feel about me, I know who I was when I was your age. There are too many similarities to discount."

Which, who knows? Maybe it was true, and he couldn't even be offended because he'd watched his dad work his ass off to provide for his family. He wasn't perfect, and there were ways he'd failed as a father.

But he wasn't a bad guy, and maybe Mia was right. Perfect solutions didn't exist, and instead of moaning about the way things weren't perfect, maybe you made the best out of them.

"It's not a choice if I can't choose this. Maybe we're alike, but this place has always been a part of me. I love it, and I know you don't think love is enough."

"It isn't. Not when it comes to hard work."

"Do you love Mom? Charlie? Kenzie? Me?"

"What does that have to do with anything?" Dad grumbled, swiveling away.

"Everything. You and Mom have been married for thirty-five years, and even though you hated this place, you..." Dell tried to find all the words, all the ways to make this right, even if it wasn't perfect. "We never felt like you hated or resented us. So something about this family had to make you happy, right?"

"All of you are everything that make me happy," he muttered, so quietly Dell wasn't half-sure it was real.

"I love this place the way you love us. The way I love you guys. The way I love..." He cleared his throat, having a hard time believing in the feeling, trusting the truth. "I love Mia, and she loves me, I think. And between the two of us, we can make sure we keep... We won't regret taking this on. All that love, it'll make it okay, no matter what."

Dad was quiet for the longest time, and Dell felt as if he was holding his breath. He couldn't see Dad's face, couldn't gauge if being open and honest had done much of anything. So he could only wait. And hope.

"All right."

Dell waited for something more, some explanation, but Dad said nothing else and didn't turn. "That's it. All right?"

"You've got some financial backing, a brain at the helm of things. This is a business plan. All that…love talk. I don't like it, but I won't stand in your way anymore. So, yeah, all right. I accept your and Mia's plan."

Dell wanted to laugh. To think he'd been talking about loving this place for as long as he'd lived and Dad couldn't see it, but you added the love of everyone else in and suddenly…

He still didn't like it, probably never would, but he *understood*. He believed. Maybe Dad would always think Mia or love swooped in and made him worthwhile, but it didn't matter.

It really didn't matter. There were farms and love and nothing else mattered, as long as he could get Mia to forgive him.

"All right. I'll tell Mia tomorrow."

Dad nodded. "Good. Can I get some sleep now?"

Dell stepped out of the way, and Dad walked toward the door. He paused there, then reached out and gave Dell's shoulder a squeeze.

"Your mother has kept me sane, afloat, more than half my life. I hope Mia will do the same for you." Then he disappeared.

Dell stood there for a few more minutes. His brain was utterly quiet. How could it argue with what was right?

IN ALL THE years she'd been working the farmers' market, Mia had never dreaded a morning more. Even in the first few weeks, where she'd been downright nauseous over the thought of talking to people and not screwing up, the not wanting to go had been real, but not like this.

Because there'd been a purpose behind it. A goal. Today her only goal was to avoid Dell at all costs, and that was not a superpositive motivator.

Maybe Cara and Anna could handle it and she could call in sick?

As if on cue, her sisters poured out of the house and toward Mia and her truck and the vegetables she hadn't finished loading.

There had been a small, stupid, completely and utterly *foolish* part of her that had stalled all morning with the hope that...

She didn't even want to think it, but there it was. There had been hope Dell would call and want to share a ride. Call and apologize. Kiss her feet and beg her to take him back.

She wanted to cry. Why did any part of her have to think that was even a possibility? This was over. She'd told him to go to hell. He cared more about people not thinking he was stupid than about her.

If he came begging at her feet, she *wouldn't* take him back. Probably. Hopefully.

"You weren't kidding, Cara. She looks like hell."

Mia shot Anna a wounded look. "Mean!"

"I'm sorry, sweetie, but we'll do some magic." She produced a makeup bag and Mia groaned, but once Anna instructed her to look in the mirror of the truck, Mia shut up and let them ply her with all means of foundation and concealer and who knew what all.

Mia felt a little silly, since it was rather obvious she was wearing makeup and she never did, but it was better than the dark-eyed death underneath.

It didn't erase any of the dread. In fact, the closer they got to Millertown, the more Mia's stomach felt like one giant, painful knot.

"Don't worry," Cara said as Mia parked the truck. "We are your bodyguards today."

Anna nodded emphatically from the backseat. "We're going to make sure you don't even have to look at him."

She wanted to argue, to say she was an adult and she could handle it, but instead she slumped in her seat and took a deep breath. "Thank you."

"And I'm going to tell Val you're not up for battle of the sexes."

Mia groaned. She'd forgotten all about that. Again, she knew she should argue, but…she didn't have it in her. She was one giant bruise of hurt, and if this was heartbreak and something everyone was supposed to experience once, she had no interest in ever doing it again.

She was a coward. Plain and simple. But she couldn't let herself talk to him now. She'd be too inclined to try to convince him he was wrong. To convince him he wasn't stupid and it didn't matter what his dad thought.

She couldn't do that. He had to be the one to figure that out for himself.

So she let Cara and Anna run the show. The first time Anna asked her to go pick up something from King Bread, which was on the opposite side of the market, Mia figured they were trying to give her a break.

The second time, when Cara asked her to go pick out some goat-milk soap for Mom's birthday, Mia stopped midstride halfway as an insidious line of thought popped into her head. She whirled around and sure enough, down the aisle, Dell was at her booth.

Cara and Anna were quite clearly telling him to go jump off a cliff, and Mia held her breath. Wondering if he'd look where she was. Wondering what he wanted. Wondering if he'd keep trying.

She felt those obnoxious tears fill her eyes and turned away from the scene. It wasn't her first impulse by a long shot. Her first impulse was to go over there and...

Well, probably fall into his arms, stupid once-a-virgin prerogative. So she walked to the soap booth and carefully picked out soap for Mom, blinking back the tears that wanted to fall.

It didn't matter what he wanted. He'd treated her as though she didn't matter, and she didn't have to stand for that anymore. She didn't have to take the crumbs someone offered. She deserved more. Someone willing to... If not sacrifice for her, at least let her in and tell her what was wrong. Let her in. Be a part of it.

Belong.

She had to swallow down the pain, breathe through it the way one might breathe through a physical injury.

She paid for the soap, trudged back to the Pruitt booth, Dell having been fended off by her sisters, who were pretending everything was normal.

Bless them.

She was quiet the rest of the morning, talking only to customers. When they were done loading up, she asked Cara to drive them back home.

She sat in the back, leaned against the side of the cab and closed her eyes. She didn't want to ask, didn't want to know, but eventually the question escaped.

"What did he want?"

Cara and Anna were silent for a few seconds.

Finally, Cara spoke. Gently. "He only said he wanted to talk to you."

"So what did you to say?"

"Well, after Cara threatened to castrate him if he came to the booth again, she said we'd tell you he wanted to talk with you and you'd be in touch if you wanted to talk to him."

Mia inhaled again, wishing breathing would make any of this stupidity go away. Stupid pain. Stupid curiosity. Stupid…life experiences.

"Do you? Want to talk to him?"

Mia let Anna's question sit in the truck, a heavy weight. Did she want to talk to him? Yes. Was she going to?

"No."

The remainder of the ride was silent. Mia dumped her unsold vegetables off at the farm. Usually they all stayed for Sunday dinner, but Mia…couldn't.

"We're coming with you."

"Mom will be suspicious," Mia said, trying to shoo her sisters back into the house.

"We'll just tell Daddy we're working on a surprise for Mom's birthday, he'll accidentally blab it to her and then she'll be thoroughly mollified. Plus, we did want to give her a little nonsurprise surprise, didn't we?"

Mia didn't feel like talking or arguing, so she let her sisters all but bundle her up into her truck and back to her apartment.

Inside, Mia went straight to her room, closed the door and crawled into bed. It was self-indulgent and pathetic, but it was totally her prerogative. She'd missed the formative years of crying over a guy. Of course, she'd been busy crying over people making fun of her. Including Dell. He'd once been among those people who'd made her cry.

Why couldn't she hate him for it?

Oh, right, because his apology, his reasoning behind it, made hating him impossible. Oh, and maybe she was too busy being an idiot in love with him. She lay there for a while, allowed herself to doze off. A rare luxury she couldn't afford, but what was one afternoon away from the farm?

Later, Mia woke up to the sounds of people. Not just Cara and Anna but a male voice. She sat straight up in bed. Not just any male voice.

Without thinking about what she must look like, Mia hopped out of bed and into the hallway.

Dell stood taking up most of the doorway, scowling down at Cara and Anna, who were playing bodyguard, blocking the door.

"Go home. She doesn't want to see you."

"Yeah. Get out of here. If you don't, I'm going to call the police," Cara added.

Dell looked up, caught sight of her and his expression softened. Oh, she was in real trouble if she wanted to keep up her resolve.

"You're not welcome here." Cara gave him a little shove.

"Don't," Mia said. "It's fine. Let him say what he came here to say." With her sisters there she wouldn't do anything stupid. She would stand her ground.

If he wanted to talk, and wasn't going to give up, this was the best place to do it.

"Fine. But we're not going anywhere." Her sisters moved a little bit. Just a fraction to let Dell enter.

He turned his attention to Mia. "I'll say it in front of them." He scowled and shoved his hands deep in his pockets. "I don't like being apart."

Her heart did not leap. It did *not* do little cartwheels in her chest. She was an immovable wall of sense and strength. "Well, you did that."

"I know. I know I did, and I was wrong and stupid." He let out an agitated breath. "I wake up knowing that you're not going to be a part of my day, and it feels like less." When his brown eyes met hers, she couldn't catch a full breath. No one had ever, ever said anything remotely that beautiful to her before.

"You get me. You see me for who I am and no one else does." He shook his head, his hands leaving his pockets. He reached out to her, but then pulled his hand back. "I don't want to lose you. The thing is…" He glanced at Cara and Anna and scowled. "The thing is…" He returned his gaze to her face and took a deep, unsteady breath. "I love you, Mia," he said quietly. So quietly she was sure she hadn't heard him correctly.

"Whoa," Cara and Anna said in unison. When Dell glared at them, Cara looked at Mia, made a subtle gesture toward the door.

He…loved her. He was here, saying he *loved* her. Mia nodded to Cara, at least as much as she could get her head to move.

Cara pulled her car keys out of her pocket. "We're gonna go." The two girls slipped out of the apartment.

Dell visibly swallowed, his gaze meeting hers again. "Your idea was perfect. It was. Working together on both our farms is perfect and I screwed it up because…" He raked his fingers through his hair and began to pace in short strides. "Because Dad got in my head."

He looked at her expectantly, but she didn't know what to say or how to say it. Even when she'd let herself think he wanted to talk because he wanted to make things right, she hadn't expected *love*.

She'd thought maybe he *could* love her, but he was *in* love with her. *I wake up knowing that you're not going to be a part of my day, and it feels like less.*

"I need to sit." She walked stiffly over to the couch and collapsed onto the cushion. Her heart was too big for her chest, and it was painful, but not that searing, want-to-be-in-bed-all-day pain.

This was like...fear, and hope, and too much feeling to be able to handle.

Then Dell knelt at her feet. He didn't touch her, but he was close enough she could run her fingers through his hair, over the growth of his beard. She could tell him she loved him and this pain would go away, wouldn't it?

But what did it solve?

"I talked to Dad last night," he began, looking at her earnestly. "I gave him your plan. Well, actually I'd made a few changes, so it was more like our plan. He agreed. He'll sell to us. For a lower price. We can do exactly what you suggested."

Mia blinked at him. He'd talked to his dad. He wanted to do the merger. He was here, in her apartment, telling her he loved her.

She couldn't wrap her mind around it.

"Maybe I should have run that by you first, but I just... I read through it, and I knew it was right. You and the farm, it's right. More right than giving a shit what my dad thinks."

She tried to swallow at the lump in her throat. He'd realized it. All on his own. She wanted to wrap her arms around his neck and squeeze and never let go, but something held her back. Fear or uncertainty or just being blown away by everything.

"If you don't love me, that's okay. Just...give me a chance to show you that you could. That's all."

"I do love you." Her voice was little more than

a squeak, but she said it. The relief on his face made her want to touch him, but she couldn't. Not yet. Not yet.

"You do?"

"Yeah."

"Okay." He grinned. "That's good." Hesitantly, he took her hand in his. "So I love you, and you love me. And we can just erase the past few days and me being an idiot and move on from this point."

Mia took a deep breath, looked at their joined hands. "I believe in you, Dell. I think we could do great things together, but..."

His hand squeezed against hers. "But what?"

She had to look him in the eye when she finished. Had to. Even though everything in her screamed to hide, she absolutely had to meet his gaze. She steeled herself and met his eyes. "You have to believe in yourself. I can't fight your dad. Or Charlie, or anyone you think believes you're not capable or smart or everything you are."

"Kind of funny I'm having to be told to believe in myself from you."

Mia smiled, leaned her cheek to his hand. "Eh, it seems about right. I'm becoming an expert."

He leaned over and touched his forehead to hers. "I get it. Took me a while, but I do." He squeezed their joined hands. "Dad said some things and I think I realized...we were both always circling each other and butting heads because we were afraid to lay it on the line, to be honest. I don't know that he really sees what I'm capable of, I don't know that he believes in me, but I know he believes in love, and…well, it's the center. It'll get us all through.

"Let's do it, Mia. Let's do the merger, let's do us. Let's take what we deserve and screw what anyone else thinks."

She couldn't get her mouth to work, her breath to force out words. "I thought it was over," she finally managed to say.

His throat moved as he swallowed. "I'm… You'll never know how sorry I am. I was just… afraid and stupid. But you, *you* were right. Being honest and putting it all out there, that changed everything. I won't doubt it or you again."

He moved so that they were all but nose-to-nose and she had to look him right in the eyes, and she could see the shadows there. That he'd suffered, too, and her heart ached even though it was his own damn fault.

"Mia Pruitt, I fell in love with you before I even know what to do with it, and I know I screwed up, but I will do everything in my power to make that up to you. I want to work with you. I want to be with you. I want to see where this goes, and if you'll give me one more chance, I promise on my newly planted corn that I won't screw it up irrevocably ever again."

It was everything she wanted. Everything.

Someone stronger or harder of heart might be able to demand more, or turn him away, but that was not her. She didn't want it to be her.

"I love you," she said again, a little stronger than she had previously. And, hesitantly, she reached out and touched his cheek, then cupped his face in both her hands.

"You've said that twice, but you haven't said if you forgive me."

She blinked, then studied his face. He wasn't perfect, but she couldn't pretend she was, either. But the thing about Dell was…he was a fighter. He'd kept trying with the farm stuff, even though his father's rebuffs had hurt him.

He'd tried with them when things had gotten complicated, when she was ready to walk away.

Why wouldn't she believe he'd…keep trying?

Forgiveness. Yes. She could forgive, and believe, and love. Being brave in the face of uncertainty had gotten her…everywhere. So here she was. "Yes, I forgive you."

He grinned, but she saw only a flash of it before he pressed his mouth to hers. She sank into the kiss, into the promise, into a future.

EPILOGUE

DELL PUSHED THE last pallet into the truck. Spring was beginning to spring, and this new season of the market was the first time he and Mia weren't just sharing a ride; they were sharing a business.

Pruitt Morning Sun Farms' stand was ready for its first season at the market. Dell couldn't help but grin. A year ago, Mia had been a blip on his radar. Now, well, he patted his pocket. Now she was a hell of a lot more.

He climbed into the truck, and then sat there, a weird nervousness battling it out in his gut.

"Going to start the truck?"

He glanced at Mia, who had her hair back in a ponytail and her big black-framed glasses on. She hadn't been able to wear her contacts all week after somehow managing to scratch her actual eyeball.

Damn, but he loved her.

"In a sec."

"What are we waiting for?"

"Kind of a big occasion. Our first official market as Pruitt Morning Sun."

She smiled and took his hand. "Yeah, I guess

it is a pretty big deal. No battle of the sexes this year. No competition."

Dell pulled her hand to his mouth and kissed her palm. "Hopefully no hail or drought, either."

"Oh, don't jinx it."

Dell rolled his eyes, but the nerves in his gut didn't let him get too cocky about it. "You know, speaking of mergers…"

"Were we?" She laughed. He'd spent a year with that laugh, almost six months officially living with that laugh, and the high of making her laugh still hadn't worn off.

Dell took his hand from hers and moved to his pocket. If he could wait to toss his breakfast until he got through with this, that'd be great. He pulled out the little gold band with a *really* little diamond on top and held it out to her.

She stared at it, comically openmouthed. He moved it back and forth so the light danced on the diamond.

"That's a ring." Her voice was little more than a whisper.

"An engagement ring, at that."

"An…" She trailed off, breaking her gaze at the ring to look at him. She swallowed, both visibly and audibly. "Engagement ring?"

He nodded. "I was thinking we needed to totally merge. Business. Us. Makes sense." His voice was casual, but the next words were a little harder to be casual over. "So, Mia, will you marry me?"

She blinked and then nodded emphatically.

"Oh, don't cry."

She sniffled. "I'm sorry. Girls get to cry when they're proposed to." Over the console, she leaned into his shoulder. "Dell."

He kissed her temple, wrapped his arm around her shoulders. "I love you, Mia."

She sniffled again. "I love you, too." She looked up. "Well, don't I get even a little bit of a kiss?"

He laughed. "Hold on. I'm trying to breathe again."

MIA COULDN'T STOP staring at it. She wouldn't have cared if it was the most hideous thing on the planet, but it was perfect. A little gold band with a diamond set in it. She could even wear it while she worked without worrying about it.

Dell pulled the truck into the parking lot. "You know, you will have to stop staring at it long enough to work today."

She gave his side a little jab. "It's perfect."

He smiled, pleased with himself. Mia leaned over and kissed him until someone started rapping on the window. She wrinkled her nose at Cara.

"Stop being gross," Cara yelled through the closed door. "I didn't wake up this early to have to watch that."

Mia pushed the door open, unable to stop grinning. "Sorry." She held out her left hand, jiggled the ring around in the light. "I was a little overcome."

Cara's screech had at least 90 percent of people's heads turning her direction. "Oh, my God. Oh, my *God*! Oh, *my* God! You're getting married!" Cara all but jumped up and down while holding Mia's hand and examining the ring.

"And now the entire town knows." Dell walked around the truck and opened the tailgate.

Cara swatted him on the shoulder. "Good. They should. So how'd you do it? Was it superromantic? Or superlame?"

"How about you help unload?"

Cara shook her head, turned back to Mia. "I need all the details. Every last one. Immediately." She started pulling Mia toward the stand, then stopped abruptly. "Oh, man, now that you're engaged, are you going to let Dell take off his shirt?"

Mia grinned. "Actually, yes. Anna and I came up with a little plan for that."

"Why am I suddenly very afraid?"

"Come here, sweetheart." Mia crooked a finger at him. He followed, shaking his head.

"I have a terrible feeling about this."

"Don't worry. It won't hurt a bit." Slowly, maybe a bit slower than necessary, she unbuttoned his flannel shirt.

He leaned his mouth to her ear. "If the idea is

to give me an erection, you're succeeding, but I'm not sure what your end game is."

Mia laughed, then shook her head. "Is that all you think about?"

"Occupies *a lot* of brain space, yes."

Mia held out her hand and Anna slapped a paintbrush and tube of black paint into her palm. "You just sit still." Carefully, she painted five large letters on Dell's chest.

TAKEN.

He glanced down and chuckled when he read it. "Taken, huh?"

"I'm too much of a businesswoman to let a prime opportunity like using the Naked Farmer to my advantage go." She grinned. "But no touching allowed."

"I see." He shook his head. "I'm not sure how exploited I'm supposed to feel."

"Well, you think about it and we can discuss it later when I wash the paint off." She waggled her eyebrows until Dell laughed.

He leaned down, kissed her nose. "I guess it works. I am very much taken."

"Good." Mia looked down at her finger, couldn't help but enjoy the little sparkle in the light. It symbolized a future, a promise. One she knew they'd both work for, well, forever.

* * * * *

LARGER-PRINT BOOKS!

GET 2 FREE LARGER-PRINT NOVELS PLUS
2 FREE GIFTS!

HARLEQUIN®

Romance

From the Heart, For the Heart

YES! Please send me 2 FREE LARGER-PRINT Harlequin® Romance novels and my 2 FREE gifts (gifts are worth about $10). After receiving them, if I don't wish to receive any more books, I can return the shipping statement marked "cancel." If I don't cancel, I will receive 4 brand-new novels every month and be billed just $5.09 per book in the U.S. or $5.49 per book in Canada. That's a savings of at least 15% off the cover price! It's quite a bargain! Shipping and handling is just 50¢ per book in the U.S. and 75¢ per book in Canada.* I understand that accepting the 2 free books and gifts places me under no obligation to buy anything. I can always return a shipment and cancel at any time. Even if I never buy another book, the two free books and gifts are mine to keep forever.

119/319 HDN GHWC

Name	(PLEASE PRINT)
Address	Apt. #
City	State/Prov.	Zip/Postal Code

Signature (if under 18, a parent or guardian must sign)

Mail to the **Reader Service:**
IN U.S.A.: P.O. Box 1867, Buffalo, NY 14240-1867
IN CANADA: P.O. Box 609, Fort Erie, Ontario L2A 5X3

Want to try two free books from another line?
Call 1-800-873-8635 or visit www.ReaderService.com.

* Terms and prices subject to change without notice. Prices do not include applicable taxes. Sales tax applicable in N.Y. Canadian residents will be charged applicable taxes. Offer not valid in Quebec. This offer is limited to one order per household. Not valid for current subscribers to Harlequin Romance Larger-Print books. All orders subject to credit approval. Credit or debit balances in a customer's account(s) may be offset by any other outstanding balance owed by or to the customer. Please allow 4 to 6 weeks for delivery. Offer available while quantities last.

Your Privacy—The Reader Service is committed to protecting your privacy. Our Privacy Policy is available online at www.ReaderService.com or upon request from the Reader Service.

We make a portion of our mailing list available to reputable third parties that offer products we believe may interest you. If you prefer that we not exchange your name with third parties, or if you wish to clarify or modify your communication preferences, please visit us at www.ReaderService.com/consumerchoice or write to us at Reader Service Preference Service, P.O. Box 9062, Buffalo, NY 14240-9062. Include your complete name and address.

HRLP15

LARGER-PRINT BOOKS!

HARLEQUIN

Presents®

PASSION GUARANTEED SEDUCTION

GET 2 FREE LARGER-PRINT
NOVELS PLUS 2 FREE GIFTS!

YES! Please send me 2 FREE LARGER-PRINT Harlequin Presents® novels and my 2 FREE gifts (gifts are worth about $10). After receiving them, if I don't wish to receive any more books, I can return the shipping statement marked "cancel." If I don't cancel, I will receive 6 brand-new novels every month and be billed just $5.30 per book in the U.S. or $5.74 per book in Canada. That's a saving of at least 12% off the cover price! It's quite a bargain! Shipping and handling is just 50¢ per book in the U.S. and 75¢ per book in Canada.* I understand that accepting the 2 free books and gifts places me under no obligation to buy anything. I can always return a shipment and cancel at any time. Even if I never buy another book, the two free books and gifts are mine to keep forever.

176/376 HDN GHVY

Name _____ (PLEASE PRINT)

Address _____ Apt. #

City _____ State/Prov. _____ Zip/Postal Code

Signature (if under 18, a parent or guardian must sign)

Mail to the **Reader Service:**
IN U.S.A.: P.O. Box 1867, Buffalo, NY 14240-1867
IN CANADA: P.O. Box 609, Fort Erie, Ontario L2A 5X3

**Are you a subscriber to Harlequin Presents® books
and want to receive the larger-print edition?
Call 1-800-873-8635 today or visit us at www.ReaderService.com.**

* Terms and prices subject to change without notice. Prices do not include applicable taxes. Sales tax applicable in N.Y. Canadian residents will be charged applicable taxes. Offer not valid in Quebec. This offer is limited to one order per household. Not valid for current subscribers to Harlequin Presents Larger-Print books. All orders subject to credit approval. Credit or debit balances in a customer's account(s) may be offset by any other outstanding balance owed by or to the customer. Please allow 4 to 6 weeks for delivery. Offer available while quantities last.

Your Privacy—The Reader Service is committed to protecting your privacy. Our Privacy Policy is available online at www.ReaderService.com or upon request from the Reader Service.

We make a portion of our mailing list available to reputable third parties that offer products we believe may interest you. If you prefer that we not exchange your name with third parties, or if you wish to clarify or modify your communication preferences, please visit us at www.ReaderService.com/consumerchoice or write to us at Reader Service Preference Service, P.O. Box 9062, Buffalo, NY 14240-9062. Include your complete name and address.

LARGER-PRINT BOOKS!
GET 2 FREE LARGER-PRINT NOVELS PLUS
2 FREE GIFTS!

HARLEQUIN®

INTRIGUE
BREATHTAKING ROMANTIC SUSPENSE

YES! Please send me 2 FREE LARGER-PRINT Harlequin® Intrigue novels and my 2 FREE gifts (gifts are worth about $10). After receiving them, if I don't wish to receive any more books, I can return the shipping statement marked "cancel." If I don't cancel, I will receive 6 brand-new novels every month and be billed just $5.49 per book in the U.S. or $6.24 per book in Canada. That's a saving of at least 11% off the cover price! It's quite a bargain! Shipping and handling is just 50¢ per book in the U.S. and 75¢ per book in Canada.* I understand that accepting the 2 free books and gifts places me under no obligation to buy anything. I can always return a shipment and cancel at any time. Even if I never buy another book, the two free books and gifts are mine to keep forever.

199/399 HDN GHWN

Name _____ (PLEASE PRINT)

Address _____ Apt. #

City _____ State/Prov. _____ Zip/Postal Code

Signature (if under 18, a parent or guardian must sign)

Mail to the **Reader Service:**
IN U.S.A.: P.O. Box 1867, Buffalo, NY 14240-1867
IN CANADA: P.O. Box 609, Fort Erie, Ontario L2A 5X3

Are you a subscriber to Harlequin® Intrigue books
and want to receive the larger-print edition?
Call 1-800-873-8635 today or visit www.ReaderService.com.

* Terms and prices subject to change without notice. Prices do not include applicable taxes. Sales tax applicable in N.Y. Canadian residents will be charged applicable taxes. Offer not valid in Quebec. This offer is limited to one order per household. Not valid for current subscribers to Harlequin Intrigue Larger-Print books. All orders subject to credit approval. Credit or debit balances in a customer's account(s) may be offset by any other outstanding balance owed by or to the customer. Please allow 4 to 6 weeks for delivery. Offer available while quantities last.

Your Privacy—The Reader Service is committed to protecting your privacy. Our Privacy Policy is available online at www.ReaderService.com or upon request from the Reader Service.

We make a portion of our mailing list available to reputable third parties that offer products we believe may interest you. If you prefer that we not exchange your name with third parties, or if you wish to clarify or modify your communication preferences, please visit us at www.ReaderService.com/consumerchoice or write to us at Reader Service Preference Service, P.O. Box 9062, Buffalo, NY 14240-9062. Include your complete name and address.

HILP15